FIRST WITH GUNS

OTHER BOOKS BY JAMES EDWARD ENGLISH

Galia's Dad Is in a Wheelchair

FIRST WITH GUNS

A NOVEL

JAMES EDWARD ENGLISH

FORT WORTH, TEXAS

TCU Box 298300
Fort Worth, Texas 76129
www.tcupress.com

Design by Preston Thomas

IN MEMORY OF
RICK MCCURRY

"Most people are other people.
Their thoughts are someone else's opinions,
their lives a mimicry,
their passions a quotation."

—OSCAR WILDE

CONTENTS

BLACKJACK

APRIL 10, 1967 – LAI KHE, SOUTH VIETNAM

Dozens of American-made Bell helicopters lined the dirt airfield inside the Lai Khe rubber plantation, fifty kilometers northwest of Saigon. The long rows of Hueys that ran parallel to the longer rows of rubber trees sat ready to take to the sky in support of Operation Junction City. It would be the largest ground campaign to date in the United States' war in Vietnam.

Standing beside the lead helicopter, Private First Class William Dougherty unfolded the weathered newspaper clipping that he almost knew by heart after studying every word of it for nearly two months. "Fire Destroys Litchfield Baptist Church," the headline from the *Sherman County Times* read. The article from 1952 described a "suspicious fire" that consumed a small wooden house of worship that once stood on the foundation of his childhood home. Dougherty was five when his family bought the property. He remembered shadowing his father during the cleanup, carrying his own little bucket of ash and rubble that occasionally included a charred page from a hymnal or Bible.

Who sent the article and why? Dougherty wondered as he stared at the plain white envelope with no return address, only a postmark from Broken Bow, Nebraska, a small town in the Sand Hills, thirty-five miles west of Litchfield.

"Jesus," Dougherty whispered. The twenty-year-old ran a hand through his brown hair as he looked across the rows of helicopters. Keith Dougherty was many things, some of them not good, but he had a difficult time believing his father, a decorated war veteran, was an arsonist.

Dougherty glanced over his shoulder at the canvas tent beside the flight line where his pilot, Colonel Nikolai Sarkis, the newly appointed commanding officer of the Twelfth Aviation Group, had disappeared more than two hours prior. Stillness. Nothing. No one had entered or departed the briefing in more than an hour. It reminded Dougherty of a magic trick he witnessed at a circus in Omaha when he was a kid. A gaggle of clowns marched single file into a colorful silk tent under the big top, and when the ringmaster raised the sides, the clowns had disappeared. Dougherty remembered being impressed by the trick and had asked his mother if the clowns would ever return. "Of course, dear. It wouldn't be a circus without the clowns," she replied, patting his hand for reassurance. Sure enough, midway through the next act, the fools stumbled back into the center ring.

"When will these clowns reappear?" Dougherty muttered as he dug a small cassette recorder out of his pocket. He had purchased a set of the devices at the Long Binh PX shortly after arriving in Vietnam. The idea was that a GI could send one home and keep one so that both parties could record and listen to cassettes, which they traded through the mail. Dougherty planned to send one of the recorders to his ex-girlfriend, Astrid Larsen, to try and win her back; however, when the mysterious article arrived, he sent the other Panasonic with a recorded message to his father, instead. Dougherty wasn't sure if the man would open up to a machine—a fear that was allayed once he received his first cassette in the post. Dougherty started listening to the lengthy recording earlier that morning but had to stop when Sarkis arrived on the flight line. He stared at the briefing tent one last time, and when he saw no motion pressed the *play* button.

...there was a church on the property that burned down in the early '50s. "Suspicious circumstances," they said. God's will, maybe (laughter and the sound of ice cubes clinking against glass). Bad wiring is my guess. The Baptists got their wires crossed, imagine that

(more laughter). Anyhow, I bought the lot for a song after that. You and I cleaned up the mess and then we built our house from the ground up, with no help from anyone else...

Dougherty pressed the *stop* button on the recorder, rewound the tape for a few seconds and listened to his father's statement about the church, again. In all the years he had lived in the house, he never considered the irony of Keith Dougherty repurposing a church for his home. Dougherty shook his head and pressed *play* on the recorder.

We needed a place closer to town. I was workin' long hours at the post office then, and you were about to start school. And your . . . mother . . . was pregnant at the time . . . although she lost the baby . . . lost? . . . hell . . . wrong word. Makes it sound like she misplaced it . . . (the sound of ice cubes clinking against glass).

Listen, you shouldn't be over there thinkin' about our house. You're fightin' a war for Christ's sake. You gotta stay focused. Keep your mind on the mission, or you'll screw up. Don't get distracted like your mother did with her California dreamin'. Look what happened to her. She ended up in La La Land with all the surfers and hippies and Barry Haller for Christ's sake. . . . (long silence).

I just want to say how proud I am that you're followin' in my footsteps . . . over there fightin' for our country. That's what a man does, and people will always respect you for that. Keep one foot on the ground, Boke. . . .

Dougherty exhaled. He pressed the *stop* button on the recorder, slipped it back into his pocket, and climbed into the cabin of his Huey. The crew chief plugged his headset into the ship's radio and took his seat at the open left door of the chopper.

"A Frenchman still owns this plantation even though the French got their asses kicked at Dien Bien Phu in '54," Warrant Officer Dan Newcomb said over the intercom. "That means the bastard is generous with the government du jour of South Vietnam *and* the Viet Cong guerrillas who really own this province," the copilot added, craning his neck toward the two enlisted airmen in the cabin behind him.

"Vat sort of monkey's business do ve 'ave here?" Oliver Hansen, the ship's door gunner said when some restless grunts further down the flight line started throwing knives at the trunks of rubber trees. Dougherty watched a blade quiver as it sank into a tree, causing the rubber to begin to bleed out.

"Who do you reckon is gonna pay for that?" Dougherty said to Hansen, who was barely eighteen and from Berlin, of all places. He had joined the US Army in exchange for a guarantee of citizenship if he made it out of Vietnam alive.

"I zink Frenchie vill just bill your Uncle Sam for zat tree, Doc," Hansen replied.

Everyone that flew with Dougherty called him *Doc*. For the first three months of his deployment, Dougherty had flown with Colonel Munro Ferguson, the previous CO of the Twelfth and the one who had bestowed the nickname upon him. "Doc, get that son of a bitch off my skid," Ferguson had barked into his helmet mic one afternoon, as a desperate South Vietnamese Army soldier, too tired to march back to camp, attempted to climb aboard their ship during lift-off. The young crew chief dutifully stomped on the ARVN soldier's fingers, then watched as his ally fell back onto the Landing Zone.

Dougherty leaned against the frame of the Huey and thought about his last flight with Ferguson, a week prior, when the old man handed over command to Colonel Nikolai Sarkis. The two officers shook hands in the company area, and then *Buffalo – 6* proceeded to the flight line for the final time.

"Prick," Ferguson muttered as he climbed into the cockpit. "Good luck with him, boys," the CO said to Dougherty and Hansen over the intercom just prior to liftoff. Twenty minutes later, after landing in Saigon, Ferguson threw his flight helmet out the door of the Huey. He shook each one of their hands, stepped into a waiting jeep, and disappeared down the flight line, leaving Dougherty feeling like a mountain climber whose guide dropped off a cliff halfway to the summit.

Dougherty keyed his mic. "I've got a bad feeling about this new CO."

"Tell me about it," Newcomb replied. "In every briefing this week Sarkis mentioned he was in the same class at West Point as Westmoreland.

That's something the man should probably keep to himself, since Westy has four stars and Sarkis is still just a full bird colonel."

Sarkis had spent the last decade one rung below the army's loftiest rank and displayed an unhealthy obsession with American generals. The colonel even incorporated General John J. Pershing's nickname—Black Jack—into his call sign, *Blackjack – 6*.

Upon assuming command of the Twelfth, Sarkis renamed Ferguson's Huey *Blackjack* and instructed maintenance to paint a King of Hearts and Ace of Spades over the buffalo head that once adorned the front of the ship. The King and Ace added up to twenty-one, but even more importantly, in the newly minted CO's mind, the King of Hearts represented his prowess as a lady killer, while the Ace of Spades, which the Vietnamese considered a sign of death, symbolized his aptitude as a killer of men. Dougherty had seen little evidence of either talent, especially the latter. Still, the diminutive commander gave each member of his crew a deck of Aces, all Spades, in case they had the opportunity to deposit one on an enemy corpse. So far, the decks had yet to be unsealed.

"I feel like a walking trash barrel," Dougherty said, adjusting the steel chest plate in his flak jacket. On his second day in command, Sarkis had ordered flight crews to resume wearing chest protection at all times during operations.

"Everybody's got to wear them," Newcomb said with resignation.

"Yeah, until they get two hundred feet in the air and then they slide the chicken plates under their seats, so they don't get their asses shot," Dougherty replied.

"I can't believe zis guy made us put our pussy poles back in ze ship," Hansen added, referring to the vertical steel shafts Maintenance recently installed in the center of each doorway, to prevent an excited gunner from firing his M-60 too close to the cockpit.

"Hansen, he's probably worried you'll shoot him in the back of the head," Newcomb said and laughed.

To kill some time, Dougherty unfolded his field map and laid it on the floor of the cabin. Military Assistance Command Vietnam (MACV), under the leadership of General William Westmoreland, divided South Vietnam into four areas known as "corps." Dougherty pointed at the seventeenth parallel, which separated North and South Vietnam, and slowly moved his finger down the length of the map, resting over III Corps. The area ran from the foothills of the Central Highlands to a line in the northern Mekong Delta, about forty kilometers south of Saigon, the capital of South Vietnam. Third Corps had a little of everything, including mountains, coastal plains, delta, some dense, triple-canopy jungle, and rubber plantations like Lai Khe—a spec on his map halfway between Saigon and the Cambodian border.

"Come on, let's get zis damn thing going," Hansen grumbled and removed his flight helmet, revealing short spiky blond hair and round wire-rimmed glasses.

Newcomb looked up from the pre-flight checklist and shook his head in dismay. "Hansen, don't let Sarkis see you in those glasses," the copilot said. "Door gunners are required to have perfect vision."

"Do you prefer I shoot vithout them?" Hansen retorted.

The forty-nine-year-old Ferguson had tolerated Hansen, whose raised eyebrows and slack-jawed expression suggested a perpetual bewilderment. Over time, the colonel even grew somewhat fond of "the kid," a nickname he assigned Hansen once he accepted the young Berliner as a bona fide member of his crew and not a throwback to the war he fought in Europe, now more than two decades in his rearview mirror.

Dougherty fished a small nylon flight bag out from beneath his seat and removed a photograph Hansen had snapped of him standing beside Colonel Ferguson on the tarmac—the old man smiling with his arm draped around his crew chief's shoulder. Dougherty could see the small book of Sir Walter Scott's poems sticking out of Ferguson's left breast pocket. "Chest protection," the colonel often joked. Occasionally, when they stopped to refuel or were waiting on the tarmac for lift-off, the old man would take the book out and read a few verses over the intercom in his thick Scottish brogue.

Pause upon thy pinion's flight;
Be thy course to left or right,
Be thou doomed to soar or sink,
Pause upon the awful brink

To Dougherty, Ferguson seemed to offer another way a man could be, even during a war, but before he could figure out how he did it, the colonel had vanished.

Dougherty and his shipmates perked up when a Vietnamese farmer with an ox emerged from the rubber trees, twenty-five meters ahead of their position, and slowly executed a ninety-degree turn to the right. The shriveled old man and his beast of burden struggled in the soft earth next to the flight line. Without emotion, the farmer flicked his ox with a switch as they approached the operations tent filled with officers.

"Doc, zis guy could 'ave a bomb," the German gunner said, nervously.

"Hansen, where the hell do you think that gook could have a bomb? Up his ox's ass?" Newcomb said as the straw-hatted farmer and his draft animal plodded by their ship. The peasant stared straight ahead, never once acknowledging the awesome display of firepower assembled on the flight line just meters to his left.

Newcomb returned his attention to the clipboard while Hansen checked his M-60 again, making sure the rounds from the box on the floor fed properly over the C-ration can attached to the side of his weapon. Dougherty's gaze followed the farmer and his ox, trudging down the long line of helicopters, until Colonel Sarkis burst out of the operations tent with two officers in tow. The CO marched toward their ship. The man was just medium height with boots on, and stout. He had the same gray hair as Westmoreland; the creases on his uniform sharp as bayonets, yet somehow one sensed Sarkis would never quite rise to the rank of general.

As the CO approached the Huey, Dougherty noticed the two ivory-handled Colt revolvers on his hips, identical to the ones carried by General George Patton, according to their current owner. Sarkis stopped at the crew chief's open door, cleared his throat, and then rested his hands on those holstered pistols. "Gentleman, in the words of General Ulysses S. Grant, 'The art of war is simple enough. Find out where your enemy is. Get him as soon as you can. Strike him as hard as you can and keep moving on.'"

The colonel motioned for the two Majors to enter through Dougherty's open left door, then he climbed into the pilot's seat on the right side of the cockpit. Dougherty knew the routine. It was his job to get each visitor buckled into the bench seat in the rear of the cabin and fitted with a flight helmet so they could listen to the new CO pontificate about the brilliance of Operation Junction City.

After a few minutes of fumbling with safety belts and radio cords, Dougherty had the officers squared away for their observation flight. He turned toward the cockpit, and Sarkis gave him the thumbs up. Dougherty returned the sign, indicating the two Majors were ready to communicate with the colonel. Then the young crew chief pivoted toward the open door to begin his preparations for lift-off. But instead of chatting up the visitors, like he normally did, Sarkis hit the ignition switch, which started pumping fuel into the combustion chamber of the ship's turbine engine. Dougherty heard the *click, click, click* of the igniters and knew it was too late for him or anyone on board to prevent what was going to happen next.

"Hot start!" Dougherty shouted over the radio before the others on board had any clue there was a problem. Sarkis was still holding down the ignition switch when the Huey's Lycoming engine burst into flames. Dougherty grabbed the fire extinguisher mounted on the cabin wall, jumped out his door, and sprayed white foam into the rear opening of the turbine on top of the Huey until it looked like it was filled with shaving cream.

Not knowing what else to do, Hansen jumped out of the ship and stood beside Dougherty. Perhaps because he was the first grunt Sarkis encountered, the colonel ripped into the young German with a tirade of expletives. Dougherty, who stood a good six inches taller than Sarkis, inserted himself between Hansen and the colonel. "Sir, PFC William Dougherty," he shouted. "I'm crew chief of this ship and it's my job to ensure the tie down straps are released before start-up."

"You bet your sweet ass it is," the colonel replied, glancing at the nylon cord running from the tip of the chopper's rotor blade to a large metal handle on the side of the tail boom that served as one of the ship's antennae. The strap prevented a grounded helicopter's rotor blades from manually turning during gusts of wind or the passing of a ship—a real threat to flight crews—but in this instance, as Sarkis powered up the Huey's turbine engine, the strap prevented the driveshaft and rotor blades from turning freely, which caused the engine to overheat and burst into flames. And now, the colonel's bird sat smoking on the runway.

"You stupid, stupid son of a bitch," Colonel Sarkis said, turning his full fury from Hansen to Dougherty. "I swear to God, you will NEVER EVER FLY IN A HELICOPTER AGAIN!" Sarkis shouted, pointing to the heavens. The CO motioned for the two Majors and Newcomb to follow him to another ship. Within minutes the flock of Hueys took to the sky, leaving Dougherty and his German gunner in their dust.

The two men looked at each other in silent disbelief as the choppers disappeared into the skyline.

"Vat do ve do now?" Hansen said.

Dougherty shook his head and said nothing, but inside his mind raced ahead to the potential fallout from the incident. He imagined spending the remainder of his year in Vietnam as a straphanger, filling sandbags and burning shitters for flight crews.

Dougherty wiped the sweat from his face with the sleeve of his fatigues. He looked back at the tent where several adjutants stood outside, and having seen what had happened, were doubled over in laughter. Dougherty spotted a small outbuilding on the far side of the runway. Without saying a word, he started across the dirt field with Hansen following him like a trained dog. After traversing the dusty makeshift airstrip, Dougherty opened the door to the hooch and found what he was looking for—a small, portable radio.

"We'll see if we can hitch a ride back to base," he said. He detached the mic from the unit and held it to his mouth for a long moment, thinking about what he could possibly say to describe the morning's events. "This is . . . PFC William Dougherty," he finally said. "We had a . . . hot start at Lai Khe this morning. The gunner and I stayed behind with the ship, over."

After a long pause, a chuckle came over the radio. Every pilot on the flight line that morning witnessed the debacle, and someone had relayed the story to Operations.

"Any chance we can catch a lift back to Long Binh? Over."

"You're gonna have to sit tight, Smokey. Could be a while before we get to you," the voice crackled.

Dougherty slammed the mic down and walked outside to where a couple of weathered crates sat beside the radio shack, meant for situations like this where some poor grunt or straphanger had to kill time waiting for a ride. The lanky crew chief dropped down onto one of the rickety wooden boxes and leaned forward. He rested his forearms on the top of his long legs and lowered his head. Hansen sat down beside him.

A few minutes later, the two young men heard a familiar jostling of reins and thudding of hooves, as the farmer and his ox sauntered back into view. The wrinkled old man with the scraggly beard stared straight ahead, never once acknowledging the airmen now just meters to his right. As he passed by the shack, the elderly man flicked his wrist and snapped the switch against the giant beast's hindquarters. Then he continued down the flight line for twenty-five meters, executed a sharp turn to the right, and disappeared into the rubber trees.

2

CLETIS BOYER

THREE AND A HALF HOURS LATER, a CH-47 Chinook appeared above the rubber trees of Lai Khe and touched down beside the smoked Huey. Two crewmen jumped out and began harnessing the damaged ship. Dougherty and Hansen walked over to the side of the large copter and signaled to the pilot to see if it was OK for them to climb aboard. The man motioned to the back of the ship with his thumb. Within an hour, the crew off-loaded the damaged Huey at Tan Son Nhut Air Base in Saigon, and then the Chinook made the short flight north to Long Binh, home of the Twelfth Aviation Group.

After stowing his flight gear, Dougherty proceeded to Headquarters Division, to find Tony Saldano, a company clerk for the Twelfth who had befriended him during his visits to drop off maintenance logs for Colonel Ferguson. Saldano got on well with Ferguson, mainly because he and Major Ricci, the Company's Executive Officer, reduced the CO's stack of paperwork each night to a handful of signature pages the old man scribbled his name on as he sipped a tall glass of thirty-year-old scotch.

Saldano was a die-hard Yankees fan from the Belmont section of the Bronx who enjoyed talking baseball with Dougherty ever since Dougherty told him about the time former Yankees shortstop Cletis Boyer spent a week hunting pheasants in central Nebraska and rented a room in the Dougherty home during his stay.

CHAPTER 2

The quiet Nebraskan often sat at the bar in the Enlisted Men's Club and listened to Saldano go on and on about his beloved Yankees. Did Mickey Mantle have one more great season in him? Could Steve Whitaker fill Roger Maris's shoes in right field? Did Whitey Ford have a shot at winning twenty games this year? Every so often, Saldano paused for a moment, shook his head, and said, "Cletis fuckin' Boyer in your fuckin' kitchen. I can't fuckin' believe it." Dougherty understood his friend's point: there was something about being in the company of a famous person that made you feel famous, too. Although the clerk and crew chief seemed like an odd pair, their friendship worked well: Tony never shut up, and Dougherty hardly said a word.

"Bill, fuckin' shame what happened this morning," Saldano said, running a hand through the thick black hair that no army barber could subdue.

"Tony, I'm done at the Twelfth," Dougherty said.

"Take it easy, Doc. Your ship will be in maintenance for a while, and by the time it gets out, the Greek Freak will be flyin' with someone else, and you can move on."

Dougherty shook his head. "The CO has it in for me. He said I'll never fly again."

"He was just hot. Give him some time. Sarkis may be an ass, but he ain't stupid. He needs every fuckin' crew chief he's got."

"I can't risk it, Sal. I have to get my transfer in now, before he permanently grounds me."

"Where the fuck would you go?" Saldano said.

"First available," Dougherty replied without a second thought.

Saldano raised his eyebrows. "You sure 'bout that, Billy? Some of those boys are fightin' a different fuckin' war out there."

"Christ, Sal, everyone in Vietnam knows what happened this morning. LBJ probably knows by now. I've got to get the hell out of here as fast as possible."

Saldano pursed his lips and stared at the despondent crew chief. "Wait here a sec," he said. The company clerk disappeared into the back room and returned a few minutes later with some papers on a clipboard. "I think this is a dumbass idea, but if you want me to, I'll fill out the

12

transfer paperwork and date it just before the old man's last day."

Dougherty shook his head. "They'll know Ferguson didn't sign it."

Saldano leaned in closer and lowered his voice. "I signed hundreds of things for him. The old man hated paperwork. Hated it more than the Viet fuckin' Cong. I got his signature down. No one will ever know. And if Sarkis finds a way to check on it, Ferguson will say he signed it just to piss off Nick, the prick."

Using his army-issue ballpoint pen, Saldano scribbled *April 1, 1967*, in the date field of the form and then signed it *Col. Munro Ferguson*. He handed the clipboard to Dougherty, who stared at the paper as if gazing into a fortune teller's crystal ball.

Dougherty considered the best and worst-case scenarios. Best-case: Leave Sarkis and the Twelfth behind, get a fresh start, see some action, maybe even become a war hero. Worst-case scenario: Dougherty and his friend get busted for forging a colonel's signature, spend time in the Long Binh jail, maybe get chaptered out of the army with a dishonorable discharge. That would be a tough blow, and Dougherty imagined having to explain it to his father. But even at this dim prospect, a story was forming in his mind: he wanted to get out of HQ division, see some action, and get away from a prick of an officer, so he and a buddy forged papers to get him reassigned to another helicopter company. Dougherty believed it was what his father would do, so he signed his name at the bottom of the form and handed the clipboard back to the clerk.

"This is dated less than two weeks ago," Saldano said. "Shouldn't raise any eyebrows in HQ. Ricci's in Saigon 'til tomorrow. I'll just tell him I found it in a stack of papers," Saldano said. "That's no fuckin' lie," he added, as he slipped the transfer form into a pile of paperwork on his desk and winked. "When Colonel Suck-Ass sees Ferguson approved your transfer before the change of command, there won't be a damn thing he can do about it except maybe give yah shit duty until the transfer is approved."

"Tony, I owe you big time," Dougherty said.

"Well, I sure as shit hope you can tell me that after this war is over and we're having a cold one somewhere."

Dougherty extended his hand and Saldano shook it. "Better get the fuck out of here before the Flyin' Sarkis gets back," the clerk said.

Later that day, Colonel Sarkis reassigned Dougherty to latrine duty and ordered a "fourteen-and-two" for the young crew chief—a formal punishment that restricted him to the barracks during off-duty hours for the next fourteen days, during which time he was also required to perform two extra hours of duty.

The next morning at five, Dougherty awoke to the loud voice and lousy breath of First Sergeant Bernard Riker, a large man from a small town in eastern Pennsylvania. "Get your goddamn lazy ass out of that bunk now, Private," the burly man shouted inches from Dougherty's ear.

Before joining the army, Riker worked for the Snyder's bakery in Hanover, Pennsylvania, where the company made its famous sourdough pretzels. Riker spent his days unloading trucks filled with heavy sacks of flour. He then loaded those same trucks with cases of hard pretzels destined for markets up and down the eastern seaboard. Throughout his workday, Riker often loaded fifty-pound sacks of flour on each shoulder and ran from the warehouse to the bakery so the pretzel makers could feed the large vats that churned out thousands of pounds of sourdough each day. After three years of employment, Riker left Snyder's looking like Mr. Universe. The day he walked into the army recruiting station in Baltimore, the sergeant on duty looked up from his desk and let out a "Sweet Jesus" before he caught himself and began his routine for the dream recruit that magically appeared in his dingy office. Riker's German roots and Aryan features earned him the nickname "The Third Riker" from those in the company who suffered at his hand.

"DOUGHERTY, ARE YOU READY TO BURN SOME SHIT?" Riker shouted in the grounded airman's face.

"Yes, sir," Dougherty replied, jumping out of his bunk and fumbling for his fatigues.

"I am not an officer, Private. You will address me as 'First Sergeant.' Do you understand?"

"Yes, First Sergeant."

"Now, are you ready to burn some shit?"

"YES, FIRST SERGEANT," Dougherty shouted while buttoning his shirt.

"Good, then follow me."

Outside the living quarters stood a balding, middle-aged Vietnamese man holding two metal poles.

"Dougherty, this is Willie, the shit-burner," Riker barked, referring to the man whose actual name was Huy Le. "Willie is going to teach you how to burn shit. You pay attention because I expect you to be the best goddamn shit-burner in the whole United States Army before this war is over."

Long Binh had rows of outhouses near the barracks with a fifty-five-gallon barrel cut in half and stuffed beneath each toilet seat. Under Willie's tutelage, Dougherty pulled each one out using a hook on the end of the metal pole, poured JP4 on the noxious human waste, and then lit the aircraft fuel on fire. The worst part of the job was that the shit-burner had to stir the flaming pools of excrement with the long metal rod. Once the human waste was incinerated, Willie nodded his approval—the signal for Dougherty to shove each ash can crapper back into place.

Sometimes for variety Riker assigned Dougherty to trenching detail. With a tiny spade, he dug narrow trenches around the barracks, placed corrugated metal over the makeshift bunkers that often filled with rainwater, and stacked sandbags on top of them. Latrine duty also included trash detail, which seemed like a holiday in comparison. Once a day, Dougherty requisitioned a three-quarter ton truck from the motor pool and hauled loads of garbage to the dump located just beyond the perimeter of the base. As he threw bags of rubbish into the landfill, Dougherty noticed dozens of Vietnamese kids, as well as some women and older men, picking through the mounds of waste. As he drove away, Dougherty watched a handful of them in the rearview mirror, racing toward the bags of trash he had just deposited in the dump.

The second Saturday night of his fourteen-and-two, while the other men were out drinking their pay, First Sergeant Riker ordered Dougherty to mop the concrete slab floor of the barracks. As he worked his way across the room with a bucket and mop, Dougherty noticed a magazine on the ground beside one of the bunks. He bent down and picked up a recent issue of *Life* magazine. The leading story was about Acapulco, a tropical paradise depicted on the magazine's cover, which showed two attractive ladies in revealing swimwear standing beside a palm tree on a sandy beach. But Dougherty's attention was caught by another headline printed on the left-hand side of the cover in a red font that contrasted with the serene blues and greens of the beach scene: "A Monstrous War," by Robert Sherrod. He flipped through the magazine until he located the article about Vietnam and scanned the piece.

> *Nothing I had read, no photographs I had seen prepared me for the immensity of the American effort. . . .*
>
> *Each American soldier carries six times the firepower he had in World War II. . . .*
>
> *This lavish use of firepower, whether effective or not, contributes to the cost of killing the enemy, which is calculated at $400,000 per soldier—including 75 bombs and 150 artillery shells for each corpse. . . .*
>
> *A colonel in the Vietnamese IV Corps in the Mekong Delta said one day, "I was one of those who told McNamara in 1964 that the war would be over by the end of 1965; I swear I thought it would be."*
>
> *. . . A private in Saigon: "The only thing to do is to kill everybody in the country over five years old."*

Dougherty turned the words over in his mind. A "monstrous war," Sherrod called it. He guessed that made him a monster. In a moment of rage, he tore the magazine in half and thrust it into the trash bag slung over his shoulder. Despite his contempt for the article and his mounting frustration over being grounded, Dougherty vowed Sarkis and Riker would not break him, each humiliating task made bearable by the knowledge that his paperwork was making its way through the system. Another helicopter company would need a crew chief soon enough. It was only a matter of time.

After Riker completed a meticulous inspection of the freshly mopped concrete slab and stormed out of the barracks, Dougherty retrieved a photograph from his footlocker and climbed into his bunk. He studied the dog-eared black and white snapshot of his father at age twenty, standing, hands on hips, on the deck of a ship, a tattoo of an eagle holding an anchor prominent on his right arm. Dougherty knew his father served as a Tin Can Sailor on a Navy destroyer in the South Pacific during World

War II. As hard as he tried, he could never get the man to open up about his time as a gunner's mate 3rd class on the USS *Charrette*. Dougherty assumed those stories were told to other veterans. It was one of the reasons he joined the service, to gain access to that club and hear his father's stories.

A familiar voice pulled Dougherty from his thoughts. "All alone on a Saturday night. That's some pretty sad shit," Saldano said from across the empty barracks.

"Do you have my transfer?" Dougherty replied without turning his head.

"Nah," Saldano said, as he walked closer to the bunk. "About that, maybe the transfer ain't such a hot idea after all. There's a ton of ways it could go south. I have a buddy over in division. I could ring him up. Make them papers disappear. No one would ever know. You could finish your time here and go home."

Dougherty shook his head. "I didn't come over here to burn shit," he said, turning to look his friend in the eyes. "Get me out of here, Sal."

The orderly nodded and started to walk away, but then turned, abruptly. "Almost forgot. You got some mail," Saldano said, handing over a letter he had been tapping against his hand the entire time.

Dougherty froze at the sight of the plain white envelope with no return address and a postmark from Broken Bow, Nebraska.

"Later, Doc," Tony mumbled and departed.

Dougherty stared at the photo of his father in his left hand and the latest correspondence from Broken Bow in his right, debating whether he should throw one or both in his first burning barrel of the morning. Instead, he opened the envelope, which contained two weathered newspaper articles from the *Sherman County Times*. The first article, also from 1952, was titled, "Keith Dougherty Named USPS Man of the Year." It lauded the work his father did as Litchfield's lone postal worker, "receiving, sorting, and delivering mail to local farmers spread far and wide, fulfilling the Postman's oath that 'neither snow nor rain nor heat nor gloom of night stays these couriers from the swift completion of their appointed rounds.'" Dougherty attended the ceremony in Chicago as a young boy; it was one of his earliest and fondest memories. His mother bought him

17

a tiny cardboard suitcase for the trip, which he carried on the train to Chicago. He remembered beaming with pride as he walked alongside the "Man of the Year." Dougherty felt a wave of relief from receiving this positive story. Perhaps the anonymous sender regretted sharing the first article, which, taken by itself, insinuated Keith Dougherty had some nefarious role in the church fire.

Without hesitation Dougherty removed the second article, which was dated less than a year later and titled, "New Postman for Litchfield." The short article implied Keith Dougherty was fired from the post office over some financial impropriety. The piece included a quote from the area's new postmaster who said, "We are going to run a tighter ship around here from now on."

What the hell is going on? Dougherty nearly said aloud to the empty room. He always believed what his father told him: that he left the post office to start his own business and be his own boss. This story suggested he was forced out for stealing money. *Was Keith Dougherty an arsonist and a thief?* Dougherty wondered. All three articles dated back to the early '50s, which suggested the person sending them had been following his father for years. Everything pointed at the mysterious sender having some connection to Broken Bow. As hard as he tried, Dougherty could not recall anyone he knew living in the Sand Hills.

A few days later, as Dougherty crouched behind an outhouse, fishing for a half-barrel of excrement with his metal rod, a figure blocked out the sun. Dougherty looked up from his work, expecting to see Willie or First Sergeant Riker. Instead, the face of his savior appeared.

"You know, you really are good at that," Saldano said. Then the company clerk produced an envelope from his back pocket. "You're free. The transfer orders just came in," Saldano said, extending the papers in Dougherty's direction.

Using the metal pole to raise himself from the ground, then holding it upright in one hand like a shepherd's crook, Dougherty reached for the papers. Saldano snapped the envelope back before his fingers touched it.

"It's the 334th, Bill. They're an armed helicopter company flyin' out of Bien Hoa. Know what that means? No ass and trash. No sight-seeing tours for politicians and celebrities. Combat. Don't be no goddamn John

Wayne out there. Just get your ass out of this fuckin' war alive. That's all that matters. You got that, Doc?" Saldano said. Then he handed his friend the envelope. Dougherty let the metal rod fall to the ground with a *clank*. Willie shook his head in disapproval while continuing to stir a nearby barrel of burning waste. Dougherty shouted in delight and then tried to shake Saldano's hand, who wanted no such contact given his friend's current line of work.

"Thank you, Sal. Thank you," he repeated.

"Don't thank me," Saldano said. "You're the one goin' from burnin' shitters to livin' in one. Better get the hell out of here before 'The Sour Kraut' throws them papers in the fire," he said, referring to First Sergeant Riker.

Saldano watched Dougherty disappear inside the barracks, then shook his head. "Cletis fuckin' Boyer in your fuckin' kitchen," he said, and walked away.

HIGHWAY 1 REVISITED

WITH ORDERS FIRMLY IN HAND, Dougherty raced through the front gate of Long Binh, feeling like a man released from prison. He stuck out his thumb, and within a few minutes an army Jeep pulled to the side of the road. Dougherty threw his rucksack into the back and climbed in. The driver accelerated onto Highway 1, which ran from Long Binh to Bien Hoa, a highway the French had called "The Dreary Road." Facing them was a big white sign with black and red letters that read:

WARNING
YOU ARE ABOUT TO ENTER
ONE OF THE MOST DANGEROUS
COMBAT AREAS IN VIET-NAM

At the bottom of the sign was another message:

A PUBLIC HIGHWAY
PLEASE DRIVE CAREFULLY

As the two men drove in silence, Dougherty recalled his arrival in Vietnam in January of 1967. He remembered how the stench knocked him back as he stepped off the C-141 at Bien Hoa Air Base. It was an unforgettable mix of shit and diesel, intensified by a heat and humidity that made being in Vietnam akin to living in a compost bin.

The Army had shipped Dougherty and a busload of other fresh-faced newbies twenty minutes down Highway 1 to Long Binh. He recalled how the vehicle had chicken wire instead of glass windows. As he was about to step off the bus at Long Binh, he turned and asked the driver, "Why?" "To keep the dinks from tossin' a fuckin' grenade in here," the man said. "Welcome to Vietnam, kid," the driver added, then snapped the door shut the second Doughtery's foot hit the ground.

When the Jeep stopped at the entrance to Bien Hoa, it occurred to Dougherty that he might not recognize the young man who boarded that bus to Long Binh three months ago. He shook off the thought and promptly reported to the 145th Combat Aviation Battalion, where he presented his orders to join the 334th Armed Helicopter Company. A staff sergeant from the Orderly Room showed the new arrival where to shit, shower, and shave, then took him to Supply for his flight gear, including a helmet, flak jacket, safety belt, and bungee cord.

"So what do you want to do?" a portly operations sergeant named Dick Swanson said to him when he reported to the 334th's Ops Room.

"I was a crew chief at the Twelfth Aviation Group," Dougherty replied.

"A crew chief," the Sergeant said without emotion. "Well, lucky you. I've got an aircraft that needs a crew chief. Follow me. There's your chopper," he said a few minutes later, pointing to a Huey on the tarmac. "Get her cleaned up. She's flying tonight."

There on the flight line sat a drab olive-green helicopter with the white diamond of the 145th on the tail and the crossed sabers of the 334th on the front. The Huey's cabin doors were removed so the crew chief and door gunner could add to the ship's firepower with their M-60s.

"We fly three types of Hueys," the Ops Sergeant said. "Hogs, which have twenty-four rockets on each side; Frogs, which have a grenade launcher on the nose and seven rockets on each side; and regular gunships like yours, with two mini-guns and seven rockets per side. In addition to your M-60s, you and the gunner will pack a box of smoke grenades for marking targets and a box of white phosphorous hand grenades or CS gas for starting fires. Some of the guys like to fly with a personal weapon, too. Maybe a side-arm or your M-16. That's up to you," the Sergeant added.

Dougherty peered inside at a floor littered with shell casings. He was about to enter the cabin when a stench hit him. "Aw . . . what the hell is that?" Dougherty said.

"Cubbins," the Ops Sergeant replied. "Former crew chief of this ship who got hit in the ass two nights ago."

Blood and shit were splattered everywhere. Amazingly, the Ops Sergeant informed him, Cubbins survived, but for the first time it occurred to Dougherty that some grunt could be cleaning his bodily fluids out of this helicopter next week.

"Hey, A. B.," the Ops Sergeant shouted to a short, fit black man dressed in fatigues and an army cap, standing beside another Huey in an adjacent revetment. "Can you help the new guy clean up this shit bird?" The enlisted airman nodded. He collected a broom and a couple of buckets filled with water, then carefully made his way over to Dougherty's ship.

"When you get your chopper cleaned up, come get me and I'll check it out," the Ops Sergeant said before leaving to complete the next task on his never-ending list of duties.

"Afton Brown," the man said after setting down his load. Using both hands he adjusted the wire rimmed glasses on his face. "Everyone calls me A. B.," he said, extending his right hand. Dougherty shook it.

"Bill Dougherty. You can call me Doc."

Brown nodded and handed Dougherty the broom. "First we gotta sweep out the brass," he said, referring to the dozens of spent shell casings on the floor. Dougherty climbed into the cabin and began sweeping shells onto the tarmac.

"Where you from, Doc?" Brown said, hands on hips, as he squinted in the sunlight.

"Nebraska," Dougherty replied from inside the ship.

"Never been," Brown said. "You're way up north. Bet you get a lotta corn in the summer and snow in the winter. My people all come from Mississippi. We got a lotta cotton and heat," Brown said and smiled.

The afternoon sun had turned the cabin of the Huey into an oven.

Sweat dripped from Dougherty's forehead as he swept. Brown peeked around the cabin door. "Can I tell you a little story to take our minds off this unpleasant business?"

Dougherty leaned against the broom and nodded, sensing he was about to receive a lecture from the spectacled and garrulous Brown.

"My great grandma was born into slavery," Brown said, as he adjusted his glasses with both hands. "She lived on a plantation 'til she was ten. After Emancipation, her family sharecropped on that same land, as did my grandparents and, for a while, my parents, too. When I was young, my mama and daddy used to bring me and my sister to the fields with them. We'd sit under a shade tree and watch 'em pick cotton. My mother hated it. All day long, she'd say things like, 'Mr. Lincoln freed the slaves nearly hundred years ago and now we puttin' ourselves in chains.' Then she'd throw another handful of cotton into that burlap sack around her neck. That fire could fuel my mother through a full day of pickin'.

"One day, when I was about five or six, my daddy said to me, 'Come over here, boy.' He started showin' me how to pick cotton. My mother marched across that field and pulled me away from him. I never seen her so mad in my life. She stuck her finger out at my father and said, 'This boy will NEVER, EVER pick cotton. Not a single boll. Do you hear me?' Then she put me back under the tree with my sister and my books. Neither of us ever picked a day in our lives. But she made us watch them, out there workin' in the hot sun, fingers bleeding, backs aching. That was our first lesson."

Dougherty passed the broom out to Brown, who handed him one of the buckets of water with a scrub brush in it. Brown picked up the other bucket and joined Dougherty inside the cabin. The two men began scrubbing the dried blood and fecal matter stuck to the floor of the ship.

"Although we didn't pick cotton," Brown continued, "there was an expectation when it came to school. My mama didn't care how long I struggled with a math problem or a book. 'Take all night if you need it,' she'd say before heading off to bed. That was the deal. Education was our field and books were our crop. *From cotton pickers to college graduates in one generation* was my mother's vision. That's a powerful vision for a colored woman to have in Mississippi," Brown said while rinsing his brush.

"I was about to apply to Jackson State when my draft notice arrived. Nearly broke my mama's heart. Before I left for the Army, she took my face in her hands and said, 'Son, you didn't get knocked down the mountain, you just have to go sideways a bit and find a new way to the top. Maybe you even find a better path than the one you was on. But whatever you do, don't you EVER stop climbing. Keep clawin' your way up that mountain until you drop. And when you're lyin' there on the side of that mountain, takin' your last breath, at least you'll know you showed others the way up and got yourself as close to God as you possibly could.'"

Brown stopped brushing and sat back on his haunches. "I've been sending all my pay home. When I get out of the Army, my sister and me are goin' to Jackson State to get our degrees 'cause in this world, if you don't have a plan, someone's gonna make a plan for you. Keep climbin', Doc," Brown said, then he dumped his bucket of dirty water on the flight line and walked away.

Dougherty watched as the last traces of Cubbins evaporated on the hot tarmac.

"Looks pretty good, DOUG . . . HERTY," the Ops Sergeant said, butchering his new crew chief's last name by reading it off a clipboard. "You're flying with Captain Schellenbacher and Mr. Kowalski tonight. Two of the best pilots in the Raiders. They'll show you the ropes. Also, Lowrie said he was your door gunner at the Twelfth, so I'm putting you guys together. You're running out of time," Swanson added. "Go get yourself some grub at the mess hall and come right back to pre-flight the ship. I want you out here when the rest of the crew arrives."

When Dougherty returned to the flight line thirty minutes later, he spotted a familiar figure inside the Huey. Though one might not guess it from the man's short, curly blonde hair and blue eyes, Victor Braveboy Lowrie belonged to the Lumbee Indian Tribe in south central North Carolina. The two men flew together briefly with Colonel Ferguson before Lowrie transferred to the 334th. Since troops often referred to the elusive Viet Cong guerillas by the phonetic alphabet name Victor Charlie, people who knew Lowrie avoided calling him Victor and instead called him Vic or Low.

A butter bar lieutenant fresh from a stateside ROTC program called Lowrie "Chief" once, but that moniker ended with a swift blow to the man's face. When the young officer appeared before Colonel Ferguson and threatened to bring charges against Lowrie, the commanding officer nearly delivered the second blow. But the old man wasn't stupid; he knew when a shitstorm was brewing. So when Lowrie appeared, hat in hand, in the colonel's office that evening and asked for a transfer to the 334th, Ferguson had him airlifted to Bien Hoa the next day. But before Lowrie left for Bien Hoa, the old man handed Saldano paperwork on two transfers; one set of papers for Lowrie's jump to the 334th, the other for the lieutenant. The colonel dealt the snitch to an old poker buddy who commanded a regiment in I Corps near the DMZ. Dougherty loved that story and couldn't wait to tell it to his father. The fact that Lowrie would be his door gunner at the 334th felt like a good omen.

"Billy Dougherty, glad you finally made it," Lowrie said. The solid young man jumped down onto the tarmac and shook Dougherty's hand. "Let me show you a few things. You'll notice some big differences from your time at the Twelfth. We're a gunship company, so it's all about the weapons. See—'First with Guns,'" Lowrie said, patting the slogan on the 334th patch covering his left breast pocket. "The 334th was born from the UTT, which came to Vietnam in '62 as the first Armed Helicopter Company, ever," he said with pride.

"Our mini-guns fire up to six thousand rounds per minute. Keepin' those ammo boxes fed is a big part of our job," Lowrie said, pointing to the containers of ammunition and access doors on the cabin floor of the Huey. "We hang our M-60s with bungee cords rather than mount them to steel supports like they do at the Twelfth," the gunner said, holding his bungee as if it was a trophy trout.

"You're gonna do a lot of shooting here. Lot of shooting. You need to be able to move around and fire. Things get hot, too, so you might have to shoot in all different directions. That's why we take out the door poles," Lowrie said, referring to the same protective metal poles that Colonel Sarkis required in the Twelfth's Hueys.

"What about chest plates?" Dougherty said, noticing his friend wore none.

"Buddy, if a 50-cal round hits you in the chest, it don't matter what you're wearin'," Lowrie said with a grin, then walked away.

"There are four platoons in the 334th," Lowrie continued, as Dougherty hurried to catch up with his friend. "Playboys, Raiders, Dragons, and the Gangbusters. We work on a rotating schedule—two weeks of daytime missions followed by one week of nighttime flying."

Lowrie pulled fourteen rockets from the depot beside the tarmac. He set seven on the ground at the left side of the ship and seven on the right side, then began arming the pods outside his door. To do this, he attached an arming wire with a detonator cap to the rear end of each rocket now resting inside one of the seven tubes. "Be sure you point this part of the cap away from the ship," Lowrie said, pointing to a spot on the back of one of the rockets. "The fins will kick out of their plastic sheath as the rocket leaves the pod and the metal cap will fly back in the direction of the arming wire and stick in your leg if you're not careful. Ever had a fishing hook stuck in your finger?" the gunner said, smiling. "You get the idea."

The Lumbee ducked under the Huey's tail boom and continued his briefing on the left side of the ship. "We have a rule on the flight line. Nobody puts rockets in the pods except the guy sitting at that door. That way if you get hit by a cap, it's nobody's fault but your own." Dougherty understood this was his cue to begin loading rockets. Lowrie nodded his approval and said, "Yes, sir," every time Dougherty turned a rocket in the pod until the arming wire faced away from the ship.

"Tonight, you're in for a real treat—Firefly. It's a nighttime search and destroy mission using three ships: a high ship with a 50-caliber machine gun, a middle ship with a spotlight, and a deck ship. We'll be the low ship tonight. When the light ship draws fire from the ground, we come in and shoot up the area. Mostly, we fly up and down the rivers and canals looking for sampans bringing in supplies from the Ho Chi Minh trail."

Lowrie and Doughtery were joined by the Huey's two pilots, who arrived at the L-shaped, sand-bag-lined revetment and started their own pre-flight inspection of the ship. "The armament system is on. These guns are live," Captain Schellenbacher said.

"Vic, who the fuck pre-flighted this ship?" Mr. Kowalski, the copilot, added. "How come the master switch for the armament is on?"

Dougherty felt his stomach turn upside down. He spent hours cleaning the ship but never once thought to check the weapons system. He assumed the previous crew had turned it off, but assumptions like that could cost lives in a combat zone. Before the situation escalated, Lowrie came to his rescue.

"Hey, get off my crew chief's ass or I'm not gonna let you guys fly in my aircraft."

Schellenbacher laughed. "So now it's *your* ship?"

"It was," the affable young door gunner replied. "I'm handin' it over to the new guy."

"Cherry boy, huh? That explains the live weapons," Warrant Officer Ted Kowalski said, extending his beefy right hand. "What's your name?"

"Dougherty. Bill Dougherty. You can call me Doc."

"Nice to meet you, Doc. Why don't you release the tie down," Kowalski said, then climbed into the left side of the ship.

Dougherty jumped out and untied the nylon strap fastened to the ship's VHF antenna. Then, using a thin metal rod, he unhooked the other end of the strap from the tip of the rotor blade. Memories of Lai Khe haunted Dougherty as he performed the task. He climbed back into the cabin and plugged his helmet's cord into the ship's radio.

"Clear right and rear, sir," Lowrie said.

"Clear left and rear, sir," Dougherty added.

Schellenbacher cranked the engine.

"They're the Firefly tonight," Lowrie said over the intercom, pointing a gloved hand at a nearby Huey with a contraption mounted to the floor on the right side of the ship.

"It's got a cluster of lights on a frame," Lowrie added. "Think of them like the headlights of a car. We'll be flying at treetops with our lights off, so we're putting our lives in their hands. If they blow the light, we're flyin' in the dark."

It occurred to Dougherty that the men in the Firefly ship were also putting their lives in his hands. They would be a big shining target up there—one not firing its own weapons and depending on the high ship and deck ship to cover them.

Dougherty watched as the copilot used a grease pencil to draw three figures in a horizontal line across the plexiglass windshield—a stick figure man, a boat, and a house.

"VC, sampans, and hooches," Lowrie said to Dougherty after switching the radio to a channel private to them. "Every time you get one, call it on the radio and Kowalski will put a tick mark next to the figure. They add 'em up at the end of the night and put it in the report."

The weight of the helicopter loaded down with armament and fuel forced the pilot to lift and slide out of the revetment onto the runway. The Army built the tarmac at Bien Hoa with perforated steel plates, so that aircraft had a firm surface for lift-off and landing, even during the monsoon season. When the ship's skids reached the runway, they clanged against the steel plates as the helicopter settled into position. Moments later, two other Hueys flanked their ship. Beacon lights on the tarmac illuminated the helmeted men in flashes of green and red light.

Next the pilots tested the different radio frequencies. "Two-four, two-two, Fox Mike," Schellenbacher said.

"Two-two, two-four check, Fox Mike," a voice called back.

After a moment of silence, the radio suddenly squawked. "Contact Gallant Ghost on 14.6," a monotone voice said. Kowalski wrote this new information on the windshield with the grease pencil.

"We're headed to Duc Hoa," Schellenbacher announced over the intercom, referring to a free fire zone in the western portion of III Corps.

"Charlie may own the night, but we control the light," Lowrie said to his shipmates.

"Roger that," Mr. Kowalski replied.

"Raider two-four requesting lift-off," Captain Schellenbacher said into his helmet mic.

Dougherty thought his heart might burst through his chest. Then a voice from the tower spoke calmly in his ear, "Cleared for takeoff. Good hunting, Raiders."

The three Hueys lifted into the pitch-black sky.

4

PARADISE LOST

THE RAIDERS FLEW FIREFLY SIX STRAIGHT EVENINGS. In the beam of their light Dougherty witnessed unimaginable sights: human beings ripped apart by gunfire, a water buffalo bursting into chunks of flesh when struck by a rocket, detached limbs floating in the water beside a sinking sampan. After each long night, a driver met the pilots on the flight line and shuttled them back to Honour-Smith Compound in downtown Bien Hoa, where they enjoyed a hot shower and some bacon and eggs while Dougherty and Lowrie remained on the tarmac, cleaning and inspecting the ship. Adrenaline pumped through Dougherty's body as he performed each maintenance task on his checklist. His hands continued to shake as he drank bad coffee in the mess hall. On these mornings, Dougherty considered that perhaps Sarkis and Saldano were right: he should never fly again, just be a straphanger in Vietnam until his tour of duty ended and forget all about this nightmare. Eventually, Dougherty collapsed into his bunk and slept until Lowrie awakened him to pre-flight the ship for another evening of Firefly.

On the sixth and final day of the rotation, Lowrie roused Dougherty from a dream state. In the dream, he and his father walked through a cemetery at night, their path illuminated by an eerie glow emanating from his father's hand. Rabbits materialized among the headstones, and when they did, Dougherty raised a weapon and fired. No matter how fast or evasive the creatures, he never missed, and he heard Keith Dougherty shouting words of encouragement after each shot.

That evening as their Huey zipped along the treetops, something clicked *off* or *on* in Dougherty's mind. He was no longer in Vietnam, firing at Viet Cong guerillas in the jungle. He was back in Nebraska, shooting at jack rabbits illuminated by the spotlight mounted atop his father's stock truck. The young crew chief no longer felt a sense of remorse as he squeezed the trigger on his M-60 aimed at frozen figures in the light. Instead, he heard the voice of Keith Dougherty saying, "Good job, son."

"Grab your helmet and follow me," Lowrie said to Dougherty the next morning after they finished a post-flight inspection of the Huey. With his own helmet wedged between his right arm and side, Lowrie led his friend across the base and out the front gate. Soon, the two enlisted airmen were moving through a sea of people in downtown Bien Hoa, whose French colonial buildings were half obscured by the wooden stalls of vendors. Lowrie turned off the main street and continued down an unmarked alley to a tiny Bohemian art gallery. Once inside, Lowrie took the flight helmet from his shipmate, placed it on the counter in front of a Vietnamese man with thick round glasses and a gray beard, then held his own helmet up for the man to see.

"Like you to paint his the way you did mine. Raider logo on the back," he said, turning his helmet around to reveal the angry little red-bearded, cowboy-hatted, Looney Toon Yosemite Sam firing pistols while riding atop a helicopter. "Put the 334th patch on the front right side and his name on the left. I'll write it for you." Lowrie grabbed a piece of paper and charcoal pencil from a nearby table and carefully wrote *D-O-U-G-H-E-R-T-Y* on it, then handed the paper to the man. "Can you have it ready in an hour?"

"Two," the artist replied, holding up his index and middle fingers, forming what was also the increasingly popular peace sign.

"Good," Lowrie said and set both helmets on the table. He nodded to the Vietnamese man who nodded back, then Lowrie turned and walked out of the shop. Dougherty followed his friend but looked back one last time before exiting. He noticed the gallery owner shaking his head as he looked down at the helmet in his hands.

"We can kill some time over at the Paradise Bar," Lowrie said. "It's a dive just around the corner."

Dougherty's first impression upon entering the dimly lit watering hole was that the Paradise Bar represented a Vietnamese entrepreneur's best stab at an American GI's idea of paradise. Paintings of palm trees, sandy beaches, and voluptuous, bikini-clad ladies covered the walls. Palm frond ceiling fans slowly turned, each slightly out of sync with the other, and none generating much airflow. Drink glasses adorned with colorful paper umbrellas littered the club's Formica tables. Young Vietnamese women in exotic silk dresses with orchids in their sleek black hair chatted up soldiers, while a juke box in the corner of the club played a continuous stream of classics from American stars like Elvis, Nat King Cole, and Frank Sinatra.

Lowrie found an empty vinyl booth in a corner and signaled to the Vietnamese bartender for two beers. A pair of Vietnamese women made their way toward the table, but Lowrie waved them away. A few minutes later, a Vietnamese waiter in a Hawaiian shirt set two cold American beers onto coasters he flicked across the table like a card dealer.

"Could we get some sandwiches?" Lowrie said. The waiter nodded and left.

Lowrie ran his hands through his blond hair as he rested his elbows on the table. "These Firefly rotations are rough," he said and yawned. "It takes you a couple of weeks to recover and then it's time to go, again. How are you settling in?"

Dougherty shrugged his shoulders and took a long sip of his beer. "Not sleeping so good," he said. "I had a strange dream the other day about hunting rabbits with my dad. We used to go out at night in a '55 pickup he bought from the Custer Public Power Company. It has a spotlight mounted on the top and metal racks in the back. I'd stand in the bed of the truck and rest my shotgun on one of those racks while he drove down old farm roads. He'd turn that spotlight on the roof with an arm inside the cab, and it would light up the fields beside the road. For whatever reason, those damn jack rabbits always ran toward that spotlight."

The waiter returned with a plate of sandwiches—ham and cheese on baguettes—that he set on the table between the two men. Lowrie picked one up and started eating while Dougherty continued his story.

"We usually got a dozen or so rabbits every time we went out. Since the cold weather kept them fresh for a while, we'd keep them in the back of the truck until one of us could drive them to the mink farm in Grand Island. They'd buy the furs for a buck a piece. My old man always let me keep the money."

Lowrie was a good listener. Dougherty liked that about him. The Lumbee had grown up in a community of storytellers and instinctively knew when there was more to a story. He waited for his friend to continue.

"It's funny," Dougherty said. "That's the happiest I ever remember him."

"What's so funny about that?" Lowrie replied with a sense that the story had finally arrived at its real point.

"It's funny that me killing something is what made him happy," Dougherty said as he peeled the label off his beer bottle, unable to confess that he now conjured this memory during Firefly.

Lowrie studied Dougherty's face for a few moments. He took a sip of beer, set the bottle down, and crossed his arms. "Sounds a lot like Firefly," the gunner said and slid the plate of sandwiches toward his shipmate. "Maybe you are being visited by the spirits of those rabbits. Or maybe you are being visited by other spirits."

Dougherty picked up a sandwich but left his friend's comment alone.

When he finished eating, Lowrie wiped his mouth and leaned back in the booth. "Did I ever tell you the story of my famous ancestor, Henry Berry Lowrie?"

Dougherty shook his head.

Lowrie leaned forward and rested his clasped hands on the table. When he spoke next, it was in the reverent tone he adopted when telling a well-practiced story.

"Henry Berry Lowrie is a legend in Lumbee folklore. Many whites in our area consider him a criminal, but to my people, he is a hero like Robin Hood.

"His story really begins in 1587, when the British sent more than a hundred settlers to the New World to start an English colony. Their ship landed on the Outer Banks of North Carolina, where they built a settlement they called Roanoke. But the Europeans arrived in the summer and soon realized they didn't have enough food to survive the winter, so the captain and his crew returned to England to get supplies for the colony. When they got home, the sailors discovered England was at war with Spain, which delayed their return to America by three whole years."

Lowrie paused and held up two fingers to the waiter. The break provided Dougherty an opportunity to consider what it must have been like for a small community of European settlers to wait three years in a strange land with no supplies or contact from their home country.

After much fanfare due to an altercation at the bar, the beers finally arrived. Lowrie took a sip of Budweiser and continued his story.

"When the British ship returned to Roanoke three years later, the colony was gone. Disappeared. Some believe the settlers died from disease or starvation, but many believe they moved inland, where they were taken in by Indians, who saved their lives by sharing their food and teaching them the ways of the land.

"Over time, the English settlers were accepted into our tribe. My people believe we are descended from the Cherokee but also those survivors from the Lost Colony. Most Lumbee I know, and many historians, say this is the only explanation for things like my blonde hair and blue eyes and Scottish names like Lowrie within our community."

Lowrie paused for a bathroom break and to let Dougherty digest these additional details of the story.

"For nearly three centuries," Lowrie continued, as he slid back into the booth, "the white man left us alone—probably because our land was so harsh. The European settlers kept pushing west in search of something better. You're okay, you know, until the white man wants what you've got," Lowrie added.

The statement seemed ironic to Dougherty, coming from a blonde-haired, blue-eyed man. But as Lowrie had told him on more than one occasion, "Being Indian is not about the color of your skin: it's a state of mind."

"There is no Lumbee language that survived," Lowrie continued. "For generations, we all spoke English and lived in modern houses. We don't have a reservation or any special status with the government, which explains why I got a draft card and my ass is here," Lowrie added with a slight grin. Dougherty extended his beer bottle, and the two men toasted and drank to Lowrie's shit luck.

"All we really have left of our Indian heritage are the stories," Lowrie said, turning serious again. He paused for a moment to reflect on his last statement. "Maybe that's all any of us has."

"Despite our English roots, we fought against the British during the American Revolution. For years, my ancestors lived peacefully as free men among the whites in North Carolina, probably because of our fair skin and European ways. That all changed by the 1800s, when thousands of African slaves and some Indians were forced to work the tobacco fields for wealthy planters. And that brings us to the story of my famous ancestor.

"Henry Berry Lowrie was born in 1845, which made him a young man during the Civil War. Like me, he had some western features, and his skin was not as dark as most Indians.

"In those days, only whites were allowed to serve in the Army. Since most Negroes were the property of wealthy landowners, the Home Guard rounded up many Indians, including Lumbee, and sent them to the coast to help build Fort Fisher and harvest salt for the Confederate troops. At the same time, whites in Robeson County started accusing Lumbee farmers of stealing their animals so they could get the Lumbee arrested and take their land. One wealthy landowner by the name of James Barnes accused Allen Lowrie's sons of stealing his hogs and threatened to kill them if they ever set foot on his land. Allen's son, Henry, didn't take kindly to that threat. He shot Barnes twice with a shotgun. Barnes eventually died from those wounds, but before he passed, he named Henry Berry Lowrie as his killer. That forced Henry Berry to live on the run in the swamps of Robeson County. Others wanted by the authorities followed Lowrie, including two of his brothers, some other Indians, a couple of runaway slaves, and even a white boy. Together they formed the Lowrie Gang, and Henry Berry was their leader.

"There was an officer in the Home Guard, a big, nasty man by the name of James Brantly Harris, who avoided service in the Confederate Army by volunteering to track down deserters and escaped Union prisoners. Harris aimed to sleep with a beautiful Indian girl who wanted no part of him. That maiden's sweetheart threatened to kill Harris if he touched the girl. Harris was furious when he heard this and set out to kill him, but he ended up shooting the wrong man, who happened to be related to Henry Berry Lowrie. To make matters worse for himself, he arrested and then beat to death the two brothers of that dead Indian man when they were home on leave from Fort Fisher, because he feared they would take his life when they found out he had not only conscripted them, but had shot their brother, too.

"Harris was never brought before a judge for the murder of the three Lumbee brothers. So you can guess what happened next: Lowrie and his gang shot Brantly Harris to death and dumped his body in a well. The Home Guard responded by rounding up several members of the Lowrie family. Some say Henry Berry was watching from the tree line when the Home Guard forced his father and brother to dig their own graves and then executed the two men by firing squad.

"After that, Henry Berry and his gang often raided the community for the food and supplies they needed to survive in the swamps, but they also took their revenge on the whites in the community who had wronged them in the past.

"Shortly after the war, Henry Berry got married, and the Home Guard used the opportunity to trap him. They arrested Lowrie at his wedding for the murder of James Barnes and took him to the Columbus County jail, thirty miles away in Whiteville. To this day, no one knows how he did it, but Lowrie escaped from Whiteville—the first man ever to do that.

"After his escape, Henry Berry resumed his life on the run until he and his men robbed and killed the local sheriff in his home. The man was known for his ruthless treatment of Indians and Negroes, but Henry Berry knew that he and his gang had probably crossed a line. Federal troops were called in, and Henry Berry became the most wanted man in North Carolina.

"Perhaps sensing the end was near, the Lowrie Gang pulled one final heist. They robbed the largest merchant in Lumberton in broad daylight and made off with twenty-two thousand dollars, which was a fortune in those days. Huge bounties were placed on the heads of each gang member and, one-by-one, they were hunted and killed for the reward money. But they never got Henry Berry Lowrie."

Lowrie opened his clasped hands to signify his ancestor vanishing like a ghost.

Dougherty sat fully upright in the vinyl booth and placed both hands on the table. "But what happened to Lowrie?" he said, demanding a better ending to the story.

Lowrie shrugged his shoulders. "They couldn't catch him and never did find his body. Some say he slipped out of town dressed as a soldier and lived a long, full life in another town. Others believe he had himself and the money nailed in a coffin with air holes that was loaded onto a train bound for other parts. And some believe he died in the swamps when his gun accidentally discharged and blew his brains out. Those folks say Henry Berry's friends diverted a small stream and buried him beneath the riverbed, then let the stream flow back over his body for all of time."

"Do you think he lived?" Dougherty demanded.

"I don't know," Lowrie replied. "For years after that people in Robeson County claimed to see Henry Berry from a distance at a funeral or in the window of a passing train. I believe he lives on in the Lumbee mind, providing hope and pride to my people."

The Vietnamese waiter approached their table, but Lowrie waved him away. "The more important question is do you think Henry Berry and his gang were criminals or heroes?"

When Dougherty hesitated to reply, Lowrie gave his own answer. "I believe their actions were justified, but the question I keep asking myself when I'm up in that Huey is am I Henry Berry Lowrie in this story or someone sent to kill him?"

Lowrie stood, counted out some script, and laid it on the table to cover the sandwiches and beer. He nodded to the bartender drying glasses with a towel draped over his shoulder. The Vietnamese man nodded back. "Time to get your helmet," Lowrie said.

On their way back to the gallery, the two men scanned their route for potential danger; every motorcycle and pedestrian a possible threat. "I'm goin' on R&R next week with Jackson," Lowrie said. "He's a crew chief who usually flies with Jester and Thompson. Jackson's a good guy—also from North Carolina. We're going to Japan. This will probably be the only chance I get. After the war, I'm headed back to Robeson County, and that's where they'll bury me.

"Word in Ops is the platoon will be going out on temporary duty next week. Every so often, they send us out in the field to support some mission. Shell and Ski will be taking the Huey to Saigon for its annual maintenance inspection and some in-country R&R. That means they'll probably put you in Jackson's spot while I'm gone. Captain Jester's got a sense of humor—maybe a little too wild for my taste—but he's a decent pilot and a pretty good guy. His gunner is the one you have to watch out for. Chuck Coffey. He was a ground pounder before coming to the 334th. Served in the 101st Airborne Division under Captain Carpenter. They were on patrol in the Central Highlands, got cut off, and ran into a full NVA Battalion. It was so bad, Carpenter had to call in a napalm strike on his own position. Coffey said he could hear people speaking in Vietnamese just before the napalm dropped. A bunch of guys in Coffey's unit got burned pretty bad. Chuck took a bullet in the arm. Somehow, most of the company made it out of there alive. After he got patched up, Coffey transferred to the 334th."

Lowrie stopped outside the artist's shop. He paused for a moment to choose his words carefully. "Coffey's a hell of a gunner, but he's a little wild. Some guys tell me he smokes weed and likes to booze it up, too. You gotta watch him, or that guy will get you killed." Lowrie waited until Dougherty nodded, then walked through the door. The shop owner looked up from his work-in-progress—a dark jungle landscape painting. When he saw the two GIs, he picked up the flight helmet and tossed it to Lowrie, who quickly examined the front and back, then nodded his approval.

"There," Lowrie said, handing the helmet to Dougherty. "Now you're officially a Raider."

There was something about seeing his name on the helmet that made Dougherty feel better. For the first time in Vietnam, he felt like he belonged—like he was part of a family that cared who he was. He was Dougherty of the Raiders from the 334th, the first armed helicopter company ever. And maybe if his chopper crashed in the jungle—long after his flesh and fatigues rotted away in the brutal tropical climate—they would find that helmet on his skull and know it was William Dougherty of Litchfield, Nebraska, who had died a hero. It would finally prove to his father that he was a man, worthy of his respect, and that was something Dougherty could draw on the next time his Huey hovered above the jungle in the dead of night while he held tightly to the spotlight that begged every enemy with a weapon to take their best shot.

5

THE TIGER MAN OF NEBRASKA

THE MORNING AFTER LOWRIE AND JACKSON LEFT FOR R&R in Japan, Dougherty watched from the flight line as Captain Schellenbacher and Mr. Kowalski climbed into his Huey, which was parked inside the sandbag-lined revetment. Within a few minutes, the rotor blades slowly started turning. Kowalski waved to Dougherty as the ship lifted off; then the helicopter turned and climbed into the sky for the short flight to Saigon.

As Lowrie had predicted, Ops assigned Dougherty to fly with Captain Jester and his crew during the temporary duty (TDY). The itinerant crew chief wandered down the flight line until he found Jester's ship, which had the name *The Joker's Wild* and an image of a smiling, white-faced joker painted on the front. Chuck Coffey sat in the door frame of the Huey holding his M-60, staring at the ground as if looking for enemy targets.

"Hey," Dougherty said, not wanting to startle the volatile door gunner. "What's up?"

"Just waitin' for you to get your ass to the flight line so we can get this show on the road," Coffey barked. "What's that you got?" the gunner asked, pointing at the nondescript box Dougherty carried.

"C-rats. Ops asked me to bring them out to the ship."

"Well open that motherfucker up," Coffey ordered. "Could be some good shit in there."

Dougherty set his flight gear and duffle on the floor of the Huey and proceeded to tear open the cardboard box. He removed one of the cans and tossed it to Coffey. The gunner stared at the tin as if it were a hypnotist's watch. "Spaghetti with meatballs," Coffey said, a smile forming across his lips. "Jackpot."

Coffey slid the case of C-rations into the center of the Huey's floor and started digging through it. In the span of a few minutes, the gunner had gone from a dark depression to a manic high. As Dougherty soon learned, Coffey's moods swung like a pendulum.

"Some of this shit is edible . . . barely, but some of the meals like Ham and Motherfuckers or Beans and Baby Dicks are just plain goddamn awful," Coffey said with a look of disgust. A case of C-rats contained twenty-four meals. With four men on the ship eating three meals per day, a case held enough food for two days. But no one working on a gunship in Vietnam had time for three meals a day, which meant the crew could eat their favorite C-rats and skip the worst.

"We keep some A-1 steak sauce and Heinz 57 on the chopper to doctor this shit up," Coffey said. He dumped all the cans on the floor of the Huey and proceeded to sort them into piles of *edible, barely edible,* and *goddamn awful.*

While in Operations that morning, Dougherty received word from Swanson that the Raiders would be providing fire support for a special forces operation to the east. The Gangbusters planned to insert small "Roadrunner" teams of South Vietnamese soldiers in civilian clothes to gather intel on enemy locations in the area. Those teams would then rendezvous at pre-arranged LZs a day or two later for extraction. Once the Roadrunner teams were out, units of US Special Forces would be inserted to engage the enemy. The Raider gunships would be on hand in case any of the follow-up teams needed more firepower.

Finally, the pilots arrived, stowed their gear, and completed their pre-flight inspection of the Huey. Captain Jessy Jester was the wild-eyed, red-haired son of a preacher from Nashville, Tennessee. His slight body seemed insufficient to contain his oversized personality. As members of the second platoon in the 334th, the eight Raider pilots each had a call sign that started with a two and ended with a number between one and eight, except Jester, whose call sign was 6-9, even though there was not a sixth platoon in the 334th and the Raiders did not have a ninth Huey.

Warrant Officer Steve Thompson flew as Jester's peter pilot and was, perhaps, the most unassuming aviator in all of III Corps. The running joke in the company was that Mr. Thompson's own family, including his wife, couldn't remember who he was. He played the straight man to Jester and Coffey's lunacy. But Thompson was so straightlaced and unassuming that in the presence of these two outrageous individuals he himself became a comical figure. Dougherty wondered what role Jackson played in all this madness. If he was friends with Lowrie, then Dougherty suspected the quiet black crew chief from Durham served as a calming influence for this ship of fools.

Once Dougherty released the tie-down strap and returned to his seat, Jester's thick southern drawl came over the ship's intercom.

"Good afternoon, ladies and gentlemen. This is Raider 6-9. I'll be your Captain for this short flight to Gookville. There's a slight chance of gunfire, today. We'll be flyin' at a thousand feet to avoid that. Please be sure your monkey belt is securely fastened. Once we get airborne, Mr. Thompson will be comin' through the aircraft with some refreshments. And folks, please feel free to move about the cabin if Charlie is lightin' up our asses."

Dougherty noticed a grin on Coffey's face beneath his dark visor as Jester maneuvered the Huey out of its berm and joined the large formation of helicopters on the flight line. Moments later, a dozen Hueys from the Raiders and Gangbusters lifted into the sky. The formation veered east and flew directly above Highway 2, the country's main artery to the coast. Dougherty watched as Coffey slid some of the *goddamn awful* C-rats over to his open door. He grabbed a can, selected a target on the road below, and tossed the small metal container at a car on the highway. After Coffey dropped a few more tins on unsuspecting locals, Jester got wise.

"Hey, Coffey, givin' those C-rats to the enemy is torture, and that's against the Geneva Convention."

Coffey grinned. "Roger that, sir. No more C-rats out the door," the gunner said as he half-heartedly released one final can toward a lone Vietnamese bicyclist on the road below.

In that moment, Dougherty recalled how Colonel Ferguson would land the Huey in a remote village and have his crew give away C-rations and chocolate bars to the Vietnamese kids who invariably swarmed their ship. He remembered gently tossing each can or candy bar to the sea of outstretched little arms while the children called out, "Chop, chop, GI. Chop, chop."

After twenty minutes, Jester and the other pilots changed course and flew due north. With no responsibility for piloting the ship and no enemy engagement, Dougherty found the steady *wump, wump, wump* of the rotors calming. He stared over the barrel of his M-60 at the verdant fields dotted with straw-hatted peasants working the land. Vietnam's patchwork of square and rectangular plots often reminded Dougherty of Nebraska. Farmers were farmers anywhere in the world, he reckoned. These people had a growing season and needed to plant and harvest a crop even if there was a war in their country. Failure to do so meant their families might not have enough food to eat or money to send their kids to school.

Chatter on the radio interrupted Dougherty's thoughts as the Hueys arrived at their destination. Like a flock of geese touching down on water, the V-shaped formation of helicopters descended onto a large grassy field beside a military outpost known as the Blackhorse Base Camp.

That evening, the pilots laagered their Hueys in a semi-circular defensive position with their cannons and miniguns all pointed toward the tree line. If the enemy attacked by ground, the pilots could return fire with their weapons, while crew chiefs and door gunners joined in with their M-60s. As the whiskey-colored sun descended in the west, Dougherty and a few other enlisted airmen dug a pit. They built a small fire, not for heat or light, but for the simple pleasure of sitting around a flame in the company of friends.

"Man, we're really in the bush," A. B. said, looking nervously at the jungle.

"I'm ready for some real bush, but you gotta be a pilot to get you some of that," PFC Louie Mancuso said. Mancuso's family owned a door factory in New Brunswick, New Jersey, which inspired the Italian-American gunner to stencil "MAKE DOORS NOT WAR!" on the back of his flight helmet.

"Look at 'em over there," A. B. said in his Mississippi drawl, referring to the pilots gathered in a circle near the Hueys. The young warrant officers laughed as they passed around a flask and occasionally slapped each other on the back or chest. "Just like a buncha frat boys at Ole Miss," he added.

"You think this is the bush?" Coffey said. "This is like a fuckin' Howard Johnson compared to the bush. Captain Carpenter used to march our asses into jungle so thick you couldn't see your dick while takin' a piss. There was shit out there you baby-sans never dreamed of. Booby traps like the Malay Whip. Charlie hangs a log from two trees with a rope and pulls that motherfucker back so it's loaded like a sling-shot. When some poor grunt trips the wire, a log comes flyin' out of the jungle and everyone gets knocked down like bowling pins."

The men gathered around the fire remained silent, their faces grim.

Coffey took a quick drag on his cigarette. "I seen more than one grunt on patrol step on a toe popper. It's a little mine Charlie buries in the dirt that's got just enough charge to blow the toes off your foot. An-other guy in my platoon got waxed by a tree mine. The gooks placed it in a tree at eye level right beside the trail. When our boy tripped the wire, it blew his fuckin' head off."

"Shit," Mancuso said.

"Yeah," Coffey replied, nodding, "Guess who had to put his head in the motherfuckin' bag?"

Coffey paused for a moment, but before anyone could say a word, he continued. "As bad as all that shit was, this jungle is the real enemy. Blood-suckin' leeches, bugs you ain't never seen before, spiders the size of your fist, and those goddamned snakes slithering around you at night. There are even fuckin' tigers out in the bush. A buddy of mine was on point one night when he shot one with his M-16 a second before it pounced on him."

Coffey took a long drag on his cigarette and stared down into the pit. It was an opportunity for someone to do something.

"Hey, Coffey, you're kinda bringin' us down here," Mancuso said, poking the tiny fire with a stick. "Doc, why don't you tell us a story? We already heard these guys' stories a hundred times."

CHAPTER 5

Dougherty looked into the faces of the men seated around him, then nodded. Coffey's tiger tale had brought a story to mind.

"I grew up in Litchfield. It's a town of about three hundred in the middle of Nebraska," Dougherty said. "Not much goin' on there, mainly farming. They got the cornfields planted right up to the edge of town. There's a lumberyard, train stop, one filling station, and a few stores on Main Street. My grandma owns the only restaurant in town—Emma's Café."

"What's Emma's specialty?" A. B. said, licking his lips.

"Well, every day she offers the hot roast beef sandwich covered in gravy. People seem to like that. But my personal favorite is her ham and beans. She takes two slices of bread and puts a scoop of mashed potatoes on there, then covers the whole thing in ham and beans. She does a mean peach cobbler, too."

The men around the fire moaned as they imagined Emma's cooking. Mancuso handed Dougherty a flask. He took a swig of whiskey, then passed it to Brown.

"When Coffey mentioned tigers, it made me think of the Old Settlers Picnic," Dougherty continued. "Every year, Litchfield holds the picnic the week of the Fourth of July. There are rides and games and different contests for the best pie or the biggest ear of corn. For years, the star of the show was always John Pesek. He was a professional wrestler in the '30s and '40s, back when they really wrestled and the outcome wasn't fixed. His nickname was the 'Tiger Man of Nebraska.'"

"Why'd they call him that?" Mancuso asked.

"Because he was so quick in the ring and incredibly strong," Dougherty replied. "Pesek's a legend in Nebraska—my dad claims to have seen him bend a horseshoe straight with his bare hands. He'd take on locals at the picnic, offering a hundred bucks for anyone who could last two rounds in the ring with him.

"Pesek has a son, Jack, who is bigger than his old man and a good athlete, too. Jack played football for the Cornhuskers in the '50s. He was drafted by the Los Angeles Rams but decided to follow in his father's footsteps and became a pro wrestler, instead. He travels all over the world. Sometimes he's even on *Heavyweight Wrestling*," Dougherty said, referring to the popular Saturday night television spectacle.

"I seen him," Mancuso said. "I seen Jack Pesek on TV."

Dougherty nodded. "When the Tiger Man retired for good, Jack continued the wrestling tradition at the Old Settlers Picnic. But instead of taking on locals, Jack decided to bring in a bunch of big-name wrestlers. This was about four years ago—the summer before my senior year in high school.

"Since my dad grew up playing sports with Jack, we know the Pesek family pretty good. That's why I got asked to drive the wrestlers around. There were three matches that night—two warm-up bouts and then the championship match between Jack and Otto Von Krupp.

"Von Krupp is a big barrel-chested guy with a shaved head and a pencil thin mustache. In the ring, he plays a Nazi villain. People in town had seen him on TV, and there was a lot of buzz about the match."

The men around the fire murmured their recognition of Von Krupp's name.

"They had a dressing room set up for the wrestlers in the basement of our high school, across town from the ring. It was my job to drive them back and forth.

"Before the matches, the wrestlers were in their dressing room, and I was sitting on a wall outside when Von Krupp came out to talk with me. He asked me my name and some basic questions about life in Litchfield. Very soft-spoken guy. He had his son with him. Just a young kid, maybe ten years old. Otto slipped me a few bills and asked me to take his son to the concession stand for something to eat.

"When we got down the hill to the carnival, two local kids came running up to the boy and demanded to know if Von Krupp was his father. Otto's kid kept saying no, but these brats wouldn't stop pestering him. They asked him if he was sure Von Krupp wasn't his daddy, and he told them his last name was Simon. They called him a liar, so I pushed them away and told 'em to get lost.

"When we got back to the school an hour later, the mayor was there—guy named Rudy Bacchus. He had helped Jack organize the matches and told me to go in and see if the wrestlers needed some beer or anything. So I walked down the stairs and into the dressing room below the stage in the school's auditorium. I remember pulling back the bed sheet curtain they had set up and seeing them in their costumes—guys who were about to fight each other, laughing and joking. A couple of the wrestlers spotted me at the door and one of them shouted something like, 'Hey, you aren't supposed to be in here. Get the hell out of here.' I thought they were going to come after me and tear me apart.

"I told them I was sent to see if they wanted some beer or soda. One of the other wrestlers shouted, 'No, now get your ass out of here,' so I turned and left. But when I got outside, Von Krupp came running out after me. He apologized for the other guys yelling at me and told me there was some rule about only wrestlers bein' allowed in the dressing room before the match. Said he was sorry, but those were just the rules.

"Later that evening, I drove Von Krupp and his son down to the field for the final match. I hardly recognized him. He had a German uniform on over his wrestling gear and seemed to be getting into his character. He spoke with a German accent and acted like the Fuhrer.

"When we got to the football field, it was packed, and of course people had been drinking all day. Everyone booed and hissed when Von Krupp climbed through the ropes. He walked defiantly around the ring, sizing up the audience, dismissing them with a nod of his head. A few times he even made the Nazi salute, which really riled up the crowd. They shouted insults at Von Krupp whenever he tried to bite Jack or jab his eyes, and they cheered like crazy every time Pesek got in a good hit. When Jack finally pinned Von Krupp, a bunch of people rushed the ring and lifted Pesek into the air. The referee helped Otto off the mat and over to the ropes where I was waiting. Mayor Bacchus and I led him through the crowd to the car. I remember having to push away some of the drunk locals who were ready to take on Von Krupp themselves.

"I opened the back door and Otto climbed in beside his son, who had waited in the car during the match.

"The boy asked him, 'Are you ok, daddy?'

"'I'm fine,' Otto told him. 'We were just pretending to fight.'

"The boy nodded and then stared silently out the window while I drove them back to the school.

"After slowly getting out of the car, Von Krupp shook my hand, then limped down the stairs to the dressing room with the boy at his side.

Mayor Bacchus paid me a few bucks and sent me on my way, so I never got to see Otto or his son again. I guess they slipped out of town during the night. For days after that, I couldn't stop thinking about them doing that same act night after night in a different town. The funny thing was . . . some of the wrestlers who played good guys in the ring that day were real assholes, and Von Krupp, who was supposed to be the villain, was probably the nicest one of the bunch."

The men stared at the flickering flame, processing the final details of Dougherty's story, until the platoon leader ordered them to put out the fire and get some shut eye.

The next morning, flight crews armed and fueled their Hueys while the pilots downed one last cup of coffee during the morning briefing. Finally, Jester and Thompson arrived at the ship.

"Boys," Captain Jester said in his southern drawl. "Today, we'll be flyin' cover for C-130s spraying the jungle with some shit called Agent Orange. Don't ask me why the hell they call it Agent Orange. It's a weed killer, and we all know how Charlie likes to hide in the weeds."

Dougherty and Coffey climbed aboard as Jester and Thompson buckled into their seats. Jester fired the igniters, and the rotors slowly started turning. After a few minutes, the pilot attempted lift-off, but the chopper struggled as if held to the ground by an invisible chain.

"Fellas, with all the weight from the armament and fuel plus the heat and humidity, I'm havin' a hard time reaching transitional lift," Jester said, referring to the point where the ship's rotor blades quit pushing air and started flying like a fixed wing.

"Doc, try dumpin' some fuel," the pilot said.

Dougherty jumped out of the Huey and opened a valve beside his door that drained JP4 out through a collection of tubes on the belly of the ship; the pungent odor of jet fuel dizzying in the morning heat. After a few minutes, he closed the valve and climbed back into his seat. Raider 6-9 attempted a second lift-off but to no avail.

"Try it again," Jester said, and Dougherty dumped some more fuel from the tank. The Huey fared slightly better on their third attempt, as if the invisible chain had been let out a bit, but still, *The Joker's Wild* could not reach transitional lift.

For whatever reason, the other armed helicopter in the Light Fire Team avoided the pitfall and hovered nearby. "Son of a bitch," Jester said, looking around the cockpit for an answer. Then the pilot noticed a red windsock mounted to a red-and-white-striped pole beside the runway, the tail of the cone barely moving, suggesting a headwind of only five to ten knots.

"Why don't you boys jump out for a second," Jester said over the ship's intercom. Dougherty and Coffey hopped down onto the tarmac, although they remained connected to the ship by their safety belts. Jester advanced the Huey down the runway, a couple of feet off the ground. The two enlisted airmen walked alongside the helicopter. After ten yards, the ship started going a little faster, so Dougherty and Coffey picked up their pace. After another twenty yards, the two men jogged beside the chopper, to avoid being dragged by their monkey belts. As Jester approached the end of the runway, the men ran at full speed alongside the aircraft. The Huey continued toward a chain link fence with rolls of barbed wire on top that lined the perimeter of the base. Beyond the fence lay a steep hill the Army had cleared of vegetation to create an open buffer zone between the base and the jungle.

At the last moment, Dougherty and Coffey jumped onto the skids, which scraped across the concertina wire. Upon clearing the fence, the ship dropped fifty feet into the valley, the Huey's rotors creating a storm of dust and debris so thick the men could no longer see through the ship's Plexiglass windshield. Certain they were about to crash, Dougherty closed his eyes and prepared for impact. But in that moment, when Raider 6-9 and his crew should have tumbled to the earth, the Huey shuddered and then lifted into the hot air.

"We made it. We made it," Jester shouted over the radio. Coffey let out a loud *Woooh* of delight.

Dougherty leaned back in his seat and breathed a sigh of relief as sweat rolled down his face—the air gradually becoming cooler as their ship climbed higher.

"I believe we just made aviation history, Mr. Thompson," Jester said.

"Roger that, 6-9," the straight man deadpanned as Jester raced after the other Huey in his Light Fire Team.

Soon, the first C-130 arrived at the designated coordinates. The two Huey gunships flew side by side, shooting up the jungle and expending some of their rockets to see if anyone on the ground returned fire. Following the all clear, the C-130, which flew much faster than the Hueys, passed between the two helicopters, releasing its payload of Agent Orange.

Dougherty felt the spray entering through his open door, misting his body as the herbicide drifted to the ground. Once the ship completed its run, Dougherty used a gun bag to wipe the beads of moisture from his helmet's visor; a chemical aftertaste lingering on his lips and tongue.

After several more sprayings, the last C-130 headed home, and the Raiders returned to Blackhorse.

During the first few days of TDY, the Roadrunner insertions and extractions proved uneventful, so the Raider gunships continued to support herbicide spraying. On the fourth morning, while Dougherty and Coffey inspected the Huey and its weapon systems, Jester and Thompson hustled out to the flight line.

"Boys, one of the special forces teams is pinned down in some dense jungle a few klicks to the north. Gangbusters dumped 'em right on top of some VC and they had to high-tail it out of there. Now they're stuck out there in the boonies. We gotta go find 'em."

Dougherty learned an important lesson on his first morning at Blackhorse. There are only two ways to lighten a gunship: reduce the armament or reduce the fuel. Reducing armament could cost lives. Reducing fuel simply meant the pilot had to refuel more often, which also provided the gunner and crew chief with opportunities to re-arm the ship. The previous evening, Dougherty only filled about a third of the Huey's fuel tank. The crew of *The Joker's Wild* climbed aboard, and in no time, the chopper lifted off.

Fifteen minutes into the search, the Raiders still had not located the friendlies or a place for the slicks to land and rescue them. The Raider platoon leader called a nearby FAC plane and requested F-4s drop some napalm to burn off an area for the landing and extraction. Jester circled a safe distance from the strike zone. Ten minutes later, two jets streaked across the sky and released their canisters.

"Holy hell," Jester said over the intercom, as the jungle in front of their hovering Huey erupted in flames.

Jester radioed the FAC plane, whose pilot confirmed the F-4s had finished their business. "Ok, we're goin' in to try and find 'em," Jester said, as he maneuvered their Huey toward the jungle canopy.

Out of the corner of his eye, Dougherty noticed the tiny silhouette of a plane on the horizon, banking around to the right. "Sir, that jet looks like he's going to make another run," Dougherty said to the aircraft commander through the intercom.

Captain Jester radioed the FAC plane to ask, again, if the F-4s were finished. The FAC plane confirmed they were in fact done and returning to base.

"Ok, keep a sharp eye on the ground, boys. We need to get these fellas out," Jester said. The pilot hovered above the dense triple-canopy jungle, as Dougherty scoured the sea of trees for any sign of the trapped men. Just then, he heard a thunderous *WUM, WUM* and looked up in time to see the underbelly of a jet streaking past their helicopter. In that instant, two five-hundred-pound napalm canisters dropped from beneath the wing of the aircraft and tumbled, as if in slow motion, toward their Huey.

They're coming through the ship, Dougherty thought to himself, but the canisters passed by his open door and descended toward the earth below.

With no time to warn the others, Dougherty grabbed his seat and let out a loud *Ahhhhh* over the ship's radio. An instant later, a fireball lifted their Huey from behind. The heat from the napalm singed the hair on the crew chief's arms and warmed the skin on his face beneath his flight helmet. Dougherty expected the blast to dump the ship upside down or send it spiraling out of control or, at the very least, cook off the rockets in the pods and blast the Huey into an even bigger ball of fire. For what seemed an eternity, the sky and earth disappeared as their ship floated through a cloud of intense heat and smoke.

A moment later, the radio erupted. The other Huey pilots in the area cried out, "6-9, 6-9, are you ok? 6-9, are you ok?" There was a long silence and Dougherty wondered if his pilot had, in fact, perished in the blast, and their ship was simply moving forward on its own inertia.

Then a familiar voice broke the agonizing silence. "Rahdger, Dahdger," Jester said in his slow southern drawl.

Napalm burned at up to thirty-six hundred degrees Fahrenheit. Coffey summed it up the best with his simple statement, "That shit will melt steel." The flames from a Napalm strike also generated a deadly concentration of carbon monoxide. If the heat didn't kill you, the CO would. It was a miracle they had survived.

Before the crew of *The Joker's Wild* could process their incredible luck at surviving the close call, the Special Forces team appeared in the newly charred clearing. Two slicks from the Gangbusters immediately dropped down to retrieve the soldiers running toward their ships.

"There's one more," someone shouted over the radio, "and he's got company." Dougherty watched as a single soldier emerged from the tree line into the clearing. The lone man, who trailed his teammates by at least fifty yards, ran toward the makeshift LZ as puffs of gunfire appeared at the far edge of the jungle. One of the Raider gunships released a salvo of rockets in the vicinity of the gunfire, but moments later a handful of enemy soldiers emerged in the clearing, unscathed, and continued firing.

"Hold up. They're too close to our man for rockets," the platoon leader said over the radio.

Without hesitation, Jester banked their Huey so that Coffey's door now faced the VC pursuers. Dougherty watched as the door gunner blasted away, a stream of spent brass shell casings spinning away from his weapon and bouncing off the floor of the cabin. Coffey maintained his intense line of fire on the exposed enemy soldiers now unable to retreat into the tree line and falling, one by one. Finally, the fleeing man arrived at the LZ and was instantly pulled aboard one of the slicks by a multitude of arms that reached out to receive him. Seconds later both choppers lifted into the air.

After the rescue team landed at Blackhorse, a big black Special Forces Captain with ammo belts strapped diagonally across his chest jogged up to *The Joker's Wild*. He was the last man out; the man Coffey had saved.

"I'd like to know who did that shooting up there."

Dougherty nodded toward Coffey, who was intently breaking down his weapon.

"You're one hell of a shot, soldier," the Green Beret Captain said to Coffey's back.

"I learned a few things in The Deuce," Coffey replied, referring to his previous assignment with the 502nd Parachute Infantry Regiment in the 2nd Battalion of the 101st Airborne Division.

"A Screamin' Eagle saved my ass?" the captain said in disbelief.

Coffey turned to face the man and smiled.

"Who'd you serve with, soldier?" the Green Beret said.

"Captain Carpenter in Charlie Company, sir," Coffey replied.

"I'll be damned. How's old Stanley Bill doin'?"

"Called in a napalm strike on the company last year. That's when I decided to try something new," Coffey said and grinned.

"I heard about that. Operation Hawthorne."

During that operation the 502nd had run into the 24th Regiment of the NVA near Dok To.

"Napalm strike on his own men sounds just like Carpenter," the Green Beret continued. "I played ball against him when he was All-American at the Academy. He used to hit his teammates harder than the other team."

Both men laughed.

"Listen, Coffey," the Captain said, reading Chuck's last name from the tag on his fatigues. "It's my lucky day you were up there. Thanks," he said, extending his big black hand. Coffey stared at the man for a moment, then accepted the handshake.

"Just doin' my job, sir," Coffey said.

"Well, you did one hell of a job today. Keep up the good work, Sergeant," the captain said. "I'll be sure to write this up for your company commander," he added, then jogged off to join his men.

Koons, a PFC from Selma, Alabama, who served as a door gunner in one of the Gangbuster slicks, walked up to Coffey after the officer departed. "Were you shootin' at the gooks, Coffey, or the niggah?" Koons said and chuckled.

Coffey ignored the comment and resumed cleaning his weapon.

"Why was you wastin' yah bullets on savin' a niggah, Coffey?" Koons said. "Shoulda' let them gooks have him, and then you could have shot the whole lot and saved us some bullets."

Dougherty watched the exchange nervously as he wiped down his own gun barrel. Coffey continued to ignore the man and remained focused on cleaning his weapon.

"You could've saved Uncle Sam some money by not savin' the—"

Before the man could finish his sentence, Coffey spun around, his arm shot out like a viper, and snatched Koons by the throat.

"I was shootin' at the gooks, Koons." Coffey said, tightening his grip on the man's windpipe. "I never miss what I'm shootin' at. You got that?"

Koons tried to nod but Coffey's grip was too tight.

"One of these days it might be your sorry ass out there runnin' from the gooks, and as much as it would pain me to save a piece of white trash like yourself, I would shoot at the gooks chasin' you. Got that, Koons? I never miss what I'm shootin' at."

Dougherty feared Coffey might kill the man and was about to intervene when the gunner released his grip on the man's neck. Koons stumbled backward, clutching his throat.

"You crazy," Koons said in a hoarse whisper. "Fuckin' crazy, Coffey," he said backing further away from the gunner. Coffey took one quick step toward the man, who turned and ran.

TDY was over. It was time to go back to Bien Hoa.

6

SOUL OF THE SAMURAI

OPERATIONS GAVE THE RAIDERS A DAY OFF after returning from Blackhorse. As Dougherty lay on his bunk, studying the article about his father's ouster from the post office, Lowrie walked into the barracks carrying a long, narrow cloth bag with Japanese characters printed on it. The gunner reached into the ornate bag and removed a samurai sword, which he handed to his friend for examination.

Dougherty drew the curved steel blade from its scabbard and let out a whistle.

"It's called a katana," Lowrie said. "The larger of the two blades all samurai warriors carried."

"Your new personal weapon?" Dougherty asked.

"It would be a more honorable choice," the gunner replied. "A katana is considered sacred, the *soul of the samurai.*"

Dougherty stood and held the sword's long handle with two hands as he imagined a samurai warrior might.

"I got you something, too," Lowrie said. He reached into the silk bag a second time and removed a twelve-gauge shotgun. "Got it from the Army PX in Tokyo. Pump action. Holds six shells. Your personal weapon for the Huey," he said, handing the shotgun to his shipmate.

Dougherty returned the sword to its sheath and laid it on his bunk so he could receive the firearm from Lowrie. "Thanks," he said, aiming the gun at an imaginary target across the empty barracks.

"No need to thank me. It's really for both of us," Lowrie replied. "If you're using it then you're probably saving my ass," he added and smiled. "Let's take a walk. And bring the shotgun."

"How was R&R?" Dougherty said, as the two men plodded along the dusty road leading from the barracks to Maintenance.

"Interesting. Jackson and I visited the Tokyo National Museum on our first day and saw a collection of samurai swords and body armor. This stuff was hundreds of years old. There was an old man working in the museum who told us all about the samurai. He suggested we take the train up to Kukonodate in the Northeastern part of Japan, to see some houses that belonged to samurai families. We rode the train all night from Tokyo, and when we stepped onto the platform in Kukonodate the first thing we saw were the cherry trees—hundreds of them everywhere, so loaded with cherry blossoms that their limbs hung like weeping willows. It was a beautiful sight."

"Who exactly were the samurai?" Dougherty said.

"They were mainly the muscle for Shoguns—great lords who ruled Japan for nearly seven hundred years. Most samurai committed their lives to keeping the Shoguns in power, and in return the Shoguns provided their food and shelter. They were great warriors who followed a strict code of conduct called *Bushido*. Obedience to the leader. Honor in battle. Suicide if defeated or disgraced."

The two men walked into the maintenance shop and found a burly corporal chomping on an unlit cigar. He held the barrel of a 40 mm cannon with a round stuck in the top in one hand and a broomstick in the other.

"Mac, how you been?" Lowrie said.

The man shrugged, then inserted the broomstick into the open end of the barrel and repeatedly rammed it against the back of the trapped round until it dislodged and bounced across the floor. Dougherty and Lowrie instinctively shielded their bodies with their arms, but the grenade did not detonate.

"Has to go thirty yards to arm itself," the surly man said to the stunned airmen, who had witnessed, on numerous occasions, the damage a 40 mm grenade inflicted upon human flesh.

"Good to know," Lowrie said, lowering his arms. "Mac, I'd like you to cut the barrel down on this twelve-gauge."

The man stared at the weapon for a few moments, then held out his hand. Dougherty passed the shotgun to the shop attendant, who wrapped the middle of the firearm in a towel, then tightened it in a vice. He instructed Lowrie to pick out a spot for the cut, then proceeded to remove half the shotgun's barrel with a hacksaw. Next, he took a metal file and smoothed the rough edges of the cut steel. Lastly, using the tip of his index finger, he inserted some emery cloth into the end of the barrel to ensure the bore was completely smooth. He removed the weapon from the vice and handed it to Lowrie.

"Good," Lowrie said, aiming the gun away from the two other men. "Would also like you to cut off the back part of the stock," he said, pointing to the wide part of the butt that rested against a hunter's shoulder for stability when firing.

The gruff corporal shifted the unlit cigar to the opposite side of his mouth using nothing but his tongue and teeth, then held out his hand. Lowrie passed the weapon back to the mechanic, who returned it to the vice. He located a skill saw amidst his tools and removed a small pencil resting between his cap and skull. He drew a curved line on the stock and proceeded to cut away most of the butt, transforming the weapon into a large, pump-action pistol. Using sandpaper, the mechanic smoothed the remaining walnut wood, then handed the modified weapon to Lowrie. "Sawed-off shotgun," Lowrie said. "Sprays a large area over a short distance. Just point it at trouble and pull the trigger."

"Might put some oil on the places I cut," the mechanic said. "Monsoon season's coming."

Lowrie nodded. "Thanks, Mac. I owe you one."

The man chomped down on his unlit cigar, then turned and walked away.

"We also visited Hiroshima," Lowrie said, as the two men exited Maintenance. "Jackson and I wanted to see where the *Enola Gay* dropped the bomb in '45. The Japanese government built a memorial park in a large open field created by the bomb blast. They opened it in '54 to honor the one hundred and forty thousand people who died. Can you imagine it? That many people alive one second, then dead the next." Lowrie paused for a few moments, to allow the magnitude of the event to register in his friend's mind.

"Inside the park is the Children's Peace Monument," Lowrie continued. "At the top of the statue is the figure of a Japanese girl with her arms stretched out, holding a wire crane above her head. Sadako Sasashi was her name. I wrote it down. She got cancer from the bomb and died of radiation poisoning. Before she passed, this little girl had a vision of creating one thousand paper cranes. According to Japanese tradition, if a person makes a thousand cranes, they will be granted one wish. Hers was to have a world without nuclear weapons. The statue is surrounded by glass cases filled with thousands of origami cranes that children from all over the world sent to Hiroshima. In the town and on the trains, you see lots of people with birth defects from the radiation. Missing and deformed limbs. Some are blind. Others seem damaged in the mind. Heartbreaking stuff," he added.

"But it helped end the war," Dougherty countered. "Probably saved a lot of American lives."

Lowrie considered the point, then shrugged his shoulders as if to say *maybe*. "Hell of a cost," he said.

Lowrie led Dougherty to an open field at the south end of the base that served as a landfill for US Armed Forces at Bien Hoa. He picked through the debris and set up some makeshift targets—cardboard boxes, pieces of wood, a crate with some bottles on top. Then Lowrie produced a handful of shells from his pocket and loaded them into the shotgun. He handed the weapon to Dougherty, who proceeded to open fire on the targets; fragments of cardboard, wood, and glass flew into the air after each shot. From his years of hunting, Dougherty instinctively worked the pump action; each empty shell casing ejected as he rapidly pumped another round into the firing chamber.

A few seconds later, after Dougherty fired the sixth and final shot, Lowrie surveyed the damage and nodded. "Yes, sir," he said.

Word spread throughout the 334th that Dougherty and Lowrie made a great team, and soon the company's top two pilots started requesting their ship.

Captain Ryan Ruby was a tall, slim, sandy-haired pilot who grew up on a cattle ranch in the Hill Country of Texas, between Stonewall, which was the birthplace of President Lyndon Johnson, and Fredericksburg, which was the hometown of Admiral Chester Nimitz, Commander of the Pacific Fleet following the attack on Pearl Harbor. Ruby, who was twenty-five years old, studied mechanical engineering at the University of Texas, Austin, and had an orange Longhorn logo stenciled on the back of his flight helmet. He seemed destined for greatness simply because he didn't give a damn about what other people thought and wouldn't bow to authority. If something was bullshit, Ruby wasn't afraid to say *bullshit*, even to a senior officer. This simultaneously pissed off and impressed the young captain's commanding officer. It also led to his selection as the Raider Platoon Leader and put him on a short list to one day assume command of the 334th.

Captain Jerry Pearle was a year older than Ruby and slightly shorter. He was a dark-haired Jew from New York City who studied political science at Columbia University. Pearle adopted a more intellectual approach to his role as a Huey pilot and rationalized his time in Vietnam as a logical step on the path to success. Pearle followed orders religiously, not because he feared authority or believed his superior officers were actually superior: Pearle recognized those men were the gatekeepers, and pleasing them increased the likelihood of his own admittance to their exclusive club of rank and privilege.

Whereas Ruby was often praised by the instructors at Fort Wolters and Fort Rucker for his intuitive flying skills, Pearle received top marks during flight school for his academic coursework related to aeronautics and meteorology. Gut instincts versus book smarts. The two men could not have been more different in their personalities and flying styles, and yet they were consistently praised as two of the best Huey pilots in the 145th Combat Aviation Battalion.

Ruby and Pearle were also rivals. In the spring of '67, the company commander informed his pilots that Bell had started construction on a new helicopter gunship that was faster, leaner, and carried more firepower than the Huey gunship. Bell's new attack helicopter was expected to be ready within months and, as the first armed helicopter company in the United States Army, the 334th was selected to test the new aerial weapon in combat. Rumor had it that either Ruby or Pearle would be tapped to lead the first platoon of Cobras in Vietnam.

When the Raiders rotated to daytime missions in the Rung Sat Special Zone in late May, Captain Ruby and his copilot, Warrant Officer Jim "Hawk" Hocking, requested Dougherty and Lowrie as their crew chief and door gunner. The day he first met Hocking, Dougherty took note of the man's long, narrow face accentuated by a beak-like nose and piercing brown eyes sunk deep in his skull. To Dougherty, this gave him the appearance of a profound thinker. Hocking's skull was so elongated that it actually had some curvature to it, like the horrified figure in Edvard Munch's painting *The Scream*.

As Ruby led the Light Fire Team southeast from Bien Hoa, the two Raider gunships crossed the Dong Nai and Saigon Rivers. Lowrie reached up and keyed the intercom to speak directly to Dougherty.

"That swampy area between the two rivers is the Rung Sat," Lowrie said, referring to miles of mud flats with tiny tributaries running through it. After giving his friend a few seconds to take it all in, Lowrie keyed the intercom, again. "In Vietnamese 'Rung Sat' means 'Forest of Assassins.' You don't want to find yourself down there," he added.

Dougherty watched as a pair of US Navy Swift Boats carved their way down the tree-lined river, a wake of white water trailing the stern of each ship.

"They call them Game Wardens," Lowrie said, referring to the boats. "They're part of the Freshwater Navy stationed at Nha Be. They go up and down the shipping channels, looking for sampans that go up these little creeks in the Rung Sat to hide or retrieve weapons and ammo."

Within ten minutes, the Hueys approached the US Naval Base at Nha Be, strategically located at the confluence of the Saigon River and South China Sea. Dougherty noticed dozens of troops on the beach.

"Navy Seals hang out at Nha Be," Lowrie said over the intercom. "The Swift Boats drop them along the river so they can sneak into the Rung Sat and look for Charlie."

The two Raider Hueys landed on a large, square concrete pad at the edge of the base. After touching down, Captain Ruby sent Dougherty and Lowrie off for some grub while he and Hocking headed to the morning briefing with the navy.

"Rung Sat is pretty good duty," Lowrie said to Dougherty while the two men waited in line at the mess hall. "Navy has good chow like real eggs, ice cream, and even lobster, sometimes. We usually come down here early and leave late so we can get at least two good meals per day. As far as flying, we spend most of our time chasing wood cutters in the Rung Sat out to bigger waters so the navy can search them."

"Why do they call them wood cutters?" Dougherty said.

"In the Rung Sat there's lots of dead timber. Every time the navy stops one of those boats, the Vietnamese on board always say they were out there cutting firewood. Sometimes we fly over these guys, and they pretend like they're chopping wood even if they don't have an ax or a saw. It's a free strike zone, so we shoot first and ask questions later. But if there's a boat already loaded with wood, then our orders are to push it out to the Game Wardens. Sometimes the navy guys find weapons or ammo beneath the sticks."

Thirty minutes later, Dougherty and Lowrie returned to the Huey. They chatted with O'Donnell and Mancuso, their wing ship's crew chief and door gunner, while waiting for the pilots to return from the morning briefing.

"Hurry up and wait," Ruby said, as he approached the ship. "Navy needs a little more time to get its ducks in a row," he added as he climbed into the right seat. While waiting for further instructions, the four men sat in the Huey and watched the Navy Seals performing calisthenics on the beach. Between the helipad and the water stood a few scattered palm trees where someone suspended a barrel between two of the palm trunks. The Seals took turns riding the barrel while two of their comrades stood opposite one another, bench pressing the ropes at their shoulders, to simulate the gyrations of an angry bull. Ruby, who grew up a real cowboy, offered running commentary over the Huey's intercom while the airmen watched the Seals take turns on their makeshift steer. Finally, around midmorning, word came down for the Raider gunships to escort an oil tanker up the river to Saigon, an action they repeated two more times that day before Dougherty and his crewmates returned to Bien Hoa.

On the Raiders' third day at Nha Be the beach was empty.

"Seals must be out kickin' some ass this morning," Lowrie said.

"Good," Hocking replied. "Just watching those assholes work out is exhausting."

Ruby keyed the intercom. "Doc, I'll bet you a case of beer you can't stay up on the barrel for twenty seconds with me and Hawk on the ropes," he said.

Hocking and Lowrie laughed.

"I'm serious," Ruby said. "If you're still in the air after twenty seconds, a case of Bud is yours."

After a few moments of silence, Dougherty keyed the mic and replied, "All right, Captain, you're on."

The other men laughed, thinking their crew chief was extending the joke until he jumped down onto the concrete landing pad and strolled over to the barrel, which rested calmly, like a cow grazing in a pasture. Dougherty placed his hands on the barrel to see how much it moved from his touch, then hoisted his long, lanky frame, stomach first, onto the steel drum.

"You have to sit on it properly," Ruby said as he and his crew approached the barrel.

Dougherty nodded and slid off. "Vic, can you give me a hand?" he said.

"Are you sure about this, Billy? Those Seals had a pretty rough go of it. Only a couple of guys ever made it twenty seconds."

"Yep," Dougherty replied.

Lowrie hoisted his friend onto the barrel while Ruby and Hocking assumed their positions within the ropes. The four men from the wing ship arrived on the beach to watch the action and cheer on Dougherty.

"Vic, you be our timer," Ruby said.

The gunner nodded and looked at his wristwatch.

"You ready, Doc?" Ruby said.

The young Nebraskan grabbed the makeshift rope reins, made one final attempt to balance himself, and nodded.

Ruby and Hocking started working the ropes, which pulled the rear end of the barrel down toward Hocking then lifted it back up toward Ruby. Dougherty gained momentum with each pass as the pilots pushed harder on the ropes.

"Ten seconds," Lowrie called out. The other men on the beach clapped and shouted.

The barrel moved faster and more erratically with each passing second, as Dougherty held tightly to the reins. Suddenly, to everyone's surprise, the rope on Hocking's right side snapped; the barrel and its rider plummeted to the ground.

Lowrie looked up from his watch. "Seventeen seconds."

"I'm still on," Dougherty said, his long legs wrapped tightly around the steel drum as he lay in the sand. "You owe me a case of beer," he shouted.

"Sorry," Ruby said. "The deal was you had to be up in the air after twenty seconds. Still, you did better than I expected." He walked over and helped Dougherty to his feet. "Forget about the beer," Ruby said. "I was just messin' with you."

"If I had made it three more seconds you better believe I'd expect my case of Bud," Dougherty said, brushing sand off his fatigues.

Captain Ruby laughed and slapped his crew chief on the back. "You're all right, Doc. We'll make a cowboy out of you yet," he said.

On the final day of their rotation, Dougherty and his shipmates flew low level up dozens of tiny tributaries in the Rung Sat, shooting anything that moved in the free strike zone. From time to time, the crew discovered a structure concealed deep in the mangroves. On these occasions, Ruby hovered the chopper above the hooch while Dougherty or Lowrie dropped a phosphorous grenade onto the thatched roof, setting it on fire; the draft from the ship's rotors fanning the flames.

The Light Fire Team expended and re-armed three times before calling it a day.

After refueling their Hueys in preparation for the return flight to Bien Hoa, a navy seaman ran across the concrete pad to Dougherty's open door. The sailor, who looked like he was fifteen, cradled a puppy in his arms.

"They're going to kill all the dogs at Nha Be because one of them had rabies," the kid said. "Will you take him with you?"

Dougherty looked at Captain Ruby in the right front seat, making sure his pilot could see the mangy, reddish-brown mutt with one folded ear and another that was missing the top half. Ruby thought for a moment then nodded. Dougherty reached out and the seaman put the pup in his gloved hands. He held the small dog to his chest in preparation for lift-off.

The sailor nodded then rushed away from the flight line.

Once the young man reached a safe distance from their rotors, Captain Ruby pulled up on the collective, and the ship lifted into the air. A few minutes into their flight, the two Raider Hueys parted company: the wing ship headed northwest toward Bien Hoa, while Ruby flew east toward the South China Sea. After motoring fifteen klicks up the coast, just beyond Vung Tau, Ruby spotted a clear stretch of beach and landed their ship in the sand.

"Go on, boys," the aircraft commander said over the intercom.

Dougherty and Lowrie looked at each other in disbelief, then quickly unhooked their safety belts and removed their flight helmets. Dougherty found the puppy nestled in the canvas mini-gun covers stacked in the rear of the cabin. He scooped the pup into his arms and hopped onto the beach. During his childhood in Nebraska, Dougherty never visited the Atlantic or Pacific Oceans. While at Fort Eustis in Newport News, he made numerous training flights over the Chesapeake Bay, where crews fired weapons into the brackish inland waters for practice. On various flights from California to Vietnam, he often looked out his window at the bright blue seas far below. But never before had he stood on a pristine beach with massive waves cascading on the shore in a warm, tropical climate. It was a gift and just unfortunate that it required a war for Dougherty to receive it.

The two pilots followed the enlisted airmen down to the water. Ruby unbuttoned his shirt and lit up a cigarette. The four young men unlaced their boots and peeled away sweaty socks. They waded into the surf while the puppy raced up to each incoming wave, only to retreat before it crashed to shore. Hocking brought a football from the Huey and the four men tossed it around for a while. After an hour of horseplay, they sat together on the beach, watching the waves in silence.

"What are you gonna name that mutt?" Captain Ruby said.

"Sam," Dougherty replied, a reference to the platoon's mascot, Yosemite Sam.

Ruby smiled and nodded. "Perfect." Then the pilot stood up and buttoned his shirt. "Vacation's over, boys," he said and walked back to the ship. One by one they slowly rose and returned to the Huey. Hocking, the copilot, was next, followed by Lowrie. Dougherty and Sam held their ground on the beach. Those few minutes alone with the puppy were the best part of his day. He savored every second as he petted the sleeping dog beside him. Knowing he could delay no further, Dougherty lifted the animal into his arms and walked back to the ship.

After landing at Bien Hoa, Dougherty and Lowrie did not complain about having to clean and inspect the ship. It had been such a good day that nothing could spoil their mood. Dougherty was about to tell Lowrie the tale of the mysterious newspaper clippings from Broken Bow, to get his friend's assessment of the situation, when the Jeep that had picked up Captain Ruby and Mr. Hocking returned to the flight line.

"Doc, Vic, we need to go back out," Ruby announced.

"What's up?" Lowrie said.

"Just get the ship ready. And arm it," he added.

Twenty minutes later, their Huey sat on the tarmac with its rotors turning.

"What are we waiting for?" Dougherty said over the intercom.

"One more passenger," Ruby replied.

A few minutes later, a Jeep screeched to a halt on the tarmac. A steel-jawed soldier wearing sunglasses and fatigues with no official markings hopped out of the passenger seat. The driver immediately pulled away. Their passenger, who crouched as he jogged to the ship, was most likely a military adviser, possibly with Special Forces or the CIA.

The man climbed aboard the Huey without saying a word. Dougherty handed him a spare flight helmet and safety harness. Their passenger knew exactly what to do with the gear, an indication he had done this before. The adviser spotted Sam nestled in the canvas mini-gun covers. Before Dougherty could remove the pup from the ship, the man picked Sam up by the scruff of his neck and tossed him out the open door. The act infuriated the two enlisted airmen, but before they could retaliate, Captain Ruby ordered them to their seats for lift-off. Sam scampered away from the Huey, barking incessantly at the large metal bird hovering above him.

The five men flew north in silence, passing over rice paddies, rubber plantations, and sugar cane fields dotted with large boulders—Dougherty's first foray into II Corps. At one point, artillery shells started falling in the vicinity of their flight path. Captain Ruby radioed in their ship's coordinates to avoid a friendly fire incident. "Raider 2-6, we copy that," a voice responded in Dougherty's headset, and, magically, the shelling stopped.

With each passing klick, Dougherty felt the muscles in his neck and shoulders tighten, as if the spinning blades above his head were winding him up like a top in the hand of an impatient child. The pressure inside the cabin mounted. The turbine whined as they clawed their way higher and higher into the thin air of the Annamite Range until finally they arrived at a tiny clearing. Ruby carefully set the ship down so that the right door, the gunner's side, faced a small village. The military adviser removed his helmet. Without saying a word, he bumped past Lowrie and jumped down to the ground.

Dougherty joined Lowrie in the gunner's open doorway. He spotted a stack of buffalo horns that reminded him of a totem pole. Gourds and thatched baskets sat on bamboo mats in front of small huts. Bare-breasted women with extended ear lobes led naked children through the village. Four young men in loin cloths, returning from a hunt, carried a thick branch with a dead pig tied to it by the hooves. Old men smoking long pipes crouched, chatted, and occasionally pointed at their Huey.

"What is this?" Lowrie said feebly over the intercom.

"Montagnard village," Captain Ruby replied over the radio. "They're the indigenous people of Vietnam. The Green Berets have been organizing their villages to make sure the enemy doesn't have a safe haven up here."

"Some of the Yards serve as guides to our Special Forces operating in the highlands, and some of them work as day laborers on the American Fire Bases up here," Hocking added.

The Lumbee stared at the indigenous village through the dark visor on his flight helmet, feeling as if the universe had opened a portal to his own history. These people, who wore beads and bone necklaces, carried baskets on their backs, and held spears, were his people, transported four hundred years into the future from the coastal plains of North Carolina to the Central Highlands of Vietnam.

A few moments later, a small platoon of Montagnard soldiers emerged from the forest and lined up in formation beside the chief. They all carried American M-14s. The military adviser nodded his approval, then produced a map. The leader of the Montagnard squad pointed to some positions on it, probably indicating enemy troop movements.

Lowrie said nothing as he took it all in. Dougherty could tell from his gunner's silence and body language that his friend was horrified. When the military adviser handed the Montagnard chief a cigar from his breast pocket, Lowrie stretched his gloved finger away, then let it settle on the trigger of his M-60, now trained on the operative. Dougherty suspected his friend wanted to rip the man to pieces. A simple squeeze of his finger and perhaps another Trail of Tears would be avoided.

"Vic, you OK?" Ruby said over the intercom, sensing his gunner's unease.

No answer from Lowrie.

"Let's keep our mind on the mission," the Raider platoon leader added.

A flying machine had descended from the sky and landed in their village. *What must they think? That a mighty god had come to deliver a prophecy?* Dougherty wondered. He understood the military adviser played the role of the powerful deity in front of the women and the innocent children, who stared in disbelief at their mechanical bird. The significance of the scene was not lost on Dougherty and the two pilots when the big white military man handed some trinkets from his satchel to the tribe's much smaller, half-naked chief.

Finally, the American adviser shook hands with the chief and sauntered back to the ship. While staring at Lowrie from behind his dark sunglasses, the man twirled his finger in the air, a signal for Ruby to crank.

The adviser hopped onboard and assumed his position between the gunner and crew chief. "Captain, whenever you're ready," he said once he secured his safety harness and flight helmet. As Ruby prepared for lift-off, the adviser keyed the mic again.

"They may be savages, but they sure can fight," he added.

Dougherty noticed Lowrie staring at the sawed-off shotgun in the holster attached to the back of his seat. As Ruby pulled back on the collective, the rotor wash from their Huey lifted dust and leaves into the air, creating a swirling sea of debris around the villagers, who stared in awe at their departing ship. Lowrie slumped against the door frame as their helicopter ascended to the heavens.

7

STAND BY ME

DOUGHERTY SPOTTED SAM IN THE REVETMENT as their Huey descended to the tarmac at Bien Hoa. He felt a sense of relief that the young dog had waited while the crew made their impromptu trip to the Montagnard village. The pup hid behind a wall of sandbags as the large metal bird approached. The moment the skids touched ground, Lowrie unclipped his safety harness, removed his flight helmet, and stormed away from the ship. Dougherty later learned that his friend proceeded straight to the Enlisted Men's Club where he downed five double shots of Jack Daniel's Tennessee whiskey in ten minutes, then picked a fight with two members of the Playboys before passing out.

Once the rotors stopped turning, the military adviser hopped out of the helicopter and into a waiting Jeep. Dougherty never saw the man again. A three-quarter ton pickup and its driver sat waiting for Ruby and Hocking, their ride back to the Villa in downtown Bien Hoa.

Captain Ruby started walking toward the truck, but then turned and called out to his crew chief, "Do you need some help with the ship?"

"No . . . thanks," Dougherty replied. "We had most of it done before going back out," he added, hoping to defray some of the impending backlash against Lowrie for walking off the job.

"Good work this week," Ruby said. "You're keepin' old 'Patches' running pretty smooth." The ship's new nickname referred to the increasing number of patches maintenance placed over the various bullet holes in the Huey's aluminum skin. One day during a pre-flight inspection, Captain Ruby joked that their ship had more patches than original metal.

"We need to see about getting you a new bird," Ruby added as he walked toward his waiting ride.

Dougherty watched the pilots climb into the truck, which quickly disappeared down the flight line. "Looks like it's just you and me," he said to the scruffy pup that sat obediently at his side, panting in the heat. Dougherty dug through a box of leftover C-rats in the back of the Huey and found a can of beef and noodles that he opened for the dog. After Sam devoured the meal, Dougherty poured some water into the empty tin, which the dog lapped ferociously. He filled the tin with water a second time and began cleaning and inspecting the ship.

Given his previously clean record at the 334th and that he was generally well-liked in the Company, Lowrie's bad day normally would not have resulted in a permanent grounding. When the gunner's bad day turned into a bad week of drinking and fighting, Operations had no choice but to remove him from flight duty.

Following Lowrie's self-inflicted grounding, Dougherty knew he would be paired with another gunner. Unbeknownst to him, Jackson had put in for a transfer to the Twelfth before he and Lowrie went on R&R to Japan, and that move was approved soon after Lowrie's grounding. The quiet crew chief from North Carolina was on the opposite trajectory as Dougherty, starting his tour with the 334th Armed Helicopter Company and jumping to the Twelfth Aviation Group, to end his time in-country in the relative calm of the Command Quarters. Jackson had survived his first nine months in Vietnam and his personal cross of flying with Jester, Thompson, and Coffey.

After the TDY to Blackhorse, word got around that Dougherty could handle working with Coffey, and since Captain Ruby was platoon leader and a *no bullshit* kind of guy, Swanson figured he had a solution—Coffey would go with Dougherty on Patches. This would give Ops a chance to wipe the slate clean and try pairing a new crew chief and door gunner with Jester and Thompson, which if done properly might tip the balance back toward sanity for *The Joker's Wild*.

In late June, the Raiders rotated to Emergency Stand By. Operations divided the eight Hueys from the second platoon into four Light Fire Teams, each consisting of two gunships and their four-man crews. These teams took rotating shifts in the Raider shack, waiting beside the tarmac, ready to crank on a moment's notice and provide fire support anywhere in III Corps.

On the first day of their rotation, Dougherty sat at a small wooden table in the corner of the Raider shack, nervously tapping a pack of Marlboro cigarettes as he studied the three mysterious newspaper clippings spread out on the tabletop. He had recently started smoking his father's favorite brand of cigarettes because the taste and smell of the smokes made it easier to conjure the image of hunting rabbits in Nebraska while on combat missions. *If my father is an arsonist and a thief, what does that make me?* Dougherty wondered as he glanced from the articles down at Sam, sleeping peacefully at his feet. Johnny Grant's *Small World*, a popular show on the Armed Forces Vietnam Network, played on a dusty FM radio propped up on a nearby shelf. When Grant introduced Ben E. King's 1962 hit, "Stand By Me," Captain Ruby lowered his magazine.

"Turn it up," he said to no one in particular. Dougherty reached over to the transistor and adjusted the volume. King's smooth and distinctive R&B voice filled the room.

Midway through the song, Swanson barged into the Raider shack.

"Doc, Major Sheffield wants to see you in his office, pronto," Swanson said, motioning toward the door with his thumb. Dougherty guessed the CO wanted to talk about Lowrie since he was the grounded gunner's crewmate and roommate and might be able to offer some insight into his breakdown. While walking from the barracks to the Orderly Room, Dougherty tried to assemble a rational account of Lowrie's behavior from a jumbled mess of thoughts about the Lost Colony at Roanoke, Henry Berry Lowrie, samurai warriors, and the Montagnard village. Each version he crafted made him sound more unhinged than Lowrie, and the best he could come up with was, "It's complicated, sir."

Major Raymond Sheffield was a paunchy, spectacled, middle-aged man who looked more like someone who might sell you an insurance policy or prepare your tax return rather than lead an armed helicopter company. When Dougherty walked into the CO's office, the major motioned for him to sit without looking up from his paperwork.

Dougherty noticed an open file on Sheffield's desk. To his surprise, it was not Lowrie's file but his own.

"Dougherty, it looks like Colonel Sarkis gave you a parting gift when you left the Twelfth," Major Sheffield said, pushing his black framed glasses further up the bridge of his nose. "He put a 'Do Not Promote' in your record."

The young crew chief remained silent.

"I know about the hot start," Sheffield said, lowering his head and looking over his glasses. "But I've also seen what you've done here. Captain Ruby speaks highly of you. We both think you're a better man than this," Sheffield said, nodding toward the file. "I'm going to remove this flag and recommend that you be promoted to SPEC-4. How does that sound?"

"Good, sir," Dougherty replied.

"There's one other thing. It looks like you're coming up on the end of your tour," Sheffield said, acknowledging the crew chief's seven months in country, which put him on the shorter end of the stick.

"Yes, sir," Dougherty replied, uncertain if he should be proud or embarrassed by the fact.

Sheffield glanced at the open file despite already knowing its contents. "I see you've got a three-year commitment with the Army. If you go home after this tour, chances are you would spend six months stateside and then be shipped back to Vietnam for another year. The problem with that," the Commanding Officer said, removing his glasses for effect, "is you could end up anywhere. There's almost no chance you would return to the 334th and no guarantee you would even be assigned to an armed helicopter company, which we both know is the top of the pecking order. If you extend with us for nine months, then you would go home next September and spend the rest of your time stateside." Sheffield's words hung in the stale, humid air of his cramped office until Dougherty realized it was his turn to speak.

"Well, sir," Dougherty said, clearing his throat. "The thought of leaving the other men has been bothering me some. I don't want to abandon them before we're done here."

"Give it some thought," Sheffield said, as if the idea of reenlisting was Dougherty's own, and now he was applying the brakes. "You know where you stand here and what you've got with the 334th." The major stood up, indicating it was time for Dougherty to leave.

"Thank you, sir, for the promotion and the opportunity to stay with the company," Dougherty said. Sheffield nodded, and the two men saluted.

When Dougherty and Coffey entered their room early the next morning, they found Lowrie passed out, face-down on his bunk. Sam, who slept dutifully beside the grounded gunner, lifted his head when the two men entered. Dougherty lay down on his cot and closed his eyes. When Sam walked over to his bunk, the exhausted crew chief extended his hand, and the dog instinctively placed his head against it. He petted the canine for a few minutes before falling asleep.

Around noon a runner notified the airmen that their team was now on alert in the barracks. Dougherty noticed Lowrie's bunk was empty. Rather than get cleaned up or head to the mess hall for some grub, the two men fell back to sleep. By four p.m., when the fourth team answered a distress call, the eight men on Dougherty's ESB crew found themselves back in the Raider shack for their second consecutive evening shift. This constant rotation of Raider Light Fire Teams continued for a week.

On their final evening of Emergency Stand By, during a fierce game of Gin Rummy, Captain Ruby walked into the Raider shack with a civilian by his side. The gentleman carried a clipboard and wore a short-sleeve dress shirt with a pocket protector and necktie. He looked as out of place in Vietnam as a grunt in jungle fatigues would appear in the offices of an engineering firm.

"Dougherty, this is Wilson T. Proctor from the Human Resources Research Organization in Dothan, Alabama," Ruby said, reading it from a business card. "He's conducting a survey of Huey crew chiefs to see why you guys earn so damn much of Uncle Sam's money," Ruby said with a grin.

"You're kiddin' me," Dougherty replied, looking up from his playing cards.

"No, he's not," the man said, adjusting his thick black-rimmed glasses. "This study is for the Office of the Chief of Research and Development. We are surveying approximately five thousand UH-1 helicopter mechanics stationed around the world, including Vietnam."

"We do get mail here," Dougherty said. "You might have saved yourself some trouble by dropping it in the post."

"We are mailing most of the surveys," the civilian replied, "but to ensure accurate results we are also conducting a small percentage of on-site surveys."

"And you drew the short straw," Coffey said, a toothpick dangling from his lip.

"I think it's important to hear directly from the man in the field," Proctor added.

"The *field*?" Coffey said. The gunner removed his toothpick and pointed it at the civilian, but before he could speak, Captain Ruby held up a hand to silence him.

"Proctor, why don't you and Dougherty use this table for the survey? I'm sure these other men wouldn't mind," Ruby said.

"How long is this survey?" Dougherty said, setting his cards down on the table.

"The full survey, including tables and appendices, is two hundred and three pages, but the questionnaire is only one hundred and thirty-seven pages."

The seven other Raiders in the room howled with laughter.

"ONLY a hundred and thirty-seven pages," Dougherty said, looking wide-eyed around the room at the other airmen in the Raider shack who struggled to contain their laughter.

"There are seven sections," Proctor said, proudly. "Part One covers your background and experience. Part Two assesses your school and unit training. Part Three deals with work conditions. Part Four..."

"Stop," Dougherty said. "In case you haven't noticed, we're fighting a war here. We don't have time for this."

"When I run the data from these surveys through the computer back in Dothan, we'll know more about you fellas than your own mothers," Proctor said, confidently. "Secretary McNamara believes, as do I, that good data is the key to winning this war."

Captain Ruby cleared his throat. "Go ahead, Proctor. Ask Dougherty your questions."

The surveyor gave a nod of appreciation for the senior officer's endorsement and sat down at the wooden table across from his subject. The other men dropped their cards and dispersed.

"Question one. What is your present rank?"

"General," Coffey whispered from a nearby table, which triggered an outburst of laughter from the airmen.

Dougherty looked at the lonely stripe on his uniform and back at Proctor. "PFC," he said dryly, declining to mention the pending promotion.

Proctor dutifully recorded the response on his clipboard then looked up at his subject. "What was your age at your last birthday?"

"Twenty," Dougherty replied, and Proctor meticulously circled the number *20* beneath the question.

"I hope that ain't your last birthday," Mancuso mumbled. More laughter.

"Only one hundred and thirty-six pages to go," Coffey added.

At that moment, Swanson raced into the Raider shack.

"Captain Ruby, Maintenance just grounded Pearle's ship. If I move a crew out here from the barracks to cover ESB, can you guys fill in on Firefly tonight?"

"I don't know, Dick," Ruby said, adopting a serious tone. "We've got some important military intelligence work to complete here, but if you really need us, we'll be happy to help out."

"Great," Swanson replied, oblivious to the running joke in the room. "I figured you'd say yes, so I had Pearle's crew drop the light at your ship."

"Doc, bring your friend along so he can see what you do. Firefly's been cool the last couple of weeks. He'll be fine," Ruby said.

Captain Ruby turned to the visitor. "What do you think, Proctor?

Want to ride along and see what a crew chief does in Vietnam?"

"Actually, that would be quite helpful," the surveyor said. "We may be able to complete part three of the survey . . . in the field," he added and smiled.

Dougherty preferred risking his life on a Firefly mission to completing the survey with Proctor in the Raider shack until a thought occurred to him: the man would see the sawed-off shotgun Lowrie had made for him. Although Dougherty had yet to use the weapon in combat, it felt like a security blanket or perhaps a good luck charm. The no-nonsense surveyor might give the crew chief poor marks for having an unauthorized weapon on his ship. The discovery might even lead to trouble for the entire crew.

"Let me make sure we have an extra flight helmet and safety harness on the ship," Dougherty said, jogging ahead of his platoonmates. When he arrived at the Huey, he reached for the gun that normally rested in a homemade leather holster on the side of his seat. It was gone. When one final frantic search failed to produce the weapon, Dougherty grabbed a spare flight helmet and safety harness.

"We're all set," he said as the group arrived at the ship.

Once fitted in an oversized flak jacket and helmet, Proctor took meticulous notes as Dougherty bolted the frame of the Firefly light to the Huey's floor at the edge of Coffey's open doorway.

After liftoff, the three Hueys flew northwest out of Bien Hoa. Dougherty operated the spotlight for Proctor's benefit while Coffey manned the M-60 hanging in the crew chief's open doorway. Not a single target appeared in the ship's light during the first Firefly mission of the evening. Proctor noted this on his clipboard. When the three Hueys landed at Tay Ninh to refuel, Dougherty's thoughts returned to the sawed-off shotgun. Perhaps whoever dropped off the light found the weapon and took it, knowing the owner could not report the theft of an illicit weapon.

Dougherty opened the fuel cap located behind his door and started refueling the Huey with a small, portable pump that sucked JP4 from a rubber bladder beside the tarmac. The evaluator stood in the left doorway, checking multiple boxes on the survey, while Dougherty monitored the needle on the helicopter's fuel gauge through the copilot's door.

CHAPTER 7

What if Lowrie removed the sawed-off shotgun? Dougherty wondered as
he refueled the ship. Lowrie was, after all, the only other person who knew
about it. And if Lowrie did reclaim the weapon, what did that mean? Was
it another act in their disintegrating friendship or was there more to it?

Dougherty and Coffey changed places for the second Firefly mission, each man returning to his designated side of the ship. After flying
ten minutes southwest of Tay Ninh, the three Raider gunships received
a distress call from Firebase Nevada, a Special Forces outpost near the
Fish Hook, a particularly desolate section of Cambodian territory that
extended into western Vietnam in the shape of the letter *J*.

"We're being overrun," a frantic voice crackled over the radio.

Captain Ruby requested coordinates from the radio operator. "Stay
alert," was all Ruby said, as the Raider Hueys raced toward the battle.
When the gunships arrived, they spotted a Douglas C-47 circling Firebase Nevada; the crew of the large plane dropping flares with parachutes
that drifted down from a thousand feet in the air, illuminating the dark
countryside in a strange but beautiful light. Dougherty understood why
troops referred to the C-47 as "Spooky" or "Puff the Magic Dragon."
When the jumbo twin-propeller plane released its flares or shot off tracer
fire, it appeared as an ominous mechanical beast in the night sky. As
each parachuted flare rocked back and forth on its gradual descent to
earth, another tropical landscape appeared briefly in the burning glow.
It reminded Dougherty of watching fireworks at the Old Settlers Picnic,
where each burst gave way to an even more spectacular sight.

When the first flares landed, dozens of VC appeared in the light—
around the perimeter and inside the wire of Firebase Nevada. Angry
gunfire from the ground struck the belly of their helicopter. Coffey fell
backward when a round knocked out one of the bulbs in the spotlight.
Dougherty unclipped his M-60 and crawled across the cabin floor to the
right side of the Huey while Coffey regained control of the light. Dougherty leaned over the edge of the ship and fired his M-60 straight down,
his finger never leaving the trigger.

"Keep it coming, keep it coming," a voice on the radio shouted. The
two other Hueys fired at targets on the ground while flying a circular
pattern around Coffey's light.

76

"Up, up, more to the left. There, there, there. Right there," Hocking screamed over the radio, trying to direct his crew chief's tracer fire toward a new stream of VC that appeared in the spotlight. Hot lead casings from Dougherty's M-60 flew through the cabin. Some bounced off Proctor, a few landed on his clipboard.

Dougherty heard the *tink, tink, tink* of rounds striking the body of their Huey. In his helmet, a voice from the ground kept shouting, "Yes, yes, yes. Keep pouring it in."

Coffey pounded Dougherty's helmet and pointed at his white-hot barrel. Dougherty released his finger from the trigger, but the gun kept firing; the rounds cooking off from the heat of the barrel. When the gun stopped firing, Dougherty slid back from the edge of the ship. He flipped the latch on his M-60, dumped the destroyed barrel, then reached into his gun bag and removed another one, which he quickly attached to the weapon. As the chopper banked wildly to evade fifty-caliber tracers from the ground, the hot barrel rolled to Proctor's feet. The surveyor nervously kicked it away, never relinquishing his grip on the clipboard.

"We've lost our rockets," Hocking shouted over the radio.

Coffey abandoned the light and grabbed his M-60, which rested beside his ammo box. He quickly fed the rounds of ammunition into his weapon and started firing from the left side of the ship.

Once Dougherty attached the new barrel to his weapon, he assumed a kneeling position at the edge of the cabin and continued firing at the ground. The search light scorched Dougherty's face and exposed him like a lone actor caught in the glow of a theater's spotlight. The other Hueys on the Firefly team had received multiple hits and announced their intention to retreat from the fight.

"I'm hit . . . in the leg," Hocking shouted over the radio. A round had entered through the plexiglass bubble on the cockpit floor and grazed his shin.

"Keep pourin' it in," the voice from the ground cried over the radio.

Amidst all the chaos unfolding around him, Ruby remained calm and piloted the ship through the storm of bullets. On previous occasions, Dougherty had witnessed this behavior from his aircraft commander.

Ruby had the ability to enter a meditative state when all hell was breaking loose—his mind in another place, his senses heightened.

After firing a burst of rounds with the new barrel, Dougherty's gun jammed. "Dammit," he cried over the radio, as their ship continued taking more hits from the ground. Dougherty emptied the chamber of his M-60 and re-fed the linked ammunition into his weapon. He resumed firing but after a few rounds, the gun jammed again.

"We're losing fuel," Hocking shouted over the radio.

Dougherty and his shipmates received one final message from Firebase Nevada. "They're coming in the front door, we're going out the back," the radio operator said, and then the line went dead.

"We've gotta get out of here," Ruby said, but he was a moment too late. A burst of heavy caliber gunfire tore through the ship's tail rotor. The tail boom of the Huey started to yaw to the right. Ruby had enough forward air speed and experience to prevent the ship from entering a death spin—a final, fatal maneuver where the tail boom rotates faster and faster to the right until the helicopter corkscrews into the ground.

"We've lost our tail," Captain Ruby announced over the radio, the implication clear to the other members of his crew. Without the tail rotor, the Huey could not land in a normal, vertical fashion. Ruby could cut the engine and autorotate into hostile territory. Or, if he maintained forward air speed of at least sixty knots, the Huey's vertical fin would keep the ship flying forward, but they would have to fly it into the ground, touching down like a fixed wing aircraft despite having no wheels. After a few minutes of experimenting with the ship's controls, Ruby discovered he could turn the nose of the ship by applying a slight amount of torque to the main rotor using the twist grip on the throttle. He used this technique to set the ship on an eastward trajectory.

"Raider 2-6, we'll escort you to Saigon," the pilot of the high ship said.

"Roger," Ruby replied. "Stay a safe distance. We're leaking fuel."

Dougherty set his M-60 down and inched his way across the cabin, careful not to slip on the hundreds of brass shell casings covering the floor. He leaned out the left door frame and, in the moonlight, spotted fuel spraying from the ship.

"Captain," Dougherty said into his helmet mic, "fuel is leaking around the turbine. We might go up in a big ball of fire. As soon as we're on the ground, we've got to get away from the ship."

Ruby radioed ahead to Tan Son Nhut Air Base in Saigon, the nearest airport of size capable of providing emergency services on the runway. The tower confirmed they would prepare for their arrival. Hocking called out readings from the Huey's instrument panel while Ruby honed his improvised method for flying the damaged ship.

As their Huey approached Tan Son Nhut from the west, Ruby reminded everyone onboard that he could not reduce speed or the ship would spin out of control. Their only option was a running landing at roughly seventy-five miles per hour. Dougherty and Coffey unhooked their monkey belts and braced for impact. If the ship caught fire after landing, a crew member still attached to the ship by his safety harness might burn alive before rescuers could disconnect him. As they descended to the runway in Saigon, Dougherty remembered the surveyor, who was now curled up in the rear of the cabin. He reached over and unclipped Proctor's belt from the wall and attached it to the clip on his own waistline so that he had the civilian on an eight-foot leash.

Through the ship's plexiglass windshield Dougherty spotted the foam-coated tarmac and an assortment of emergency vehicles with flashing lights parked beside the runway. Ruby descended lower and lower until the ship banged down hard, bounced, and skidded forward through a wall of white foam. The flame-retardant material worked its magic as the ship's metal skids and aluminum body scraped along the runway. Once the Huey ground to a halt, the gunner and crew chief jumped from the ship and waded through the foam to open the cockpit doors for their pilots. Then everyone ran from the wreckage with Dougherty dragging Wilson T. Proctor by his safety belt. The men, covered in white foam, dove into a drainage ditch beside the runway, expecting an explosion at any moment, but none came.

After crawling out of the berm, Captain Ruby noticed the surveyor still tightly clutching his clipboard. "Well, how did Dougherty do?" he said to Proctor, who seemed catatonic.

"Not so fuckin' good," Coffey said before the man could reply. "Look at his ship."

"Yep. That's one hell of a mess you've got there, Doc. Good luck with that clean up," Ruby said, slapping his crew chief on the back.

At daybreak, Dougherty's shot up Huey was hosed down and slung back to the maintenance hangar at Bien Hoa. An initial inspection with the mechanic on duty revealed that three enemy rounds had pierced the floor boxes, which caused Dougherty's M-60 to jam. Another round severed the fuel line, which resulted in the spray of JP4. Multiple rounds destroyed the tail rotor gearbox. The hard landing mangled the skids and scraped the paint off the bottom and right side of the Huey's body. "Patches" was filled with an assortment of new bullet holes.

"Any idea when she might be ready to fly?" Dougherty said.

The mechanic laughed and walked away. Swanson stepped up beside the crew chief and stared at the demolished Bell Iroquois helicopter. "That bird ain't flyin' anytime soon," he said, shaking his head. "Come with me." The Ops sergeant led Dougherty to the revetment where his ship normally parked. A different helicopter sat there now. Dougherty recognized it as the Frog.

"O'Donnell's only got ten days and a wake-up left," Swanson said, referring to the Frog's former caretaker. "He's so short a turtle might fuck him if he puts on his helmet. I'm keepin' Big O in Operations until we ship his ass back to Bean Town. The Frog is yours."

The door of the Huey featured a cartoon image of a frog wearing a Boston Red Sox hat while holding a grenade launcher over its shoulder. The chunker's big round metal cover also had the frog's face painted on it, with the barrel of the grenade launcher sticking out like a tongue protruding from the amphibian's mouth. The ship received its nickname, *The Green Monster*, from O'Donnell, a lifelong Red Sox fanatic who grew up in the blue collar Catholic Irish neighborhood of South Boston. And now the Southie was going home.

The ship was in good shape. O'Donnell prided himself on that. It was not lost on Dougherty that the Frog was special and only entrusted to the best crew chiefs in the platoon. This validation meant more to Dougherty than the promotion that Major Sheffield had recently recommended.

When Dougherty returned to the barracks that afternoon, he noticed someone had removed Lowrie's possessions from his room. Dougherty

— STAND BY ME —

spotted Afton Brown in the hallway.

"Hey, A. B., have you seen Vic?"

"Yeah, man. He's gone," Brown said, solemnly.

"Gone?" Dougherty repeated, thinking the worst.

"Not dead and gone. Gone as in goin' home gone."

"They chaptered him out?" Dougherty said, referring to a dishonorable discharge, which was not a stretch considering Lowrie's recent behavior.

"Emergency Leave," Brown replied. "I was sitting with Low in the club when Swanson gave him the news. Red Cross sent word through the chain that Vic's old man had a heart attack and died. Sarge handed Low some orders and told him to pack up ASAP and head to the Air Force side, to catch the next bird back to the States."

"Damn," Dougherty said. "How'd he handle it?"

Brown shook his head. "Strangest thing, man. Vic didn't get upset. When Sarge told him the news, he just stared down at his glass and said, 'I could sense his passing.'"

Dougherty nodded. That sounded like the Lowrie he knew, *sensing* his father's death from halfway around the world.

"I'm sorry you didn't get to see him 'fore he left," Brown added. "I know you guys were tight."

Dougherty nodded and walked back into the plywood room. Lowrie had been his best friend in Vietnam, and now he was gone. It wasn't just Lowrie's sudden departure that bothered him, but the direction his friend's life was moving and the way their friendship had unraveled at the end. When Lowrie really needed a friend, Dougherty felt he had not delivered.

Exhausted from the ESB rotation, Dougherty pulled the blanket back on his bunk. There, on his thin, Army-issued mattress, rested Lowrie's samurai sword in its ornate scabbard, laid vertically, perhaps ceremoniously, on the white sheet. He picked up the katana and retracted the ancient weapon a few inches until his face reflected in the steel blade. He stared at it for a few moments, then clicked the sword back into its sheath.

Dougherty noticed something else on his bunk—a folded note, which he slowly opened.

Good luck to you, Billy. I hope you make peace
with the spirits that visit you in the night. – Vic

The note was the first communication Dougherty received from
Lowrie since their trip to the Montagnard village. Lowrie's few words on
a piece of paper and his parting gift of the sword provided some confir-
mation that their friendship had been real. But true to his nature, Lowrie's
final gesture also raised more questions than it answered.

If his friend took the sawed-off shotgun and left the samurai sword,
what did that mean? Lowrie called the katana a "more honorable" weapon. Dougherty wondered if his friend took the shotgun to spare him
from performing more dishonorable acts and left the sword to remind
him of Bushido, the samurai warrior's high moral code of conduct.

Or perhaps Lowrie felt himself to be the disgraced warrior, undeserv-
ing of the sword after aiding the white man in an unjust war that used
the indigenous people of Vietnam to fight against the colonized people
of Vietnam. And the sword he would one day fall on was not a sword at
all but the weapon of his great ancestor—the shotgun.

Dougherty also considered Lowrie might be trading the sword for
the gun because he needed the shotgun to become Henry Berry Lowrie.
Perhaps this was Vic's way of telling him that honor was not possible in
this lifetime, and the only option was to fight for oneself, even if it meant
living as an outlaw in the swamps of Robeson County.

The passing of Lowrie's father would prove to be his reprieve from
Vietnam. Dougherty soon learned that Victor Braveboy Lowrie was
granted an honorable discharge from the US Army for personal hardship.
The United States government had used Lowrie as a cog in its war machine, and he had performed acceptably for most of a year. The Lumbee
warrior's elite masters were willing to let him go. The decision was not a
particularly compassionate one. A logistician weighed the cost of returning a man to Southeast Asia for less than two months of service. Included
in that calculation was some acknowledgment that a soldier who recently
lost his father might be unproductive, and with that, Lowrie's tour of
duty was over.

For Dougherty, he lost more than a friend: Lowrie served as his moral compass, someone who seemed to be pointing him toward a path through this war—a path that might even lead to his adult self. But now, just as his father had predicted, another important figure in his life was gone. "In the end, they'll all go except for me," Keith Dougherty said to his tearful son the day his mother left. "Just stick with me," his father added, leaving him alone at Candace Dougherty's burial plot.

8

GODBOLT

AFTER A MONTH OF FLYING WITH COFFEY, Captain Ruby had enough: the volatile gunner from Arkansas tested the easygoing Texan's last nerve. A solution to Ruby's dilemma appeared to present itself in the form of Jack Godbolt, a tall, square-jawed kid from Wapakoneta, Ohio, who had recently joined the company. Godbolt cropped his blondish hair so tightly that it looked as if he had a scrub brush balanced on top of his head. He was something of a local hero to the folks in Wapakoneta—a star pitcher for the town's baseball team, a record-setting point guard in basketball, and an all-state running back for the Wapakoneta Redskins. Even Godbolt's lofty name hinted at divine intervention, as if their golden child was sent, like a bolt of lightning, from the heavens. When the good people of Wapakoneta discovered their native son was headed to Vietnam, the consensus was that Uncle Sam was putting in the A-team. After all, what chance did the lowly Vietnamese have against Jack Godbolt, the young lion who mowed down opposing defenders like they were cardboard cutouts?

Wapakoneta was also home to a well-known astronaut by the name of Neil Armstrong. On March 16, 1966, while serving as Command Pilot of Gemini 8, Armstrong made history when he performed the first successful docking of two vehicles in space. That same week, Jack Godbolt and his

84

teenage bride welcomed their child to earth. Jack had impregnated his high school sweetheart the summer before their senior year, and the fruits of their labor arrived the spring before graduation. Instead of heading to Ohio State on a football scholarship, Godbolt took a job in a metal fabrication plant in Wapakoneta, stamping out parts for the auto industry to support his new wife and baby girl.

Armstrong and Godbolt, two young bucks from the same small town in Ohio who both seemed destined for greatness. Why then was it that one man soared into space while another man landed in the GAMCO factory? It was the question that vexed Jack Godbolt during his early adult life.

The day his draft notice arrived in the mail Godbolt believed he had received a course correction from the gods. Vietnam represented another shot at glory, his second chance to show the world what he was capable of in the field. With that frame of mind, Godbolt attacked soldiering with the same tenacity and determination he showed in sports. He received top marks in basic training and at door gunnery school, which he completed at Schofield Barracks Army Base in Oahu, Hawaii, home of the legendary 25th Infantry "Tropic Lightning" Division. Godbolt was given his choice of assignments, and when he asked a gunnery instructor, recently returned from Vietnam, which armed helicopter company was the best, he was told the 334th. The decision was made.

Some of the Raider pilots swore Godbolt was a genius with his personal weapon, the M-79 grenade launcher, which fired a relatively slow-moving explosive round on a curved trajectory toward its intended target. Effective use of the M-79 from a moving helicopter required the user to aim ahead and slightly above the target. Everyone flying with Godbolt watched in awe as his shots curved into hooches and sampans that burst into flames when the rounds struck. Godbolt once fired the M-79 from the skid of a banking Huey and hit a running VC in the back from three hundred meters, blasting the man to pieces. Word spread throughout the Company: the kid had a gift.

The Raiders lost a crew chief when Godbolt's shipmate, Bernie Dietz, accidentally shot himself in the eye with the M-79. Perhaps because his gunner made the weapon look so easy, Dietz decided to try his luck. His first shot out the left door of their Huey hit the tops of some nearby trees and exploded. A piece of shrapnel from the 40 mm round flew back into the cabin and lodged directly in the center of the crew chief's left eye, causing it to burst. Ironically, Dietz had raised the protective visor on his flight helmet moments before firing the weapon so he could see better.

Ruby seized the opportunity. The platoon leader suggested Operations pair Godbolt with Dougherty, an experienced crew chief in need of a gunner since Lowrie's departure. Swanson thought that was a splendid idea, and with the stroke of a pen, the deed was done.

"How did Pearle do yesterday?" Captain Ruby said to Dougherty when he arrived on the flight line for his maiden voyage with Godbolt.

"Four VC, two sampans, and a hooch," Dougherty replied.

"We can do better than that," Ruby replied, as he climbed into the pilot's seat.

After they'd flown twenty minutes north of Bien Hoa to Dau Tieng, the jungle gave way to a beautiful landscaped property with a mansion. "Pretty nice place," Godbolt said over the intercom.

"That's Frenchie's place," Ruby said. "This whole area is a giant rubber plantation owned by a wealthy Frenchman. The tires on your Chevy back home were probably made with rubber from these trees. Here, let me give you a little tour. Maybe his daughters will be out sunbathing."

Ruby maneuvered the helicopter over the stately colonial mansion, which Dougherty had only seen from a distance. The property featured a large grassy yard, manicured gardens, tennis courts, an airstrip, and even a swimming pool.

"Looks like nobody's home," Ruby said over the intercom. "That's too bad. Means something's probably up. What I heard from the guys stationed up here during Operation Manhattan was that when Frenchie took off in his little plane, the shit was about to hit the fan. They say he pays the VC protection money. Now if Frenchie drains his swimming pool, then you're really in trouble. That means Charlie is planning to be around for a while. How's it look, Doc?"

"Water in the pool, sir, but no sunbathers," Dougherty replied. To his surprise, Captain Ruby continued to descend and landed the Huey at the edge of the large yard behind the mansion while his wing ship continued to circle the area.

"Frenchie has a pineapple grove back here," Ruby said over the intercom. "Doc, go grab us a couple of nice pineapples, will you?"

At first Dougherty thought his pilot was joking. Did Ruby expect him to leave the ship for some fruit? Was this another of his pilot's dares, like riding the barrel at Nha Be, designed to test his mettle while entertaining the crew? And why didn't Ruby ask Goldbolt to go? Now, if he refused the challenge, he would look like a chicken in front of the new guy. Dougherty slipped out of the safety harness and removed his flight helmet. He hopped down onto the grass lawn that felt soft and squishy beneath his feet.

As he entered the grove through a crumbling stone wall, Dougherty noticed small piles of pineapples throughout the field; the fruit hacked away from the knee-high cabbage-like plants. Dougherty leaned over and picked two pineapples from a stack. He studied each one for a moment then held them up for Ruby to see, expecting a thumbs up or thumbs down on his selection. Instead, the pilots waved frantically at him.

"Get back!" Hocking shouted from the cockpit door. "We're taking fire."

Dougherty turned in time to see a puff of smoke at the edge of the rubber trees. Godbolt chunked a grenade from the M-79 over Dougherty's head as he raced back to the ship. He heard the round explode behind him as he tossed the pineapples into the cabin and jumped through his open door. Ruby immediately lifted off and turned the ship away from the gunfire to present a smaller target. The Huey climbed over the mansion, then ascended away from property at an angle, gaining altitude and distance with each second. Once out of small arms range, the wing ship joined the lead ship, and the two helicopters flew toward the free strike zone in western Vietnam.

With Godbolt as their gunner, Dougherty and his shipmates watched in disbelief as their numbers of VC, sampans, and hooches increased with each mission. Sometimes Godbolt's shooting required Hocking to make so many tick marks on the windshield with his grease pencil that Dougherty wondered how the warrant officer could see to pilot their ship. Godbolt was so spectacular in combat that Dougherty occasionally found himself following the gunner's performance rather than firing his own weapon. While he had to admit, as he did privately to Captain Ruby, that Godbolt made them all look better, Dougherty found the gunner's confidence maddening, while the man's energy and drive appeared limitless. At the end of a long day of flying, Godbolt often stowed his flight gear and headed out on a two- or three-mile run, while Dougherty collapsed into his bunk. Even at night, while Dougherty and Coffey watched TV and drank beer, their new roommate performed sit-ups and push-ups beside his bunk.

One hot afternoon, Dougherty sat on a stack of sandbags and smoked several Marlboros while he watched Godbolt shooting free throws, trying to figure out what made his gunner tick. The man had erected a sheet of plywood beneath the crude metal hoop mounted to the side of the barracks that kicked the ball back to him if he made the shot. If he missed, which rarely happened, he hastily retrieved the ball and jogged back to the free throw line. Dougherty finally grew bored of the monotonous drill, flicked his cigarette butt in the dirt, and sauntered off in the direction of the mess hall with Sam following closely behind, wagging his tail in anticipation of the scraps that might fall his way.

Soon, however, the first chink appeared in Godbolt's armor: Dougherty caught the man sitting on the edge of his bunk, shoulders slumped, staring at a photo of the baby girl he had fathered. That little seven-pound bundle of pink flesh seemed to present more of an obstacle to his new gunner than any linebacker ever did. After a while, Godbolt cleared his throat, which caused Dougherty to look over from his bunk. "Captain Ruby said you were a star quarterback in high school. Is that true?"

"Yep, starting QB for the Litchfield Trojans," Dougherty said and laughed. "We had a hard time coming up with eleven guys, so we usually lost to schools that had enough players for an offense AND a defense. They always wore us down in the fourth quarter," Dougherty added and flashed his crooked smile.

"Would you mind tossin' me some passes?" Godbolt said, holding out his football.

Dougherty stared at the pigskin, wondering if Captain Ruby had talked Godbolt into pulling his chain. "Sure," he finally said.

After playing catch for thirty minutes, during which time Godbolt never dropped a single pass no matter how poorly thrown, Dougherty walked toward his roommate—the universal sign for "bring it in."

"Everything ok?" Godbolt said.

"There's somethin' I got to ask you," Dougherty said. "You always seem so sure of yourself, whether you're shootin' a free throw or shootin' at Charlie. How is that?"

A perplexed expression crossed Godbolt's face.

"I mean, you just do everything so naturally and without hesitation," Dougherty said.

Godbolt thought for a moment and nodded. "I guess it's like football. If the quarterback hands me the ball and there's an opening in the line, I don't stop and think, 'Well, there's a fine hole. Should I go through it?' If I did that, I'd get tackled. Probably for a loss. When I see that hole, I race through it. I guess that's how I see life. When that hole opens up, you have to go through it, or the hole will close. Maybe forever."

Dougherty considered the response, then nodded. "Go deep," he said. Godbolt took the cue and immediately sprinted in the direction of the barracks. As he watched his gunner breeze past non-existent defenders, Dougherty realized that Godbolt and Coffey had something in common. Coffey was always in the moment, too, but only in the way a weather-vane mounted atop a barn was—one moment pointing east, then west, depending on which way the wind was blowing. Dougherty let loose a long spiral pass that Godbolt gracefully hauled in, then he raced across an imaginary goal line. As the young lion raised his hands in celebration, Dougherty concluded there was a consistency to Godbolt's actions that gave him his sense of purpose—he was always running toward an endzone, while Coffey was just running all over the field.

Still, there was that little seven-pound linebacker, capable of bringing Godbolt down all by herself, Dougherty thought as he jogged to catch up with his gunner. In running through a hole to Vietnam, Godbolt had also run away from his wife and baby girl, and that dilemma, Dougherty believed, was the reason for his gunner's perpetual motion—to forget the past by intensely engaging in the present.

When the two men got back to their room, Dougherty opened his locker. Inside, the two pineapples from the Frenchman's plantation flanked Lowrie's samurai sword. "Hey, Jack," Dougherty said.

Goldbolt turned and Dougherty tossed one of the pineapples to his gunner, who instinctively raised his hands and deftly caught the lateral pass.

"Thanks," Godbolt said, admiring the tropical fruit.

"You earned it. You saved my ass at the plantation."

Godbolt nodded and smiled.

"What's her name?" Dougherty said when he noticed Godbolt had turned his attention back to the photo of his daughter attached to the front of his locker.

"Penelope. My wife calls her Penny. I call her my little Pea."

When Dougherty spied a tear sliding down Godbolt's cheek, he wondered if his mother had similar moments of anguish, after leaving him to run through a hole to California.

THE RED BARON

IN MID-JULY, ANOTHER CASSETTE ARRIVED IN THE MAIL.
Dougherty refused to play his father's recording in the barracks with Coffey
offering running commentary, so he took the Panasonic to his revetment,
to listen in the Huey. Dougherty settled into his seat on the left side of
the cabin, took a deep breath, and pressed *play*.

> *Greetings, Boke. I got your last cassette. Sounds like you landed*
> *in a good spot there with the 334th. First armed helicopter company*
> *ever. That's something. Glad you asked my opinion about reenlisting.*
> *I definitely think you should. If you come home after one tour, they'll*
> *just ship you back for another one. And who knows what kind of*
> *crap assignment they'll give you. Might as well finish the job with the*
> *334th. Besides, the war might not even last that long. I can't imagine*
> *the slopes holding out against you boys much longer* (the sound of ice
> cubes clinking against glass).
>
> *Be good to see you when you're home at Christmas. Maybe we can*
> *do a little hunting. I'll take you to the VFW for a beer, introduce you*
> *to some of the other vets. I'll bet you have some good stories.*

Next, Keith Dougherty gave a lengthy account of a laundromat his
company was building at the state penitentiary in Lincoln. Dougherty

watched helicopters arriving and departing on the flight line as he half-heartedly listened. His ears perked up when his father abruptly changed subjects.

You asked about why I left that dead-end job at the post office. I'll tell you why. They hired a real jerk to be our new postmaster. That asshole from Broken Bow rolled into town like some big shot know-it-all and tried to change everything.

Dougherty nearly fell out of his seat at his father's mention of *Broken Bow*. He pressed stop, rewound the tape, and listened to the line about Broken Bow again. He hastily retrieved the newspaper clippings from his pocket, found the one with the quote from the new postmaster, and scanned the article for the man's name—Lonnie Slocum. The clipping made no mention of Slocum's hometown, but the postmaster's disdain for Keith Dougherty was apparent and could be a motive for sending the articles, particularly the one about his father's dismissal from the post office. After all, what better way to get back at an enemy than by knocking him down in front of his son? Dougherty wondered how Slocum knew his address in Vietnam, but concluded that if the man served as postmaster, it was information he probably had access to. Dougherty felt he had his first solid lead on the mysterious articles. He pressed the play button on the recorder.

Anyhow, we had a big falling out one day. I told him to shove it and quit. Best decision I ever made. Started the construction company after that. Now I'm my own boss and nobody tells me what to do. Best feeling in the world.

Hey, I bumped into Max Larsen the other day. He said Dag joined the Air Force and is over there in Saigon. I guess he's at West-moreland's headquarters. Pretty impressive. I always thought that Dag was a bit of a squirrel, but he must be doin' something right if he's workin' for the top dog. If you ever get to Saigon, maybe you can look him up. Who knows, maybe you'll get to meet Westmoreland.

I guess that's it for now. Keep one foot on the ground, Boke.

Dougherty leaned back in the seat and closed his eyes. The word *Boke* hung in the air of the cabin. His father assigned him the nickname as a young boy. He said a *boke* was a type of white snake and his son was so long and lean at birth that he reminded him of that snake. Years later, when Dougherty enrolled at Kearney State College, he asked his biology professor about the boke snake. The herpetologist dismissed the question, saying no such thing existed.

"Doc, what are you up to?" Captain Pearle said, leaning into the Huey.

Pearle's sudden presence startled Dougherty. Not wanting to go into a long explanation about the articles and recordings from home, Dougherty said the first thing that popped into his head. "I wanted to inspect the ship before we fly tonight."

"Great idea," Pearle said. "Let's do it together."

Once the initial shock of the pilot's offer wore off, Dougherty handed Pearle the ship's logbook so he could document the inspection.

The designers of the Huey placed a couple of small steps in the body that provided access to the top of the ship. Spring-loaded doors concealed the steps. The crew chief pushed down on one of the small panels and peered inside, looking for any dirt or wet spots on the floor of the engine compartment. "Clean and dry," Dougherty said. Pearle noted it in the logbook.

"Every nut and bolt on this ship has a paint mark to show if it's tight. If you see a nut that's away from the paint mark, then we know it's loose," Dougherty said, as he walked around the nose of the ship, looking for structural damage. Next, he crouched down and inspected the Huey's undercarriage. "Everything looks fine, here," he said after emerging from beneath the ship.

Pearle followed Dougherty as he inspected the drive shaft from the transmission to the tail rotor, looking for any bullet holes or other damage.

"You and Godbolt have been flying with Ruby a lot lately," Pearle said, while Dougherty checked the tail rotor for signs of cracking. "How's that going?"

"Fine, sir," Dougherty said, then used the spring-loaded steps to climb on top of the Huey and inspect the push-pull tubes that ran from the swash plate to the rotor blades. These tubes, which changed the pitch on the rotors and caused the helicopter to lift or descend, had Teflon bushings that occasionally wore out and needed to be checked daily.

The talkative pilot followed the crew chief onto the roof of the helicopter. "I'll tell you one thing," Pearle said, as he looked across the flight line at the rows of gunships parked in their revetments, "flying Hueys over here has helped me understand how those old aviators felt about their Sopwith Camels and Albatros two-seaters. Those were the first armed airplanes, and we're over here flying the first armed helicopters. We're making history, Doc. First with guns," Pearle said, nodding at their ship.

Dougherty examined the push-pull tubes in silence.

"When I was a kid," Pearle continued, "my mother gave me a book about the top aces from the First World War. I spent hours reading about those famous pilots and their dogfights over northern France and Germany. For Hanukkah that year, my uncle gave me an old aviator's cap and a pair of goggles that I wore everywhere, even to bed," the pilot said and laughed.

"In the back of the book, it listed the top fighter pilot for each country," Pearle continued. "Manfred von Richthofen was the top ace in the war. You probably know him by his nickname, 'The Red Baron.' The Baron downed eighty Allied planes before he was shot down by Captain Roy Brown, a Canadian flying for the RAF. Rene Fonck, the great French pilot, had seventy-five 'victories,' as they called them. Mick Mannock flew for the RAF and shot down seventy-three. Eddie Rickenbacker was the top American ace. He had twenty-six.

"I lived inside that book. I loved the chivalry and romance of it all. Those pilots had a real style with their leather flying jackets and scarves. They dueled their enemies in the skies over the frontlines, then flew back to base in time for drinks and dinner at the chateau.

"The book had quite a few pictures. God, those planes were beautiful," Pearle said. "The Baron's red Fokker triplane with its black Iron Cross. Can you imagine seeing that on your tail? Or if you were a German pilot, imagine seeing Fonck's Nieuport with the French cockade on its wings suddenly dropping out of the sky.

"The things they did with those planes—loops, barrel rolls, forced stalls—they were fearless pioneers of aviation. That's us, Dougherty. We're doing the same thing here with the Huey gunships. Who knows, maybe one day they'll write books about us."

Dougherty chuckled at the thought of such a book as he checked the head on the collective collet that provided friction and gave the stick some feel by transferring pressure from the rotor blades back into the stick.

Determined to get a response from his quiet crew chief, Pearle continued his tale. "When I was growing up in New York, all I really knew about my old man was that he died in Europe during the Second World War. I guess I got this idea in my head that my father was a pilot, and that's why my mother gave me the book. So one day I asked her if he was an aviator. She laughed and then she cried, but that's when I found out he was a professor of mathematics at the University of Prague. The man had a real head for numbers, I'm told.

"I don't tell this to many guys in the company, Doc," the pilot said to his crew chief's back, "but my father died in the Holocaust. He was politically active during the Nazi occupation. When my mother got pregnant with me at the end of '40, he took every penny they had and sent her to live in New York with her sister. I was born in the Big Apple in '41. Not long after that, the Nazis started rounding up Jews in Czechoslovakia and shipped them to a camp north of Prague. They were loaded into train cars and moved to concentration camps in Germany and Poland.

"I only have one photograph of my father," Pearle continued. "He's standing beside my mother on their wedding day. I know every detail of that picture. I can close my eyes and see that curly hair beneath his Kippah. He's holding a pipe down at his side, trying to hide it from the camera. He's got a little notebook in his breast pocket. Probably for calculations. Doing math on his wedding day," Pearle said, shaking his head.

"Do you know much about the Holocaust, Dougherty?" Pearle asked.

"Not much, sir," Dougherty replied. He was checking all four bolts of the pillow block. "My old man served in the South Pacific."

"The Nazis killed six million Jews during the war. Six million. It's hard to wrap your head around that number. My father died at Auschwitz in 1944. More than a million Jews were murdered there. When prisoners arrived in the camp, the first thing the Nazis did was shave off their hair. My father's beautiful curly hair. . . . They sold it to companies that made slippers and mattresses."

"I'm sorry, Captain," Dougherty said, turning to face Pearle.

"The thing about genocide, Doc, is that it goes much deeper than killing. The Nazis tried to take everything from us—our religion, our communities, our property, our hair, even our names. They tattooed a number on each Jew's arm, and that's how you were known in the camps—by your number, not your name. I think about that a lot. My father loved numbers, and then the Germans tattooed a row of them on his arm. They even killed his love of numbers."

Wanting to change the subject, Dougherty pointed at the large bolt that held the rotor blades on the Huey's body. "We always check the Jesus nut," he said.

"Why do you call it that?" Pearle replied with a perplexed look.

"When you're five hundred feet above the jungle, taking enemy fire, you start prayin' to Jesus for that one nut to hold you up," Dougherty said.

Pearle laughed. "Jews don't pray to Jesus. Maybe I should pray to the Adonai Nut."

Dougherty smiled and nodded. "We'll take any help we can get, sir."

"I hope we'll get to fly together more often," Pearle said as they climbed down.

"That would be fine, sir. Appreciate your help with the inspection."

Captain Pearle returned the logbook to Dougherty, then extended his hand. The enlisted airman wiped his hand on his pant leg to remove any oil or grease before he shook it.

As Pearle walked away from the flight line, Dougherty felt more deeply ensnared in the rivalry between the departing pilot and Captain Ruby. He believed Pearle respected his skills as a crew chief, but he also knew the man was smart enough to sense his loyalty to Ruby. In the end, only one man would receive command of the Cobras, and Dougherty wondered if he would live long enough to see which one triumphed.

BIG IRON

IN EARLY AUGUST Dougherty earned his first out-of-country R&R, while Coffey qualified for his second one. After weeks of careful deliberation and heated debate, the two men chose Hong Kong over Bangkok. It wasn't Hong Kong's British colonial status or its proximity to mainland China that lured them. Neither man had read Richard Mason's *The World of Suzie Wong* nor seen the film version starring William Holden. For Dougherty, the allure was the fact that his father had taken shore leave in Hong Kong during the Second World War. Coffey, on the other hand, was drawn by its bars, brothels, and high-quality tailored suits.

At the R&R departure center, the two men changed into civilian clothes, exchanged their military script for a stack of Hong Kong dollars, and received a briefing on proper conduct for US servicemen on leave. That afternoon, the two men walked onto the tarmac at Bien Hoa and up a rolling flight of stairs leading to a Pan-Am commercial airliner. Dougherty and dozens of other GIs in line gawked at the beautiful American stewardess greeting each soldier at the door of the cabin—a pleasant distraction from the parallel row of palletized gray steel coffins staged on the tarmac, awaiting transport back to the United States.

During the flight, the two airmen ate steak and ice cream and chatted with their stewardesses. When the pilot announced their descent,

Dougherty stared in disbelief at the mountains and skyscrapers surrounding Kai Tak Airport's runway, which extended into Victoria Harbour.

Their first stop in Kowloon, after checking into their cheap, one-star hotel on Nathan Road, was a bar across the street aptly named the Happy Bar. After they downed a couple of drinks, an elegantly dressed older Chinese woman made her way to their table.

"You look like nice American boys," she said. "First time in Hong Kong?"

"Yes, ma'am," they replied in unison.

"You like two nice girls show you around the city? See some sites. Do some shopping. Maybe get nice suit. They get you good deal."

Before either man could respond, the woman motioned across the room. Two beautiful young women in silk dresses made their way to the table.

"This is Suzie, like Suzie Wong," the woman said pointing to the girl nearest Coffey. "And this is Mae, like Mae West," she added, pointing to the girl beside Dougherty.

"Hi," they said, slightly out of sync, then giggled shyly and waved.

"Would you girls like to show these nice boys around Hong Kong tomorrow?" the older woman said.

"Sure. That would be fun. We meet you in hotel lobby tomorrow morning at ten," one of the girls said. Then they shuffled away.

"Don't run away, girls" Coffey said, craning his neck to catch a final glimpse of the beautiful young women before they disappeared into the back room.

"These no yum-yum girls," the elderly woman said, using a common phrase for Hong Kong's prostitutes. "These good girls who show you around, keep you safe, help you shop. Only one hundred Hong Kong dollars for one day," the woman said.

Coffey did some quick math in his head.

"About ten bucks each. We'll take 'em," Coffey announced, then reached into his pocket and extracted a fistful of bills. "My treat," he said to Dougherty as he handed the money to the woman. "We're in the four-star hotel across the street," Coffey added, sarcastically.

The woman smiled and nodded. "Remember," she said, wagging her finger at Coffey, "no yum-yum."

The next morning Suzie and Mae arrived at the hotel wearing different silk dresses, their long dark hair held in place by ornate porcelain combs. From the hotel, it was a short walk to the Star Ferry, which transported passengers from the Kowloon Quay across Victoria Harbour to Hong Kong Island. Dougherty and Coffey leaned against the rails of the ferry and watched old wooden junks with square sails maneuvering around commercial freighters and naval ships from the U.S. Seventh Fleet.

In Hong Kong's commercial district, red double decker buses, motorcycles, cars, and rickshaws all jockeyed for position on the overcrowded streets while a flood of human traffic, mostly well-dressed residents of Hong Kong, filled the sidewalks beneath high-rise buildings and neon signs. Dougherty recognized some western brands like Lucky Strikes and Coca-Cola, but most of the advertisements featured Chinese characters.

Suzie and Mae insisted they all ride the tram to the summit of Victoria Peak, the highest point on Hong Kong Island. As the metal car slowly ascended the steep hillside, it afforded passengers an increasingly spectacular view of the various islands that comprised Hong Kong and the hundreds of ships jockeying for position in Victoria Harbour. Upon arriving at the final stop, Coffey suggested the two couples walk in opposite directions around the summit. He and Suzie went left, while Dougherty and Mae took the path to the right. On the tour, Mae pointed out Buddhist temples and mountain steppe farming in the steep rocky cliffs above the city.

After a couple of hours, the two couples reconnected at a quiet outdoor café. They spent the rest of the afternoon together—the men drinking beer and laughing, the girls sipping tea and giggling—before they finally rode the tram back down to sea level.

After returning to Kowloon, Mae and Suzie took Dougherty and Coffey to a tailor's shop near their hotel to get measured for their suits. The tailor informed his new clients that their suits would be ready on Tuesday, the day before they were scheduled to leave Hong Kong.

"What's next, girls?" Coffey said once they exited the shop.

Suzie and Mae quietly conferred with each other and then took the two young men by their hands and led them down a series of narrow alleys in the Tsim Sha Tsui District of Kowloon, where they saw no other

GIs or British civilians. The two Americans sensed a hostility in the stares they received from pedestrians and street vendors but did not realize they had arrived in Hong Kong in the midst of labor strikes and pro-Communist demonstrations against British Colonial rule.

Dougherty and Coffey followed the young women into a five-story building with a red and white striped awning over the front entrance. The ground floor of the apartment building served multiple purposes, including shelter for street vendors, storage for the residents, and parking for dozens of bicycles and motorbikes. An old woman who sat behind a large basket of rice that she sold by the cup shook her head disapprovingly at the sight of the Americans. Suzie and Mae raised the wooden door to a large service elevator. The four of them entered the lift and rode slowly up to the fifth floor to the girls' apartment. Inside the small flat, a slightly older woman, presumably a third roommate, chatted with a US Marine on the sofa. After a terse exchange with Suzie and Mae in Chinese, the woman and her companion disappeared into a side room. The young escorts cooked Dougherty and Coffey some traditional Chinese food and then tried to teach the Americans how to play Mahjong, a Chinese board game with connecting tiles that reminded Dougherty of dominoes.

After ten minutes of Mahjong, Coffey abruptly tossed his tiles down on the board. "I'm tired of this fuckin' game. And I'm tired of this tourist shit," he said. "I came to Hong Kong to fuck and drink, not to play dink dominoes."

"Calm down," Dougherty said.

"I won't fuckin' calm down. I want to go in the back room like that Marine. Yum yum time," Coffey said to Suzie, who looked confused and horrified at her date's sudden transformation.

"No yum yum," Mae said. "Just tour guide."

"Bullshit," Coffey barked. "I know how much a whore costs in Hong Kong. I paid my money, and I want yum yum."

Coffey flipped the Mahjong board aside, sending tiles flying across the room. The girls screamed, but before Coffey could grab Suzie, Dougherty wrapped his long arms around the gunner's chest.

"Let go of me, goddamn it," Coffey said, twisting against his friend's grip.

Following Coffey's outburst, the marine and his female companion emerged from the other room while several neighbors suddenly appeared at the door.

"Chuck, let's go back to Nathan Road," Dougherty said, struggling to contain the outraged man. "I saw a place near the hotel that has booze and girls, but we need to get out of here."

"Listen to your buddy," the marine said.

"SHUT UP, YOU FUCKIN' JARHEAD," Coffey shouted.

The marine's eyes widened then narrowed while his posture stiffened, as though Coffey's words had flipped a switch in the soldier's brain. The devil dog charged at the gunner still wrapped in Dougherty's arms. As the marine approached, Dougherty released his friend to block the approaching man, but there wasn't enough time for Coffey to defend himself. The leatherneck delivered a blow to Coffey's face that sent him tumbling backward into the sofa. Before the marine could continue his assault, Dougherty stepped in and shouted, "ENOUGH! WE'RE LEAVING." Once Dougherty established that he was prepared to fight, the marine calculated his odds against two men and lowered his fist.

"Get the fuck out of here before I kill both of you," he said.

Dougherty grabbed Coffey by the arm and dragged him to the door. He bumped past several locals, desperate to get his friend out of the apartment before he could scuttle the truce. Dougherty refused to release his grip on Coffey's arm until they were back out on the busy street and headed in the direction of Nathan Road. He looked over his shoulder several times to see if the marine or any of the locals were giving chase, but no one was in pursuit. A tiny stream of blood trickled from Coffey's nose, over his lip, and onto his clothes. At first, Dougherty thought Coffey was crying but, in fact, he was laughing—a barely audible chuckle that swelled to a cackle.

"I can't wait to tell the guys about this," Coffey said, wiping the blood on his face with his arm. "Let's go get a drink."

When Dougherty finally spotted their shabby hotel on Nathan Road, he felt the same sense of relief he often experienced upon returning to Bien Hoa following an intense combat mission. Dougherty had no desire to go out again that evening. Instead, he purchased a bottle of Jim Beam and two six packs of beer from a small shop next to their hotel and suggested they order some room service. The fifth of liquor served as an effective tranquilizer, and by nine that evening Coffey had passed out on his bed.

On Monday, the two men spent the entire day at the Oriental Bunny Club on Cameron Road. The bar's scantily clad waitresses served drinks while wearing rabbit ears and faux bunny tails. Coffey seemed to enjoy the combination of beautiful women, cheap drinks, and loud music. To Dougherty, intoxication seemed like the only viable option for keeping Coffey in check until they returned to Vietnam.

By Tuesday morning Coffey had enough of the Oriental Bunny Club and wanted a change of scenery. He picked out a bar further down Nathan Road called The King's Crown. As he downed one drink after another in the pub, Coffey started talking in a fake British accent. At first, Dougherty found the shtick humorous, but after an hour he begged Coffey to can it.

When Coffey noticed several British sailors at a nearby table, he started talking loudly again in his awful British accent.

"It's the bloody Queen's Navy," he said.

The men sneered at Coffey.

"They look jolly good in their sailor suits," Coffey said when the men returned to their conversation.

The largest of the three sailors got up and walked over to their table.

"Is there a problem, mate?" he said to Coffey.

"No problem, MATE," Coffey replied, snickering. "Jolly good. Right as rain."

"Chuck, shut up," Dougherty said. "He didn't mean anything. Here, the next round is on us," Dougherty said, holding out a bill. The man ignored the offer and walked away.

"Cheerio, old chap," Coffey said loudly.

The sailor turned and charged toward the table, but this time Chuck was prepared. He lunged up from his chair and delivered several blows in rapid succession that sent the man toppling backward into a table of American sailors. When the British sailors rushed to the aid of their fallen comrade, the Americans assumed they were under attack and started swinging at the Brits. All hell broke loose in the club as barmaids and boozehounds raced for the exit.

In the melee, Dougherty pushed Coffey out the door of the club and across Nathan Road. He dragged his friend, who was again laughing hysterically, toward the Star Ferry. He wanted to get as far away from the scene as possible.

When Dougherty spotted two MPs on shore patrol racing toward The King's Crown, he pulled Coffey into the first available shop, which happened to be a record store. The two young Americans tried to compose themselves and started flipping through stacks of vinyl records in a bin marked *A – E*: the Beach Boys, the Beatles, Buffalo Springfield, the Byrds, the Doors, Bob Dylan.

After a few minutes, Dougherty moved to the other side of the stall, which offered a view of Nathan Road, and flipped through records from bands whose names started with the letters R through T: the Rolling Stones, Barry Sadler, Nancy Sinatra, Percy Sledge, the Supremes, the Trogs.

The men soon forgot about the MPs and started to feel like twenty-year-old Americans again. Coffey held up the Beatles' newest release, *Sergeant Pepper's Lonely Hearts Club Band*. The inebriated gunner shook his head while pointing at the album's colorful jacket and said in his faux British accent, "Tell me, Gov, ooze gonna buy this hippie shite from the Beat Holes?"

Dougherty snorted loudly, causing the other patrons to look up from the stacks. Once they spotted the drunk Americans, they left the store, one by one.

The young Chinese shop owner, who wore a striped shirt and sported a Beatles mop-top haircut, walked over to the GIs.

"Fellows, you scare away all my customer. That no good."

Coffey tried to contain his laughter and, instead, blew raspberries in the man's face.

"Here's the deal, fellows. I know those MP outside prob-lee look for you guys. You spend some money in my shop, I not call shore patrol."

A crazed look suddenly appeared in Coffey's eyes, as if he might snap the man's neck, but some measure of common sense still functioned in the gunner's alcohol-riddled mind. He realized that beating the man would most likely result in his being jailed in Hong Kong. Besides, Coffey wanted to purchase a record player while on leave, so he could "drown out the crap" his platoonmates listened to in the barracks.

Coffey smiled and patted the man on the chest. "Ok, boss. We spend some money in your shop."

Coffey sobered up while the salesman explained the different stereo systems to him. He eventually settled on an American-made Magnavox Stereophonic Portable Record Player. Packed away, the Magnavox looked like a suitcase, but upon opening the latches, the turn table could be lowered, and two speakers opened like cabinet doors. The shop owner reminded Coffey that he needed something to play on his new stereo. Dougherty rolled his eyes when the gunner chose Marty Robbins' 1959 release *Gunfighter Ballads and Trail Songs*. The album's first song, *Big Iron,* had been adopted by the 334th and was a standard on the juke box at the Enlisted Men's Club.

Coffey spent his last Hong Kong dollars on the record player and Marty Robbins record.

With the shore patrol no longer in sight, the two GIs left the record store and returned to the tailor's shop to pick up their suits. The tailor complimented the young men on how handsome they looked, sold them each a pair of dress shoes that matched their suits, and smiled when Dougherty paid for everything.

Later that evening, while Dougherty picked at some leftover Chinese food in their hotel room, Coffey stepped out of the bathroom wearing his new suit.

"It's our last night in Hong Kong. I'm goin' out," Coffey said, then bummed some money for one final trip to the brothel.

"There's a good dink band at the club two blocks down on Nathan Road," Coffey said before closing the door. "Meet me there later for a drink. And enjoy yourself for a change. You're on vacation, goddammit."

Dougherty nodded, relieved Coffey had finally given him a moment of peace. While in Hong Kong, Dougherty had witnessed his friend's personality change by the hour. Guessing who the man was at any given moment was like spinning a roulette wheel. One moment Coffey was helping a little old lady across a busy street and the next he was picking a fight in a bar. Initially, Dougherty found himself drawn to the gunner's unpredictability. It could be fun and entertaining, but by the fourth day, he felt exhausted.

After shaving and showering, Dougherty studied his body in the mirror on the closet door. He didn't have access to a full-length mirror at Bien Hoa, and it had been months since he had looked at himself. He appeared as thin as he did during his freshman year in high school, but his upper body was now muscular and tight, the skin on his face, neck, and arms turned brown and leathery by Vietnam's tropical climate.

Before leaving for R&R, Dougherty had packed a stack of mail in his bag. For days, he imagined himself sitting in the lobby of a nice hotel in Hong Kong, freshly shaved and showered, wearing a new suit, sipping a good cup of coffee at a table covered in white linens, and going through his mail. He told this idea to Mae while they walked around Victoria Peak, and she suggested the Peninsula Hotel.

Two prostitutes working opposite sides of Nathan Road immediately spotted Dougherty when he exited the hotel.

"Hey, rich American, you want yum-yum girl?" one called out from across the street.

"Hey GI, souvenir me," the other prostitute said playfully as the American approached her, a suggestion that he court her with some gift.

"Maybe later," Dougherty replied.

"Hey GI, why wait? Get lucky now," the prostitute shouted as he continued down Nathan Road. After a few blocks, Dougherty turned left onto Salisbury Road near the Star Ferry. There, at the edge of Victoria Harbour, sat the massive, horseshoe-shaped white colonial structure of the Peninsula Hotel. A fleet of Rolls Royce sedans lined the entrance to the four-star hotel, their drivers neatly dressed in black suits and caps, standing at attention like soldiers in formation. The owners billed the Peninsula as the finest hotel east of the Suez Canal. When Dougherty walked into the immense lobby wearing his tailored suit and with a pocketful of Hong Kong dollars, the young American felt like he might just pass for an international businessman. An impeccably dressed British concierge directed him to the hotel's impressive restaurant.

Dougherty ordered a coffee and set his mail on the white linen tablecloth. He skimmed a letter from the US Army confirming his recent promotion and pay increase. Next, he reviewed his latest bank statement—$6,134.31 in the Litchfield Bank and Trust. Each month, he had most of his pay deposited in his bank account back home.

After the waiter replenished his coffee, Dougherty reached for the letter he had waited so patiently to open. There were countless times in the days leading up to R&R when he nearly opened it. Once or twice, after a difficult mission, he even had his finger on the corner of the envelope from California, ready to tear it open. But each time he refrained, opting instead to read the letter from his mother while on leave in Hong Kong, clean and rested, sipping a cup of good coffee in a beautiful hotel. Now that moment had finally arrived.

He picked up the almond-colored envelope with a return address in Santa Monica and slowly unsealed it with his finger. As he removed the note from inside, Dougherty thought he detected a faint scent of his mother's favorite perfume. He slowly unfolded the note with impeccable handwriting.

Dear William,

It must be quite a shock for you to receive this letter. I know it's been seven years since I left, and you must hate me. There's a reason I didn't write or visit all those years. I promised your father I never would if he agreed to let me and Barry go without a fight. That must sound cowardly to a soldier, but I had to get away from Litchfield or I was sure I was going to die there.

Barry's family occasionally sends us copies of the Sherman County Times, so I saw the article about you serving in the helicopter company in Bien Hoa. I called the Army to get your address. I guess they're not supposed to give out that information, but I was able to convince a nice young man to help me. I wasn't sure whether I should write, but I finally decided to because you're a grown man now and you can make your own decisions. I want to be a part of your life again, William, if that's something you want.

I can never go back to Litchfield, but I know that soldiers going to and from Vietnam often fly through California. Maybe you

could come visit me in LA sometime. We need to talk. There's
so much I need to tell you, and I'm sure you have a million
questions for me. I wouldn't blame you if you threw this letter in
the trash and never thought of me again. But I hope you won't.
I never stopped loving you or thinking about you. My number in
Santa Monica is 464-3895.

Love always, Your Mother

Dougherty stared out the hotel's large glass windows toward Victoria Harbour, not knowing how to feel about his mother's invitation. For seven years, she did not exist in his life, and now, out of the blue, she wanted to see him. Did she really believe she would have died if she had stayed in Litchfield or that she would have to fight his father if she had tried to stay in touch? Like the mysterious newspaper articles from Broken Bow, his mother's letter suggested Keith Dougherty was not the man he believed him to be.

When Dougherty read Candace Haller's letter a second time, her line about Barry's family sending them the *Sherman County Times* caught his attention. He briefly considered the possibility that his mother or Barry was the one sending him the articles in Vietnam. They certainly had a motive for disparaging Keith Dougherty. But if Candace had just obtained his address at Bien Hoa, then she would not have had his address at Long Binh where Dougherty received the two envelopes. Also, there was the issue of the postmarks from Broken Bow, which ruled out his mother and Barry. Postmaster Slocum still seemed the more likely culprit.

As he was about to motion to the waiter for his tab, Dougherty noticed one final piece of mail on the table—a smaller letter with an Omaha return address. He opened the envelope and removed the note.

Dear Bill,

You don't know me, but my name is Lena Weiss. I'm a nurs-
ing student at Duchesne College of the Sacred Heart, an all-girls
Catholic school in Omaha.

My hallmate, Connie, has been writing to soldiers in Viet-
nam. The other day, I walked into Connie's room, and she was
working on some letters. She picked the next name on her list

*and said, here Lena, you should write to this guy, Bill Dougherty.
So that's what I'm doing. (Connie is very persuasive!)*

*I'm from Grand Island, so not too far from Litchfield. I'm
studying to be a nurse. I'm just one year in, but so far, I like it.*

*Anyhow, I just wanted to say thank you for your service to
our country. If you like getting letters, let me know and I'll keep
writing.*

Take care,

Lena

Dougherty returned the letter to the envelope and tucked it inside his
coat pocket. The young American enjoyed one final cup of coffee, savor-
ing every drop, then paid his bill and left the Peninsula Hotel. Dougherty
knew, as he walked past the luxury cars, that he had reached his furthest
point from Vietnam, and now he was beginning his journey back to the
war. He still had one piece of unfinished business before leaving Hong
Kong. He slipped into the red-light district of Kowloon and wandered
the streets until he found what he was looking for.

When Dougherty returned to the hotel later that evening, he found Coffey
passed out, face down in bed, still wearing his suit, a half-empty bottle
of Jim Beam on the nightstand. Dougherty stared at the black telephone
beside the bottle, debating in his mind something he had considered
since the day they checked into their dingy little room. He picked up the
receiver. A cheerful operator with a British accent helped him place a call
to a number in Nebraska. After the phone rang half a dozen times, it occurred to him that midnight in Hong Kong was ten in the morning back
home. As Dougherty prepared to hang up, his father answered the call.

"Hello?" the gruff voice said, sounding confused and angry. "Who is
this?" Keith Dougherty demanded. "Who the hell is this, goddamn it!"

Dougherty didn't know what to say, so he gently lowered the phone
onto the cradle. After quietly undressing in the red and green glow from
neon signs flashing on Nathan Road, Dougherty neatly placed his suit

trousers and jacket on a coat hanger in the closet. He stared at himself again in the mirror on the closet door.

In the weeks leading up to R&R, Dougherty had found it increasingly difficult to imagine he was shooting rabbits with his father while flying combat missions in his Huey. Smoking Marlboros and drinking Jim Beam—his father's favorites—had helped him in the final days before his leave. But he'd felt he needed a stronger connection to Keith Dougherty to cope with the killing. Dougherty touched the gauze on his right arm where his skin still burned intensely. He peeled back the bandage and studied the ink-black image of an eagle with outstretched wings, clutching an anchor in its talons—a replica of the tattoo Keith Dougherty had etched onto his right forearm in Hong Kong more than twenty years ago. Now, when Dougherty flew in the Huey with his sleeves rolled up, he would see the image of his father's tattoo as he fired his weapon.

Dougherty retaped the gauze, then lay down on his bed and stared up at the ceiling fan slowly rotating above him. Four days in Hong Kong hardly left him feeling rested and relaxed, but tomorrow, he and Coffey would be back at Bien Hoa, and the day after that they would be flying combat missions. In a strange way, Dougherty missed it all—his shipmates, buzzing along treetops in his Huey, the adrenaline rush from firing his weapon. Dougherty remembered something Lowrie once told him—if a wooden bow lost its tension, it would no longer fire arrows properly and might even break when restrung. Perhaps Coffey shared that belief and was making certain they didn't lose their tension while on leave.

Dougherty's thoughts were interrupted by the crackling sound produced when a needle is lowered onto a spinning vinyl record. *Big Iron* by Marty Robbins started playing for what felt like the hundredth time in two days.

Coffey laughed in the dead of night. Dougherty laughed, too.

11

YEAR OF THE SNAKE

A WEEK AFTER DOUGHERTY RETURNED FROM R&R, he and Godbolt watched as the first twelve Cobras were unloaded from the bellies of four Cargo Master planes. "We're going to be out of a job soon," Dougherty said to his gunner, referring to the ship's sleek body that only provided room for a pilot and copilot, who sat in tandem in the narrow cockpit. The new design made it harder for the enemy to strike the helicopter but eliminated the crew chief and door gunner who manned M-60s in the cabin of each Huey.

Dougherty soon learned more about the Cobras from the Playboy crew chiefs he played cards with in the enlisted men's club. To compensate for the loss of door gunners, Bell opted to increase the ship's firepower. The Cobra's pods carried nineteen rockets per side while its twin six-barreled machine guns held two thousand rounds of ammunition each. These four thousand rounds could be expended in one minute of continuous fire, an action that produced a shrieking noise akin to a mill saw ripping into an oak log.

Major Sheffield chose Captain Jerry Pearle to lead the first platoon of Cobras. As a student of combat aviation, Pearle recognized the Cobra's arrival in Vietnam marked a significant new chapter of that history.

He and his men were going to be in the spotlight—briefing dignitaries, conducting interviews, and being filmed by news crews. The Bell Cobra was the army's baby, and all eyes, both military and civilian, would be on his unit.

Dougherty suspected the brass chose Pearle because he displayed a certain panache that fit well with the image the army sought to project with its new gunship. Drawing inspiration from the World War I Aces he so revered, Pearle ordered custom-made black nylon flying suits for every pilot in the First Platoon—a bold but inappropriate choice for the savage heat of Southeast Asia. He designed a new patch for the Playboys that featured an ominous cobra behind the iconic Playboy bunny. The local sweatshop that produced the patch misspelled "helicopter" as "helcopter," which required Pearle to manually insert an "i" into each emblem with a black pen. For headgear, the pilots had their choice of a black baseball cap with aviator's wings and their rank insignia, or, for special occasions, each pilot also received a black Stetson cavalry hat.

Pearle instructed maintenance to paint the Playboy bunny logo on the platoon's six Cobras. He also ordered business cards for each of his pilots to drop over III Corps. His own small white card featured the silhouette of the famous bow-tie clad rabbit in the center and read:

THE VC IN YOUR AREA HAVE BEEN KILLED
COURTESY OF PLAYBOY 1-6.
334TH ARMED HELICOPTER COMPANY.
BIEN HOA – VIETNAM.

Shortly after the arrival of the first Cobras, Dougherty's ship developed compressor stall problems. Dougherty detailed the problem in his logbook, and maintenance grounded the Huey until mechanics could resolve the issue. A day later, maintenance returned the Frog with a note in his logbook saying the Huey was fine, "no mechanical problems detected." When Captain Ruby attempted to lift-off that day, he immediately set *The Green Monster* back down as the Lycoming engine fluttered under the weight of the fully loaded ship. Upon emerging from the cockpit, he grabbed the logbook from his crew chief's outstretched hand and stormed off in the direction of the maintenance hangar.

Swanson gave the two men the next day off, to try and pinpoint their problem. When Dougherty arrived on the flight line, Captain Ruby handed him a box.

"What's this?" Dougherty said.

"Walnut shells," Ruby replied, nonchalantly. "After I crank, toss a few handfuls into the intake."

Dougherty stared at Ruby in disbelief, wondering if the man was having some fun at his expense, again. When the pilot climbed into the cockpit, Dougherty realized he was serious, so he scaled the side of the Huey and straddled the turbine with the box between his legs.

The crew chief threw handfuls of walnut shells into the turbine's intake; the gears instantly pulverized them and presumably knocked some of the dirt and carbon off the teeth. When the box was empty, Dougherty climbed down, and Ruby killed the engine.

"Take all the armament off the ship and dump half the remaining fuel," Ruby said. When Dougherty completed these tasks, the pilot invited his crew chief to sit next to him in the co-pilot's seat. With minimal weight, Ruby easily lifted off. He hovered at two hundred feet, flew a circular pattern around the base, and then returned to the tarmac.

"Ok, let's add some armament," Ruby said. Over the next twenty minutes, he and Dougherty placed rockets in pods and ammo cans on the floor of the Huey. The two men returned to the cockpit and again lifted off with no trouble. After hovering and flying the same circular pattern, the pilot set the ship back down in the revetment.

"Ok, now let's add about four hundred pounds to the cabin to account for a crew chief and door gunner with their gear," Ruby said. The two men estimated each sandbag that formed their L-shaped revetment weighed approximately twenty-five pounds. They loaded sixteen sandbags into the cabin, eight on each side of the ship. Again, Ruby achieved transitional lift with no difficulties.

"Final test," the pilot said. "Let's add some fuel. Take her up to half a tank."

Dougherty pumped the prescribed amount of JP4 into the ship and then climbed in beside the pilot. As the Huey started to lift, the turbine engine coughed and sputtered. "SHIT," Ruby shouted, quickly setting the ship back down in the revetment.

After ten minutes of studying the compressor, Ruby pounded his wrench against the side of the helicopter. "God damnit! Pearle's flyin' Cobras, and we're stuck with this shit bird," he said. "I'll be damned if I'm going to take a crew out over the jungle with a Huey that might stall. It's suicide."

"I'll write it up in the logbook and walk it over to maintenance," Dougherty said.

Ruby put his hands on his hips, looked toward the west, and nodded.

"Hey, I'm sorry you didn't get the Cobras. It should have been you," Dougherty said to Ruby's back.

Ruby shrugged. "I don't give a damn. What's wrong with the Cobra is what's wrong with this army. Too much emphasis on technology and firepower and not enough on teamwork and common sense. Just having a helicopter that flies faster and shoots more rounds isn't going to win this fuckin' war." Ruby hurled the wrench at the sandbag-lined revetment and stormed away from the tarmac.

It occurred to Dougherty that he had never seen Ruby lose before. He wondered if it would change the man. Deep down, Dougherty was relieved his pilot was not chosen to lead the Cobras. If he had been, he would have shifted to the Playboys, and Dougherty would never fly with him again. Ruby's reputation as one of the best Huey pilots in Vietnam had elevated Dougherty's status from shit burner to rising star, and the thought of losing that terrified him.

LBJ

THE NEXT DAY IN OPERATIONS Dougherty failed to locate his name on the mission board.

"Doc," Swanson called out, as he approached the Raider crew chief from across the room. "Maintenance can't figure out what's wrong with your bird. You and Captain Ruby are taking the Frog to Saigon so the Bell reps can have a look. You might be gone for a few days, so go pack a bag ASAP and get your ass to the flight line. The Captain's waiting for you."

What Swanson had described sounded like an in-country R&R. Dougherty raced back to the barracks and quickly stuffed some fatigues and his shaving kit into his duffel bag. He decided to grab his mail on the way to the flight line, since he would have plenty of time to read it in Saigon. After retrieving a single item from his box, Dougherty stopped dead in his tracks, frozen by the sight of another plain white envelope with a postmark from Broken Bow, Nebraska. As much as he wanted to tear open the envelope and discover the latest revelation about his father, Dougherty stuffed the letter inside his duffel bag and hurried to the tarmac. As he approached the revetment, Dougherty spotted Captain Ruby leaning against the Huey like he didn't have a care in the world.

"Doc, since it's just the two of us, why don't you ride up here with me," Captain Ruby said, motioning to the copilot's seat. Dougherty tossed his rucksack into the cabin and climbed into the cockpit beside him. A few minutes outside of Bien Hoa, Captain Ruby keyed the intercom. "Did I ever tell you about the time I met LBJ?"

"Negative, sir," Dougherty replied.

"Met him face to face at a little church on the Pedernales River. It's near LBJ's ranch, so he and Lady Bird go there, sometimes. I'll never forget that day. It was in the fall of '66. A warm Sunday. We were a few pews back of the president. Somehow, without saying a word, the man gave you a sense that he cared deeply about everything but didn't give a damn about anything. It was his magic," Ruby said, turning toward Dougherty.

"After the service, my mother approached Lady Bird and told her I was about to go fly helicopters in Vietnam. The First Lady whispered something in her husband's ear. He nodded, then walked straight over to me. Guess what happened next?"

"No idea, Captain," Dougherty said.

"LBJ puts his big hand on my shoulder, looks me square in the eye and says, 'I hear you're about to deploy to Viet-Nam.'

"'Yes, sir,' I said. I'm frozen at that point. I can't move. And Johnson's a tall guy. About six foot four. He stretches up to his full height and then says in a real loud voice, 'You listen to me, son.' I think everyone in that church turned and looked at us. Then he leans in real close and says quietly, "'You give Charlie hell, but then you get your ass back here to Hill Country. That's an order from your President.'"

"'Yes, sir,' I said. I almost saluted," Ruby added and laughed. "He shook my hand. Firmest handshake I ever had. Then he patted me on the shoulder and walked off to greet another member of the congregation."

"That's impressive, Captain," Dougherty said into his helmet mic, and he meant it.

After a few minutes of silence, Ruby keyed the intercom. "One day I'm gonna meet up with LBJ again, probably at that same little church on the Pedernales River, and tell him that I gave Charlie hell and returned to the Hill Country."

"I'm sure you will, Captain," Dougherty replied, having witnessed, on numerous occasions, the *hell* Ruby had inflicted on the enemy.

Ruby received instructions over the radio from the tower at Tan Son

Nhut. When the exchange ended, he switched to the intercom, again. "Doc, there's something big in the works at the 334th, and I want you to be a part of it. When the time is right, Major Sheffield will be talking to you. This is the kind of thing that if we pull it off, we'll be heroes. That's all I can say for now, but I hope you'll consider it when the time comes." Ruby turned and looked at Dougherty, who nodded.

For the rest of the flight, the young Texan talked nonstop about Lyndon Johnson's prized Herefords, his attractive daughters, and his collection of classic cars. When Ruby landed the Frog at the Bell maintenance hangar beside the runway at Tan Son Nhut airbase, Dougherty keyed the intercom. "That's a little smoother landing than the last time we were here," the crew chief said, referring to their crash landing in Saigon following the shoot-out at Firebase Nevada.

"Roger that," Captain Ruby replied and laughed.

When one of the Bell tech reps informed the two men it might be a day or two before they even looked at their ship, Ruby told Dougherty to go enjoy himself.

Dougherty recalled that Dag Larsen was serving as an Air Force clerk at Tan Son Nhut. Dougherty played baseball with Dag on the Ravenna Blue Jays and was the team's starting catcher and cleanup hitter, while Larsen spent most of his time on the bench, occasionally playing right field or serving as a pinch runner. Larsen didn't really care about baseball. There wasn't much else for a young man to do in that part of Nebraska during the summer, particularly when his friends all played ball, so he joined the team. Dag preferred warming the bench where he could cut up with his teammates during the game, then go out with them afterwards for a few beers and some more laughs.

One day after practice, Larsen invited Dougherty to his house for a sandwich. That's when he met Dag's sister, Astrid.

After asking around, Dougherty finally located the Orderly Room and found someone who knew Larsen. It was the beauty of a name like Dag: people rarely forgot it.

"That Dag is a real card," the nondescript clerk said, then pointed out the window at two white buildings in the distance. The young clerk reckoned Larsen could be found in the one on the left.

When Dougherty walked into the room, he spotted his friend among a bevy of office personnel, stabbing at a typewriter with his index fingers, occasionally stopping to slide his thick black glasses back up on his nose. Dag was the first person from home Dougherty encountered in Vietnam, and even before saying hello he felt a kinship with his fellow Nebraskan.

"Can I help you," Larsen said without looking up from his typewriter.

"Larsen, we need you to go out on patrol tonight," Dougherty said in his best drill sergeant's voice.

Dag looked up abruptly. "Sweet Jesus," he said. "Bill Dougherty. You scared the shit out of me." Larsen extended his hand, and Dougherty shook it. "I didn't think a rear-echelon motherfucker like me would ever bump into the war hero from Litchfield. What brings you to civilization?"

"Our gunship is in the shop," Dougherty said with an intentional nonchalance. "I might be here a couple of days. Mind if I bunk with you?"

"Hell, yes, I mind, but I suppose we can find some space for you."

Larsen informed one of his coworkers that he was taking a break to show his friend where to stow his gear. He led Dougherty to the enlisted barracks where the clerks in Larsen's company slept. Dag directed Dougherty to an empty rack near his own and invited his friend to relax until he got off work.

After Larsen departed, Dougherty studied each photograph Dag had posted in his area, eager for any connection to home. Amid the smiling images of people he knew well, he found what he was looking for—a snapshot of Dag's beautiful sister, Astrid, pinned up on a wooden post near Larsen's bunk. Dougherty removed the photograph and studied it. His former girlfriend's infectious smile and natural warmth radiated through the photograph. In that moment, he felt that leaving Astrid to join the army was the biggest mistake of his life.

After a few minutes, Dougherty carefully returned the snapshot to its original spot, then returned to his bunk with the latest letter from Broken Bow. He carefully slid a finger into the seam of the envelope and opened it. Inside, he found a single article from the *Sherman County Times* dated less than three months ago. "Dougherty Construction in Dispute with City of Kearney." According to the article, Keith Dougherty's company had poured every driveway in a new development too close to the adjacent property's driveway, violating a local ordinance. The city inspector for Kearney had issued a citation and a ten-thousand-dollar fine. The man was quoted as saying he would take Dougherty Construction to court if they didn't fix the driveways or pay the fine.

"Holy shit," Dougherty said aloud. Ten thousand dollars was a fortune—one that his father surely didn't have. And moving half the driveways would likely cost even more. When Dougherty read the article again, it occurred to him that Postmaster Slocum's territory would include Kearney. The man would be well aware of the driveway issue from his postal workers in Kearney. Perhaps Slocum contacted the city inspector and demanded action, since the awkward driveways would impact the placement of mailboxes. Clearly, the man had it in for his father. Perhaps he resented Keith Dougherty's selection as "Man of the Year." But what was Slocum hoping to achieve by sending the articles to his former employee's son in Vietnam?

When a few of Dag's fellow clerks returned to the barracks, Dougherty discreetly returned the article to the envelope and slid it into the top of his duffel bag. As Larsen entered the living quarters, he announced that a real soldier was on the floor. Dag then introduced his fellow Nebraskan to every single person he knew, making sure they understood his friend was a decorated crew chief from an armed helicopter company, which made Dougherty a celebrity among the clerks.

That evening the two men caught a taxi into downtown Saigon— Dougherty's second visit to the capital. The first was a short day trip soon after he arrived in country. He took an overpriced taxi from Long Binh to the Cholon District to purchase some tacky souvenirs that he sent home. Dougherty distinctly remembered the crowds of people packed everywhere, as if the city was about to burst its seams. During the war, Saigon doubled in population to more than two million residents, the influx mostly refugees who fled rural areas controlled by the Viet Cong or destroyed by the Americans. These refugees lived like sardines, packed in squalid, makeshift slums that blighted the affluent colonial city once known as the "Mistress of the Mekong" and the "Pearl of the Orient." Some of the refugees eked out a living by hustling in the city's booming black market, while others turned to prostitution or begging.

Dougherty stared in disbelief at the fancy colonial building where their taxi dropped them. Larsen was fond of good food and wanted his friend to try his favorite French restaurant.

"I'm a Rear Area Pussy," Dag said as he sipped a glass of French Bordeaux. "A total house cat, if you know what I mean. I work eight to five, get three square meals a day, have time to mess around in Saigon, and when this is all done, the Air Force is going to pay for me to go to college."

Dougherty smiled. Larsen had a heart of gold, and despite growing up in rural Nebraska, the gentle soul could never bring himself to take the life of a fish or animal, let alone a human being. Dag had no business in a war zone, and Dougherty was relieved his friend had landed in the relative comfort and security of MACV headquarters.

"How's Astrid doing?" Dougherty said, not wanting to sound too interested in his friend's sister and not sure if he even had a right to ask.

Larsen set his wine glass down and took a moment to compose himself. He expected the question at some point during the evening and had rehearsed his answer.

"When you two broke up last year, Astrid lost it. Instead of going back to school in the spring, she returned to that dig up in the Sand Hills. Said she wanted a gap year to think about her future. I doubt she'll find the answer buried in the ground with a bunch of old Indian bones," Dag said, and then finished his last sip of wine. "I heard she's shacked up with some guy in Broken Bow, so maybe that's the future she's thinking about."

Dougherty looked up at his friend. "Did you say Broken Bow?"

Dag nodded and signaled to the waiter for the check. "Yeah, Joey Petersen. Remember him? Blond-haired guy who played centerfield for the Broken Bow Indians. I think you two had a collision at the plate once."

"He knocked me on my ass, but I held onto the ball, and he was out," Dougherty said.

Dag laughed. "That's the guy."

"Broken Bow," Dougherty said aloud, confident his former girl-friend, and not his father's former boss, was the sender of the newspaper articles.

"Yep, who would ever want to live in that one-horse town? Not me, brother."

With Dag's revelation, Dougherty started connecting the pieces in his mind. As an archeology major, Astrid Larsen was always digging into the past to understand the present. He hated it when Astrid would lie on top of him in bed and interrogate him about his mother, trying to un-earth the real reason for her departure from Litchfield. Astrid had spent the previous summer at the archeological dig, earning academic cred-its, while Dougherty worked construction with his father. His only visit to the Sand Hills came after he enlisted in the army, something Keith Dougherty had talked about all summer. He could easily imagine Astrid using her gap year to dig up articles about his father, just to prove her point that Keith Dougherty was leading him astray.

"Hey, let's get outta here," Dag said, tossing his napkin on the table.

As they left the restaurant, Larsen put his hand on Dougherty's shoulder. "Life is short, my friend. We better make the most of it while we are still here." From that point on, Larsen made it his mission to give Dougherty a few hours of fun in Saigon. He knew enough of the war to understand what life in an armed helicopter company must be like, and if there was one thing Larsen could offer his friend, it was a good time.

Dag flagged down two human-powered trishaws so they could race across Saigon to Larsen's favorite bar. A trishaw was like a rickshaw, but rather than being pulled by a human on foot, the passenger sat in a large basket at the front of an oversized tricycle. The design was brilliant, as it afforded the paying customer an unimpeded view of the road ahead, and a human pedaling could go much faster and longer than a human run-ning. The two Americans cheered the Vietnamese men powering their respective trishaws as if they were thoroughbreds in the Kentucky Derby. The men traveled through darker parts of the city, past crowded bars and cheap hotels that now served as drug dens and brothels. Street orphans periodically sprinted beside the two men, their outstretched hands im-ploring the rich Americans to offer some charity in exchange for their departure. In these instances, the trishaw drivers pedaled faster to spare their fares the unpleasant scene. When they finally arrived at the bar, Dag handed the two drivers a handful of piasters and dropped a few coins into a metal can beside a legless beggar on the sidewalk.

Dougherty and Larsen spent the remainder of their evening drinking and reminiscing about life in central Nebraska, recalling the place as if it were Shangri-La.

The next afternoon, after sleeping off his hangover, Dougherty walked to the Bell maintenance hangar while Dag worked his normal shift. When he entered the repair facility, Dougherty spotted Captain Ruby talking with the technician in charge of a team of mechanics working on their ship. Ruby waved him over and introduced him to the Bell rep, who reported that the Frog would be ready to go in the morning.

The next day, Dougherty arrived on the flight line with Dag Larsen in tow. He introduced his friend to Captain Ruby and asked if he would give Dag a short ride in the Huey. Dougherty was certain his request violated multiple army policies, but if anyone might agree, it was Ruby.

The maverick pilot thought for a moment, then nodded. "Sure. Be happy to. Besides, I want to make sure they really fixed our bird before we go all the way back to Bien Hoa."

Dougherty fitted Larsen with a flight helmet and safety harness, then positioned him in the right door, as if he were their gunner for the flight. Instead of joining Ruby in the cockpit, Dougherty rode in the cabin, in his normal left-door position. He chatted to Dag over the intercom as Captain Ruby flew a fifteen-minute semi-circular route from the north of Tan Son Nhut to the west and then to the south.

"Not too far from here are the free strike zones," Dougherty said, pointing to the west. "Out there, we shoot anything that moves." From their vantage point in the sky, the area looked peaceful and beautiful in the early morning light.

After an uneventful flight, Ruby set the ship down at the same spot on the tarmac.

"Unbelievable," Dag said of the view and the adrenaline rush, then handed his friend the flight helmet. "I don't think people back home have any clue about what you do."

Dougherty nodded and shook his friend's hand, but Dag pulled him in close for an embrace.

CHAPTER 12

"Be careful out there," Larsen said.

"You bet," Dougherty replied. Then he climbed into the copilot's seat. When Captain Ruby hovered at two hundred feet, Dougherty waved to his friend one last time, then Ruby banked the Huey dramatically and raced north toward Bien Hoa.

JEST

DURING OCTOBER, WORD FILTERED DOWN through the Company that the Raiders had been tapped for a covert mission in Thailand that would almost certainly involve going into North Vietnam. Dougherty recalled the first time he heard mention of *Thailand*. It was like an initial drop of rain brushing an exposed cheek on an overcast day, so faint it makes one question whether a droplet of water had, in fact, fallen from the sky.

Soon, however, the droplets turned into a light rain that increased to a steady shower of conversation all centered on Thailand. There were just enough details leaking out of HQ to make him suspect that no grunt could fabricate the Thailand story. Dougherty also recalled how Captain Ruby had alluded to "something big in the works at the 334th." Speculating on the nature of the top-secret mission became a favorite pastime in the Raider shack. Several leading theories soon emerged, including liberating American POWs from camps, attacking remote sections of the Ho Chi Minh Trail in Northern Vietnam and Laos, and even invading Hanoi.

Then one day, another piece of information flowed down the pipeline: the man chosen to lead the mission was none other than Captain Ryan Ruby. Pearle got the Cobras, and now Thailand was Ruby's plum from the brass.

CHAPTER 13

The army knew something about its human resources, Dougherty thought as he watched the two captains engaged in a heated debate one morning on the flight line. The flamboyant and ambitious Jerry Pearle was ideal to serve as the face of the army's new gunship, while the daring and independent Ryan Ruby was the perfect choice to lead a covert mission into North Vietnam. He imagined the company's senior officers perched on their bar stools in the Villa, listening to Ruby go on and on about "taking the war to Hanoi" and saying to themselves, *here's our man*. Thailand also represented their opportunity to resolve any lingering bitterness Ruby may have harbored over Pearle receiving command of the Cobras.

One morning when Dougherty returned to the barracks after an intense evening of Firefly, Swanson rapped on the door to his room, just as the exhausted crew chief's head hit the pillow.

"Sheffield wants to see you in his office right away," the Ops sergeant said through the homemade plywood door. For a moment, Dougherty thought he was dreaming until Swanson poked his head into the room and repeated the order with several expletives added.

Major Sheffield was no fool. During the summer, he had planted the seed about Dougherty reenlisting, and now it was time to harvest the crop. If the commanding officer failed to secure Dougherty's commitment to stay with the company before he returned home for Christmas, he suspected he would lose one of his most experienced crew chiefs.

Sheffield motioned for Dougherty to sit, then ran a hand through his thinning salt and pepper hair. His face was puffy with fatigue.

"Dougherty, this is top-secret, classified information," the major said, lowering his voice and leaning forward to bring the young man into his confidence. "But since it potentially involves you, I'm going to share something. Can you promise me this will remain confidential?"

Before Dougherty could respond, Sheffield continued.

"At the end of the year, half the second platoon will be going north to Thailand. They'll be staying in nice rooms, wearing civilian clothes, no tail numbers or unit markings on their ships."

Dougherty leaned forward in his seat. After weeks of speculation about Thailand, he felt he was on the cusp of receiving some sacred knowledge of the universe. Sheffield took his time, knowing he had the enlisted man on the line and only had to reel him in.

"Captain Ruby is going to lead the mission in Thailand while I fill in as acting Raider Platoon Leader here at Bien Hoa. Ruby's going to need experienced men to pull this thing off, and he specifically requested you. I can't tell you more than that now, but it's going to be different and exciting.

"I'll throw in a couple extra weeks of leave so you can spend the holidays with your family and get rested up. When you get back from the States, I'll send you up to Thailand to join the team. What do you say?" Sheffield said, sliding a paper across the desk for Dougherty to sign.

A week later, Dougherty and three other members of the Raiders boarded a transport plane and flew across the South China Sea to the Philippines for three days of Jungle Environment Survival Training (JEST). The JEST camp taught flight crews how to find food, water, and shelter in the jungle should they unexpectedly find themselves on the ground in hostile terrain. Completing the survival course was a prerequisite for those pilots and enlisted airmen participating in the Thailand mission.

As their plane approached the Philippines from the west, Dougherty noticed hundreds of tiny green formations jutting out of the ocean—a collection of the archipelago's more than seven thousand islands.

"Like a bunch of fuckin' boobs stickin' outta the sea," his seat mate, Louie Mancuso, said—a typical response from the Italian-American door gunner who had plastered the walls of his room in the barracks with Playboy centerfolds. Soon, a larger body of land appeared on the horizon, which someone on board announced was Luzon, the country's largest island and home to the capital, Manila.

The Philippines hosted two of the US military's largest overseas installations—Clark Air Force Base and the Subic Bay Naval Station, jewels of the American empire that greatly augmented the Filipino economy and elevated the small nation's status on the global stage. After landing at Clark, the four Raider airmen squeezed into a taxi for the journey across the island.

"Where you fella headed," the Filipino taxi driver asked in decent English. The pudgy middle-aged man had parted his dark hair neatly and wore a white, buttoned-down dress shirt with tan slacks.

"Subic Bay," Lieutenant Balfour Chalfant of Amarillo, Texas, deadpanned. Chalfant was the tallest and skinniest member of the platoon, and it was laughable to see him folded into the front seat of the small taxi. He had a cropped mustache that covered his thin upper lip, and he spoke in a dry monotone voice that never changed pitch or pace so that it was impossible to discern if the man was serious or joking. Chalfant had the tiniest gait for a tall man Dougherty had ever seen. It was maddening to watch the string-bean pilot shuffle down the flight line, knowing if the tall Texan just extended those long, lanky legs he could cover the distance in half the time.

"My name is Joe," the taxi driver said and smiled. "Like DiMaggio," he added, holding his hands up as if he were about to swing a bat. "You fella like baseball?"

"Sure," the men answered half-heartedly, weary from the long flight.

As they traveled south on Highway 1, Joe talked incessantly about American sports, recent Hollywood films, and every family member he had living in the United States, offering up the popular topics in the hope his passengers connected with at least one.

"You guys know Magellan, the explorer?" Joe said when there was a lull in the conversation. "He come here in 1500s. Got hacked to pieces by local tribe that didn't want to be Catholic," the driver said and laughed. "Spain rule us for three centuries, until you guys kick them out. When you ask Filipino about our history, we say, 'Three hundred years in a convent and fifty years in Hollywood,'" the driver said, and laughed again.

"When did the Americans arrive?" Warrant Officer Lenny Briggs asked from the backseat. "I studied some history in college, and I don't remember that."

"1899," Joe said, grinning at Briggs in the rear-view mirror. "You guys sunk Spanish Armada out there in Manila Bay and they call it quits. America take over. Your President McKinley call it 'Benevolent Assimilation.' We had American Governor, American troop, American teacher, and American missionary, all trying to make us into mini-America."

When there was another lull in the conversation, Joe looked at Dougherty in the rear-view mirror and asked him where he was from.

"Nebraska," he replied.

"Really? Guy from Nebraska start war in Philippines," the driver said, referring to Willie Grayson, a US soldier who shot a Filipino soldier in 1899. "About two hundred thousand Filipino die after that. Some tortured. Some watch their village burn. So we say Benevolent Assimilation OK. We give it a try. Just stop killing us," he said, laughing again.

"Hey, DiMaggio, since you're such an expert on history, tell us about MacArthur," Chalfant said, deadpan.

Joe nodded and thought for a few moments. "The day after Japan bomb Pearl Harbor, they invade Philippines. MacArthur was here with about ninety thousand troop on Bataan peninsula. Your President Roosevelt told Mac to go. He and his family get away in small boat to Mindanao. Then they take plane to Australia. That's where Mac say, 'I shall return.' And he did."

"Damn straight," Chalfant said. "I bet MacArthur's a big hero down here."

"Oh, yeah," Joe replied. "Corn cob pipe. Dark sunglass. 'I shall return.' Filipino love him."

"Hey, Joe," Briggs said, leaning forward from the backseat. "Tell us about YOUR President Marcos."

The Filipino driver smiled. "Young guy. Good talker. Kind of like JFK of Philippines. His wife Imelda kind of like Jackie, but she famous for her fancy clothes and closet full of shoes."

The Filipino driver proceeded to explain in his broken English that Imelda and Ferdinand Marcos courted Lyndon Johnson during his recent visit to Manila and cemented that relationship by committing Filipino troops to the US War in Vietnam. Of course, Marcos required the United States to underwrite the cost of those Filipino troops, an expense Johnson reluctantly agreed to bear to demonstrate to the world that the US had allies in Southeast Asia who also feared the "falling dominoes" his war in Vietnam aimed to prevent.

Joe announced to his passengers that he lived on the island during World War II and was one of the more than sixty thousand American and Filipino POWs the Imperial Japanese Army made take the infamous Death March from Central Bataan to Camp O'Donnell in Capas, an eighty-mile journey north that claimed the lives of an estimated ten thousand men from disease, malnutrition, and torture.

"Really?" Chalfant replied in his monotone voice when the man said it was a miracle he had survived the ordeal.

"I show you," Joe said. Their driver proceeded to stop twice, at Hermosa and Orani, to point out stone markers on the route of the Death March. "Tough time," he said over and over, as he made the sign of the cross at each site.

"I'll bet every taxi driver haulin' GI's to Subic claims he was on the Death March just to get a bigger tip," Chalfant said to Dougherty as the Filipino man hurried back to the cab.

"Great, more fuckin' jungle," Mancuso said when their taxi entered the pristine Roosevelt National Park. The reserve consisted of thirty-three hundred acres of old-growth forest that sat adjacent to the massive naval station at Subic Bay, where the navy maintained ten thousand acres of preserved jungle ideal for training US troops for the conflict in Vietnam.

As they drove through the JEST entrance, Briggs informed the group that the US Army supervised the camp, but the guides were all indigenous tribesmen known as Negritos, a fact he learned from two other Raider pilots who had already completed their JEST training.

"*Negrito* mean 'little black person' in Spanish," Joe said. "Good luck, fella," he added, smiling when the group handed over their fare plus a generous tip.

As the four men watched the taxi pull away from the camp, an army captain followed by a Negrito approached the group.

"Gentleman, welcome to the JEST camp. This is Datu," the solemn-looking officer said, pointing to the tiny but muscular man at his side. "In the local tongue, Datu means 'Chief.' Datu will be your Chief for the next three days. At JEST, you are all the same," he said, pointing at the two officers and two enlisted men. "We have no rank here. The jungle doesn't care if you are a general or a private. You're all dead men until you learn the skills that just might keep you alive. You will treat Datu as if he is your Chief. If you're smart, you'll treat him like the Father, Son, and Holy

Ghost, because he is the only one who can save your soul in this living hell. This is not R&R, gentlemen. There are things in this jungle that WILL kill you. If you screw up here, you could die. It has happened. Just remember that what you learn over the next three days could very well save your life one day."

When the Captain marched off to give his speech to the next group, Datu stepped forward. He pointed his bolo knife at their rucksacks and then pointed at a nearby tree, a clear signal for the men to leave their bags. Then their instructor confidently sauntered off into the jungle.

That afternoon, Datu showed the Americans how to harvest snails from small mountain streams, using the tip of a bolo knife to scrape them from the rocks along the riverbank. Their instructor sharpened a tiny bamboo stick, which he used to pry the fleshy body of each snail from its shell. He handed all four Americans a slimy treat, then popped two in his mouth. The airmen looked at each other in trepidation, then simultaneously tossed the snails into their mouths. Dougherty swallowed his whole, knowing he would gag if he bit into the cold and clammy mollusk.

The men attempted to make fire by rubbing two pieces of bamboo together until the friction produced a spark that ignited fine bamboo tinder packed inside a piece of wood. Despite their best efforts, the Raiders only produced thin wisps of smoke, a result that caused Datu to shake his head in dismay.

When Datu grew bored, he walked further into the jungle, then stopped and slowly turned. To the men's surprise, the man intentionally cut his left arm with the tip of his bolo knife, causing a tiny rivulet of blood to trickle across his brown skin. Datu scraped the stock of a strange plant with his bolo blade, gathering a mushy paste. He covered the cut with it, and it clotted his blood and stopped the bleeding. Next, Datu pulled up the root of another plant, which produced a kind of soap when he rubbed it in the water of a nearby stream.

At one point in the afternoon, Datu stopped in the jungle, reached up and pulled down a vine snaking around a tree. He cut one end of the stem with his bolo knife and drank water from inside the plant. He repeated the act for each of the thirsty airmen. Finally, at the end of a long, hot day, Datu directed his four charges to a cabin at the base camp where they bunked down for the night.

The next morning at dawn, Datu led the four Raiders out of the base camp and into the jungle, but in a new direction this time. The Americans were only allowed to carry the salt tablets they brought from Bien Hoa and one bolo knife each provided by the JEST camp. The objective for the day was to build a shelter, create a fire, and find something to eat and drink before nightfall. At one point, while cutting bamboo for their shelters, Dougherty and Mancuso hacked into the wrong grove of trees, and Datu came running.

"Nooh, Nooh," he shouted. The warning arrived too late. A shower of large black ants rained onto the men as they struck the bamboo with their machetes. Chalfant and Briggs laughed hysterically when, moments later, the insects commenced biting any piece of exposed flesh on the two men's arms and faces, which caused Dougherty and Mancuso to dance wildly.

"That why so much bamboo here," the instructor said to the two men, as he wiped ants from their bodies. "We no cut these trees."

Once Datu was satisfied with the amount of bamboo his students harvested, he located a specific tree in the jungle. Using his bolo knife, he cut strips of bark that he braided into twine. His pupils then used the makeshift string to fasten the bamboo poles together. They each built a platform resembling a bedframe that would provide a resting place above the venomous insects and snakes. Datu instructed the men to lay palm fronds on top of the bamboo frames to soften them for sleeping.

When Datu sent Dougherty and Chalfant out to forage for food, Dougherty spied what he believed to be an egg or white mushroom. He held it up for Chalfant to see. "Don't suppose the Chief could cook this up for us," he said.

Chalfant grabbed the Titleist golf ball from Dougherty's outstretched hand. "Follow me," he deadpanned and shuffled forward. The two men hid in the jungle foliage and watched from the tree line as a foursome of naval officers hacked their way down a lush fairway.

Once the group played through, Chalfant announced he was going to find something to eat and stepped onto the golf course. Both men knew leaving the jungle was against camp rules, but Dougherty wasn't about to tell an officer what to do. There might not be any rank at JEST, but when they were back at Bien Hoa with the privilege of rank fully restored, Captain Chalfant would make him pay for any disrespect. Dougherty watched as the stick man slowly made his way down the fairway. Chalfant stopped once at a sand trap, briefly looked back, then continued shuffling until he eventually disappeared beyond the tee box.

About twenty-five minutes later, Dougherty spotted Chalfant coming back up the fairway with a box under his right arm. When the tall pilot stepped into the tree line, Dougherty realized the pilot had a case of Snickers bars.

"I walked a few holes back to the clubhouse. It's the Camp John Hay Golf Course for the navy brass. All they had to eat was candy bars, so I bought a whole box. Want one?"

"Sure," Dougherty replied.

"They're a buck apiece," Chalfant said, quoting a price ten times higher than what he paid for each bar. Dougherty handed the Lieutenant a dollar in script. The pilot handed him a candy bar and shuffled away.

On their third day, Datu informed the group that their final task was to spend a night alone in the jungle. He sent each man away from the relative comfort of their bamboo beds, pointing his bolo knife in the four directions of the compass. Dougherty walked north and eventually found himself climbing an elevation. Rather than stop to build a shelter or look for food, he continued his ascension, most likely out of the ten-thousand-acre reserve. Finally, the enlisted airman arrived at the top of a steep bluff several thousand feet above Subic Bay. He located a grassy area near the edge of the precipice and decided to spend the night at the scenic overlook. Instead of honing his survival skills, Dougherty rested in a bed of wispy grass and watched US Naval ships coming in and out of Subic Bay while he ate the Snickers Bar. With his R&R in Hong Kong and now the survival training in the Philippines, Dougherty was literally following in his father's footsteps, as Keith Dougherty spent time in both ports during his war years.

Following a stunning sunset, Dougherty quickly drifted off to sleep. During the night, he dreamed of his father as a young man standing on the deck of a navy destroyer. In the dream, Keith Dougherty's hands clutch the railing at the front of the ship. His sleeves are rolled up, revealing the tattoo of the eagle and the anchor on his right forearm. A battle rages. Guns on his father's ship are blazing as incoming shells explode all around him. Undeterred, his father stares straight ahead . . . at the church that once stood on the Dougherty property. It is engulfed in flames, and Dougherty knows his mother is trapped inside. If she leaves the church, she will be gunned down by the destroyer. If she remains inside, she will burn alive. The flames are growing higher, more intense. They are blinding.

Dougherty instinctively raised his hands to shield his eyes, waking himself from his deep slumber. For a moment, he expected to be engulfed in flames; then he recognized the intense light as the sun rising over Subic Bay. After a few disoriented moments, Dougherty remembered his long hike the day before, the JEST training, and his platoonmates. He retraced his steps in double time, and before long arrived at the bamboo bedframes. From there, he followed the path back to base camp where the three other men waited, suggesting they had not strayed far from their previous night's lodging.

"Where the hell you been?" Chalfant shouted when Dougherty emerged from the jungle.

"We all got captured by Charlie," Briggs added, referring to the Negritos who played the role of a Viet Cong patrol.

"Couldn't get enough of those snails," Dougherty replied and smiled.

While waiting for an Army truck to take them into Subic Bay, Dougherty and Mancuso watched two Negritos at a fiery forge, heating and pounding a piece of steel from a truck's leaf spring. They worked the flattened piece of metal into the shape of a knife blade. A third Negrito stood at a nearby display table, selling finished bolo knives to the GIs who completed JEST training. Each machete was fitted with a handle made of guava wood and came with a thin, flat wooden scabbard. One particular knife caught Dougherty's eye. He picked it up and examined it. The bolo felt slightly heavier than the one he used during training, and he reckoned it would easily slice through a mature bamboo tree and perhaps even bone.

"How much?" Dougherty said.

"Ten US," the man said. Dougherty handed him the script and walked off with his purchase.

"I don't want any fuckin' souvenirs from this place," Mancuso said, shaking his head at the knife. "I had bugs and shit crawlin' all over me last night."

Before climbing into the deuce-and-a-half that shuttled GIs from the camp to the base, an adjutant handed the Raiders their JEST completion certificates signed by the officer-in-charge, whose subordinate wished them good luck.

When the truck dumped the men off, Chalfant and Briggs announced they were going to get cleaned up and then head to the Officer's Club. Dougherty and Mancuso decided to find a place where they could get a drink. They walked to a bar adjacent to the base that a passing sailor recommended.

"This joint is a dive," Mancuso said upon entering the dimly lit club, which had a similar vibe to the Paradise Bar in Bien Hoa. "Did you see that piece-of-shit door?" Mancuso continued, as the two men sat down at an empty table. "Every door at our factory is made of solid hardwood. None of that veneer shit," Mancuso added, sneering at the cheap portal through which they had just passed. The two men ordered some beers, but Mancuso couldn't let it go. "Cherry, maple, oak, and ash. Take your pick. We got 'em all. Ash wood is tough as nails. That's why they make baseball bats out of it. Ain't nobody gonna kick down a Mancuso door made outta ash. But that piece-of-shit door over there," Mancuso said, nodding toward the offensive entrance, "a little old lady could trip through that son of a bitch and knock it over."

Dougherty smiled. "I never met anyone who cared more about doors than you," he said, then took a long sip of beer.

"Bro, I was born to make doors," Mancuso said and smiled. "My grandfather made doors in Italy. My old man makes doors in Jersey. I'm gonna make doors when I get home, and my kids will make doors one day. Suits me fine. Somebody's gotta make the doors. Could you imagine a world without doors? That would be a fuckin' nightmare."

The two men downed a second round of beers and then ordered a third, which they nursed. "Whatcha thinkin' about, Doc?" Mancuso said when there was a lull in their conversation.

Dougherty removed the bolo from its sheath and studied the blade for a few moments.

"I started working for my old man when I was thirteen."

"No shit?" Mancuso said, impressed someone had logged some hours in their family's business at a younger age than him.

"Yeah, my mom left us that year, and he started takin' me along to job sites. He built all kinds of stuff—grain bins, houses, barns, post offices, laundromats.

"I was pretty tall for my age, and even though I was just thirteen, my old man would say, 'Get on that dozer and push up that pile of gravel.' Of course, he never trained me to operate a bulldozer, so I would have to play around with the controls until I figured it out.

"When I turned fifteen, he made me drive a truck in the convoy whenever the crew went to a new job site, even though I didn't have a driver's license. The old man gave me a cushion to sit on, so I rode higher in the cab. He even bought me a gray fedora to make me look older. He always put my vehicle in the middle of the caravan, so I was less likely to be spotted if a patrol car passed us."

Mancuso laughed as he drained the last of his beer.

"That first summer I worked for him, my father landed a job up near the South Dakota state line. Every night, we ate our dinner at the town's only bar, so my old man could drink while I had a sandwich and some chips.

"When I saw those Negritos makin' the knives it got me thinkin' about this one night," Dougherty said, turning the knife around in his hand. "Earlier in the day, my father fired a local for bein' late two days in a row, and that night, the same guy happened to be at the bar, sitting across from us, drowning his sorrows for getting sacked. The SOB started swearing out loud while staring at us. My dad calmly said to him, 'Hey, if you don't mind, my son is sitting here.'

"This guy couldn't believe that the same cat who fired him had the nerve to show up at 'his' bar and tell him to be quiet. So the asshole starts swearing again, but louder this time. My dad stayed surprisingly calm. He just politely asked him to watch his language. This really pissed the guy off. He's boiling over at this point. So my father gets up and walks over to where this jerk is sitting and when he does, the man pulls out a switchblade. When that blade clicked open, the whole bar got as quiet as a church."

"Damn," Mancuso said, his sleepy eyes perking up a bit.

"My father turned to me and said, 'Boke, step away from the bar,' which I did. Everyone in that place had their eyes on my old man. He turned back to the guy, and I'll never forget this 'til the day I die. He calmly and clearly says to the guy, so the whole room can hear, "You better put that fuckin' knife away before I take it from you and shove it up your ass."

"Holy shit," Mancuso said, his sleepy eyes as wide-open as ever. "What happened?"

"The bastard turned and ran."

"Damn, your old man's one tough son of a bitch," Mancuso said and laughed.

"Yeah," Dougherty replied, then looked at his watch. "We better get going. Don't want to miss our flight back to Bien Hoa."

After they passed through the bar's cheap faux-wood door, Mancuso stopped and turned toward Dougherty. "I shall not return," he said—his own variation of General Douglas MacArthur's famous declaration.

14

CHRISTMAS SPIRITS

IN LATE NOVEMBER, Dougherty and a handful of Raiders stood on the tarmac and waved as a cluster of Hueys led by Captain Ruby lifted off and turned north for the long trip to NKP Air Base in Thailand. As the helicopters grew smaller on the horizon, Dougherty felt as though he might never see his platoonmates again—the discarded airmen like playing cards, once held tightly in the hand of the company commander, but now laid onto a table where more experienced gamesmen sat. With every passing klick, the departing men faced longer odds of returning to the 334th.

Dougherty's two roommates were among the Raiders who remained at Bien Hoa. Godbolt didn't go north because he was a short-timer and, despite Sheffield's best efforts, had no interest in re-enlisting—the pull of his infant daughter more powerful than the Major's praise. Coffey, on the other hand, tried to volunteer but was considered too unstable for Thailand, given the discipline and discretion required by the secret mission. One evening in early December, as the three men watched Dougherty's black and white television, a prerecorded news clip showed Robert McNamara announcing that he intended to resign as Secretary of Defense.

"Good riddance," Coffey said. "Never liked that arrogant prick."

Godbolt simply shrugged and dropped to the floor for another set of push-ups. He was going home in a couple of months and didn't give a damn who ran the Department of Defense.

With half the second platoon in Thailand, the remaining Raiders had to pick up the slack until Sheffield could beg, borrow, and steal personnel from throughout the battalion. Dougherty flew around the clock for the next two weeks until, exhausted and emotionally drained, he boarded a Pan Am 747 to Guam, the first leg on his long journey back to Nebraska.

After fastening his seat belt, Dougherty closed his eyes and recalled the last time he was home. It was the previous December, when he completed advanced training at Fort Eustis and received his orders for Vietnam. He had a few weeks of leave before he had to report to Oakland, so he planned to fly home to see his father and attempt to repair his relationship with Astrid. He was making some progress with his former girlfriend, but it all ended one night after he showed up early at the Larsen house for their date. When Astrid called out from her bedroom that she needed more time to finish getting ready, her father Max asked Dougherty if he wanted to grab a quick beer at Karl's Tavern.

"This guy's going to Viet-Nam," Max Larsen announced when they walked into the crowded tavern. "I wanna buy him a beer." Dougherty had not yet reached the legal drinking age in Nebraska, but Larsen reasoned that any young man going off to risk his life in a war damn sure had the right to drink a beer before he went.

"If we get caught, it's your ass," Karl shouted from behind the bar, as Larsen led Dougherty into the stock room where the owner stored extra cases of beer and empty kegs.

Of course, one beer turned into many, and the two men didn't return until much later. Astrid had fallen asleep on the couch, but she awoke when the two drunk men staggered into the house. She was still dressed for their date. She looked beautiful, and even intoxicated, Dougherty knew he had messed up.

"You're ready," he slurred.

"I was ready three hours ago. Now I'm going to bed," Astrid said tersely, then marched upstairs and slammed her bedroom door.

"Don't worry, boy. She'll get over it," Max Larsen said, as he slapped Dougherty on the back, then staggered off to bed himself.

But that was his last date with Astrid. Before leaving for Vietnam, Dougherty stopped by the Larsen house to apologize. Astrid wished him well and promised to write, but she never did. Now that he knew Astrid lived in Broken Bow, Dougherty was certain she was the one sending him the articles about his father. It seemed unlikely that his old flame was trying to win him back; rather, her likely motivation was to inflict some pain on the person who had wounded her.

An announcement from the captain pulled Dougherty from his thoughts. As the jet taxied down the runway, an eerie silence settled over the cabin. The grunts on board who spent countless days patrolling South Vietnam and the desk jockeys who battled on their paper trail stared nervously out the plane's tiny windows. Once the commercial airliner completed its ascent and leveled off, safely out of range of enemy fire, the cabin erupted in cheers. That's when it occurred to Dougherty that this was the Freedom Bird for many on board who had survived their year of war and were leaving Vietnam permanently. In that moment, Dougherty felt a tinge of regret for extending with the 334th, but then he reminded himself of what Sheffield had said in their meeting—with a three-year commitment to the Army, he would almost certainly be shipped back for a second tour if he left now. This plane could never be his Freedom Bird, and so he vowed to push such thoughts out of his mind.

When his fourth and final flight landed in Omaha, Dougherty waited for the other passengers to exit, then descended the stairs to the runway and assumed his place at the end of a line of uniformed soldiers. Dougherty spotted his father smoking a cigarette and pacing at the fence that separated the terminal from the runway.

"Welcome home, soldier." Keith Dougherty said, shaking his son's hand as he came through the gate. "You couldn't get a seat closer to the front of the plane?" he added, then walked away, leaving his son no choice but to follow in his father's footsteps.

Two hours later, Keith Dougherty's green Chevy Impala pulled up in front of the family home. The younger Dougherty's thoughts turned to the first newspaper article. As he watched his hulking father lumber up to the front door, he tried to imagine a church where their house now stood. And then he tried to imagine his father setting it on fire. When Keith

Dougherty noticed his son frozen in the front yard, he flashed a look from the porch that conveyed *What the hell?*—his cue to get in the house.

Once inside, he barely glanced at the drab living room, which had lost all its life when Candace Dougherty walked out seven years ago. Dougherty dropped the heavy canvas duffel bag in his bedroom and stepped into the bathroom across the hall. He stared at his reflection in the vanity mirror, recalling the last time he stood in that very spot, on the day he left for Vietnam, and how he looked like a boy dressed up in a soldier's uniform. Now, a year later, the image of a much older man stared back at him. Dougherty touched the stubble on his face to confirm that he was, in fact, the man in the mirror.

Later that day, when Dougherty grew restless, his father extended the keys to the stock truck. "Maybe we can get some rabbits while you're home," he said.

Dougherty stared at the keys dangling from his father's index finger and wondered if his coping mechanism worked in reverse, and shooting real jack rabbits from his father's stock truck might conjure images of killing Viet Cong guerrillas from his Huey.

Keith Dougherty grew impatient and tossed the keys at his son, who caught them against his chest. Then the elder Dougherty walked into the kitchen and poured himself a drink.

Dougherty drove to the sawmill on the edge of town. He parked the truck on the side of the road and walked over to the weathered wooden fence where he used to linger on his way home from school. As a teen, he found himself mesmerized by the mill hands cutting logs into cants. Each pass a log made through the spinning blade peeled away another layer of skin, revealing a square edge of pure, hard lumber that had been there all along, just concealed beneath bark and sap. The ripping of those logs into lumber was how Dougherty imagined his journey into manhood. Some parts of the self were ripped away by life. But over time, after enough cuts, something more formed and useful existed in place of the log. Lumber was strong and level. You could build with it: a foundation that supported a home, stairs to climb higher, a roof to shelter you from storms. It was still the same wood, yet different. He came to see his mother leaving as that mill saw ripping away a part of him. Astrid breaking up with him, too, and going to war—all cuts shaping him into a man.

After leaving the mill, Dougherty proceeded to his grandmother's restaurant on Main Street. Emma Dougherty appeared busy in the kitchen, so he seated himself at his favorite table, where he drank coffee and stared out the window, waiting for the family matriarch to finish with the lunch crowd. Occasionally, locals walking by the restaurant spotted "Keith Dougherty's boy" through the big glass pane and stopped to chat with their hometown war hero, who was featured twice in the *Sherman County Times*. Sometimes they reminisced about football games Dougherty quarterbacked. On these occasions, Dougherty tried to be cordial with his friends and neighbors, but if the conversation dragged on too long, he found himself irritated and made some excuse to end the dialogue so he could be alone with his thoughts.

The scrape of a chair pulled back from the table interrupted Dougherty's reverie. His grandmother wiped her hands on the apron she always wore and sat down at the table across from her grandson.

Emma Dougherty was born in the late 1890s in Sartoria, Nebraska, a small settler community on the South Loup River in Buffalo County. She was not far removed from the generation that arrived in wagon trains and lived in sod houses. Emma was cut from the same cloth as those people, her persona toughened further by surviving the Dust Bowl and the Great Depression. For twenty-nine years she worked in her restaurant from sunup to sundown, six days a week, and she still found time to grow violets, which she crossbred to create new varieties.

"How you doin', kiddo?" she said.

"I'm ok," Dougherty replied.

"We missed you," Emma said, touching her grandson's hand for a moment. "Town feels empty without you."

"I missed you, too. How's Grandpa?" Dougherty said, referring to Norris Dougherty, who ruptured a disc in his back when Dougherty was five.

"Not good," Emma said. "Still bedridden. That back surgery they tried a couple of years ago didn't pan out. I've taken him to see specialists in Lincoln and Omaha, but they all say the same thing—he's partially paralyzed and will never walk again. He's up at the house propped up in bed. Maxine still checks on him during the week while I'm down here. Maybe you could go see him one day."

"Sure, I'll do that."

"I've been watching you sittin' over here," Emma said after a long silence. "Reminds me of when your father came back from the war. I think he may have sat at this same table," she said and smiled. Emma looked out the window and squinted, perhaps trying to see what her son and grandson hoped to see. "Big war ships and helicopters are a lot more exciting than tractors and pickups, but that's what we got here. I don't know the answer to the question that's in your head right now," she said. "I don't know if it's out that window, either." Emma pushed herself up from the table. She was a strong, formidable woman, even at seventy years of age. "Maybe there's something you could learn from your father on this one. Might be worth askin' him. Just my two cents," she said, then returned to the kitchen to start preparations for dinner.

The next morning after his father left the house, Dougherty carefully removed the sock drawer from his dresser and placed it on his bed. The previous day, after unpacking, he pinned the newspaper articles about Keith Dougherty to the back of the wooden drawer, for fear his father might discover them.

Dougherty poured himself a tall glass of Jim Beam from one of the many bottles his father kept in the pantry. The cheap Kentucky bourbon was now his drink of choice, too. Having the familiar bottle in his locker at Bien Hoa provided some comfort before going out on combat missions. Dougherty plopped down in a seat at the kitchen table and stared at the newspaper clippings spread out on the faded checkered tablecloth. When he finished his drink, he poured himself another and then another. Around noon, he staggered to his father's Chevy Impala and started driving northwest, toward Broken Bow.

When he reached Highway 2, Dougherty rolled down his window to try to sober up. Train cars loaded with coal from Wyoming rolled eastward on the tracks to his right. The endless stream of railcars passing in the opposite direction had a hypnotic effect on him, and he caught himself drifting over the center line of the highway from time to time.

Forty-five minutes later he pulled up in front of a nondescript white house on a side street in Broken Bow. Dougherty had gotten the address from Dag in September.

"Twenty-three Elm Street, Broken Bow," Dag said over the intercom the day Captain Ruby gave Larsen a ride in the Huey. "Don't tell her I gave you that," Dag added.

Dougherty had requested Astrid's address earlier in the visit, but Dag, the protective brother, declined to provide it. Following Larsen's revelation, he wrote the address in his logbook and copied the number onto a scrap of paper shortly before heading home on leave.

Dougherty pounded on the door of the modest, one-story box home that appeared identical to so many others built in this part of Nebraska after the Second World War. A few seconds later, Joey Petersen opened the door.

"Bill Dougherty. What the hell?" the stocky, blond-haired young man said.

"Is Astrid here?" Dougherty slurred. "I need to speak with her."

At that moment, Astrid Larsen appeared from a back room of the house, wearing a thick wool sweater, blue jeans, and work boots. She was tall, with Nordic features, and had her long blonde hair pulled back in a ponytail.

"It's ok, Joe. He just got back from Vietnam," Astrid said, touching Petersen's back. "Give us a few minutes," she added, then stepped onto the porch, pulling the door closed behind her.

"I can't believe Dag gave you my address," Astrid hissed, shaking her head in disapproval.

"He's worried about you," Dougherty mumbled.

"He should be worried about himself and this stupid war," Astrid replied, staring across the street.

"I saw him a few months ago in Saigon," Dougherty said, trying his best to sound reassuring. "He's doing fine. He's in the safest place in Vietnam he could possibly be."

Astrid shook her head in disagreement while keeping her arms crossed. "Why are you here?"

"Dag said you're working on the dig, again. How's it going?"

"You're kidding me, right?" Astrid said, shaking her head. "You drove all the way up here to ask me about the Apache village? All the times I begged you to come up here last summer, and you never did because you had to work for your father!"

Dougherty decided to abandon the small talk and try the direct approach, which is what his father would do. "Look, I know you're the one who's been sending me the articles. Why are you doing it?"

Astrid shook her head; a perplexed expression clouded her face. "I have no idea what you're talking about."

"You're the only person I know in Broken Bow, and every envelope I got in Vietnam was posted here. You're still mad that I enlisted because of my dad."

Astrid turned and looked her former boyfriend in the eyes. "I am mad that you enlisted because of him. Your whole life you've been a follower. You followed Dag home and met me. You followed me to college. Then you followed your father to the recruiting station, and now you're following orders in the army. Stop following, Bill, and start leading."

"Fair enough, but why not just tell me that straight up? Why send the articles with no note or return address?"

Astrid shook her head. "You're drunk, Bill. Go home and sleep it off. You have to move on. I have. I'm with Joe now, and we're having a baby. I pray this child will keep him out of the draft, but if it doesn't, I swear to God, the three of us are getting in that truck and driving to Canada, and we're never coming back."

Astrid stopped, realizing she may have shared too much information. She wiped a tear from the corner of her eye with the back of her hand.

"Listen to me, Bill," she continued with a trembling voice. "When you get back from the war, find a nice girl, get married, and settle down. This will all be over soon enough."

Astrid stomped back inside the house and slammed the door, her words more sobering than the cold Nebraska air that slapped Dougherty's face on the drive to Broken Bow.

A few days later, Dougherty sat at his favorite table in Emma's Café, staring out the window and drinking coffee. Big, fluffy flakes started falling from the gray sky and soon covered the town in a soft white blanket of snow. It reminded him of an incident when he was twelve. That year his mother attended classes in Kearney to become a beauty operator. Barry Haller, who lived in town, was also going to Kearney to complete a graduate degree in engineering, so he and Candace rode together in one of the pickup trucks from Keith Dougherty's construction company. Coming back from Kearney one night in a snowstorm, Barry skidded off the road and rolled the truck several times beside the highway. Someone called the house to tell Keith one of his pickups was upside down on Highway 10, just south of Hazzard.

"Did you stop?" his father barked into the handset.

"No," the man said. "I just wanted to get to a phone and call you."

"You stupid son of a bitch," Keith shouted and slammed the phone onto the cradle. "Grab your coat," he ordered his son.

While driving out of town on Main Street with the snow falling harder, Dougherty spotted his mother and Barry in the window of Emma's Café at the very table he now sat.

"Dad, there they are," he shouted, pointing at the restaurant. Keith Dougherty slammed on the brakes, which caused the truck to slide for nearly ten yards down the center of Main Street. His father shoved the gear shift into reverse and backed up to the restaurant, parking parallel to the sidewalk since the storm had driven most people home for the evening. Keith Dougherty shut off the engine and raced inside, not waiting for his son to join him. Dougherty watched from the sidewalk, through the restaurant's big glass window, wondering if his father was going to blame Barry for the accident, maybe even beat him up. Instead, his father grabbed his wife by both arms and pulled her toward him for a long embrace. In retrospect, it was that moment that he knew from the way Candace Dougherty looked over her husband's shoulder at Barry that his mother would be leaving them.

That evening Keith Dougherty ordered his son to grab his coat and follow him to the stock truck parked out front. When he climbed into the passenger seat, Dougherty noticed the shotgun his father had given him—his only present on the first Christmas after his mother left home. A box of shells rested on the seat beside a dented thermos and his father's flask. The two men drove in silence down familiar dirt roads surrounded by farmers' fields. Keith Dougherty pulled the truck off to the side of the road and turned on the spotlight—the cue for his son to assume his position in the bed of the truck. The late December air swirling across snow-covered fields chilled Dougherty to the bone. He tried to steady his shaking hands as he loaded the shotgun, then rested his body and the weapon against the frigid metal racks. Keith Dougherty slowly pulled forward—one hand on the steering wheel, the other on the mechanical arm that turned the spotlight mounted on the roof of the truck. His father swept the field beside the road with the light until it revealed the first rabbit of the evening. When his father returned the beam to the frozen creature, Dougherty fired without hesitation, then watched as a crimson rivulet seeped into the pure white snow.

After Dougherty tossed his ninth and final rabbit into the bed of the truck, he joined his father in the cab.

"Nice shooting. I don't think you missed one all night," Keith Dougherty said and handed his son the flask. "I drank all the coffee," he added and laughed.

Dougherty took a long pull of Jim Beam and handed the flask back to his father, who downed a bigger gulp of whiskey.

"In one of your cassettes, you asked about my war stories," Keith Dougherty said, staring straight ahead, as if reading the story he was about to tell from the truck's windshield. "You know I was a Tin Can Sailor on the USS Charrette," he continued. "This one time, we were part of a small fleet that was shelling some islands in the South Pacific. Nimitz had us clearing the way for the island hoppers. We were the closest ship to shore that night. All the sudden, the wind changed, and all the smoke and cordite from our own battle ships washed over our deck. Made me sick as a dog. I left my post on the twin guns and ran to the railings and started puking my guts out over the side. An old navy chief

145

came running up to me in the middle of the battle. He gets right in my face and yells, 'Are you scared, boy?' I told him I guess I was. Then he shouts, 'Are you worried about goin' to hell, boy?' I told him I guess I was. Then the old salt leaned in closer and screamed in my face, 'Don't worry, son, you're already here!'"

Keith Dougherty chuckled at his own story until he started coughing. A few moments later his father continued. "Our ship had the record for takin' on the most Jap prisoners. We got most of 'em when we sank a bunch of their ships near the end of the war. We brought the Japs on board. They were half-starved because the war was goin' so bad for them by that time. All I remember was that we fed the Nips ice cream to keep 'em from starvin' to death. Can you imagine it, a bunch of Japs, sitting on the deck of a destroyer, eating bowls of ice cream in the middle of the South Pacific?" Keith Dougherty shook his head at the absurdity of his own tale, then he took a swig of Jim Beam from the flask.

The two men sat in silence as the unabated prairie winds whipped their truck. Finally, Dougherty asked his father the question he had pondered since joining the 334th. "Did you ever have a hard time with the killing?"

Keith Dougherty remained silent. "We did what we had to do," he finally replied, looking over at his son. "You don't think about it. You just do your job. I didn't start that war, and you didn't start the one you're in now. We have to do what our country asks us to do."

Keith Dougherty took another long swig of bourbon from the flask and then passed it back to his son. "Honestly, your mother hurt me more than any Jap ever did," he said, moving the conversation to the place it always ended. "I could make sense of the Japs tryin' to end me, but not her. And Barry Haller? Christ, you lend a guy your truck, and he drives off with your wife. Just remember that, Boke—a man is at war every day."

Dougherty nodded. "I went ahead and extended with the 334th before I came home. I'm going to do the extra nine months now, so I don't have to go back for the last year of my enlistment."

"Good decision," Keith Dougherty said.

The two men sat in silence, passing the flask back and forth until it was empty.

The next morning, Dougherty and his father sat on stools at the Ravenna Drug Store, drinking coffee and nursing hangovers. An older but fit gentleman dressed in a long cashmere overcoat and black bowler hat walked by the large glass window.

"That's John Pesek," Keith Dougherty said casually, which caused his son to perk up a bit and crane his neck for a better look.

The distinguished gentleman stopped when he noticed a black sedan with rear wheels spinning on a patch of ice while attempting to pull forward out of a parking space on Main Street. Dougherty then watched in disbelief as the old man lifted the rear bumper of the car and moved it to a different spot that offered greater traction and allowed the vehicle to escape. The driver waved as he fishtailed onto Main Street. The older gentleman patted his gloved hands together to remove some snow and then continued walking, as if he had done nothing more than stopped to pick a penny off the sidewalk.

"Holy shit that is Pesek," Dougherty said. "He just lifted that car off the ground!"

"That's a world champion wrestler right there," his father said, not surprised by the feat.

"You'd have to be strong as an ox to do that," Dougherty said, knowing he had just witnessed greatness. He already imagined telling the story to his platoonmates back at Bien Hoa.

As the Tiger Man of Nebraska performed his miracle in Ravenna, the clock approached midnight in Vietnam. Jack Godbolt operated the searchlight for a Raider Firefly team that evening when his high ship suddenly dropped from the sky and passed through the beam of Jack's light. At first, Godbolt thought he imagined the sight of the motionless Huey falling through the night sky, but moments later, the ship exploded as it struck the ground.

There were no signs of enemy fire before the incident and no survivors after the crash. The crew in the high ship didn't even have time to make a distress call. Maintenance later blamed the crash on a failure of technology. This conclusion horrified Godbolt, as it lay bare the stark fact that his fate was not in his own hands. It was an epiphany. Even if Jack Godbolt was "the best damned door gunner in South Vietnam," as Major Sheffield often told him, his Huey could still drop from the sky at any moment, simply because some small part in his devilishly complex flying machine had failed.

Before the crash, there was never a doubt in Godbolt's mind that he would survive the war, but after he witnessed that fatal failure of human technology, the game changed for the young warrior. The feeling reminded him of the state championship football game during his senior year of high school: his team fell behind by two touchdowns in the fourth quarter, and then one of Godbolt's teammates fumbled the ball on their own twenty-yard line. Some deficits could not be overcome; some burdens too great even for a golden child, and this led Godbolt to the only logical place where his faith could reside—with God. And since religion was the pathway to God, Jack Godbolt got religion that evening.

In the days after the crash, the Bible verse that resonated most deeply with him was 1 Corinthians 13:11—"When I was a child, I spoke as a child, I understood as a child, I thought as a child; but when I became a man, I put away childish things." In Vietnam, at five hundred feet, as a helicopter dropped through the glow of his spotlight and exploded in the jungle below, Jack Godbolt became a man. In an instant, he no longer cared about scoring touchdowns or making baskets or throwing a ball or playing war. Those endeavors were all childish pursuits. Godbolt had a wife and a daughter, and most importantly, his Lord and Savior Jesus Christ, all waiting for him in Wapakoneta. But first, he would have to fight his way back to Ohio.

15

DEAD WATER

DOUGHERTY SAT IN THE IMPALA near the entrance to Prairie Village West, studying the newspaper clipping about the dispute between the City of Kearney and his father's company. Following his confrontation with Astrid, he doubted she had sent him the articles. It also appeared unlikely Slocum was the mysterious sender, since Mayor Bacchus informed him the day before that the postmaster had retired a few years ago and moved to Florida. A new theory was taking root in Dougherty's mind—perhaps a member of the Haller family was sending him the articles. Barry's relatives all lived in the Litchfield area, so they would have easy access to both the *Sherman County Times* and Broken Bow. He suspected the entire Haller clan resented Keith Dougherty for threatening Barry and his mother. Perhaps they were trying to turn him against his father, which might facilitate Barry's safe return to Litchfield.

Whoever the mysterious sender was, the message with this latest article seemed crystal clear—disputes like the one with the city inspector were endemic to any future he might have with Dougherty Construction. Dougherty left the car and walked beneath the ostentatious stone arch that read Prairie Village West—an ambitious name, in his opinion, since it seemed unlikely Kearney could also support a Prairie Village East. Once inside the development, Dougherty quickly spotted the violation that led to the citation. *How the hell did this happen?* Dougherty wondered, hands on hips, as he stared at the odd sets of cement driveways, as far as the eye could see.

When he returned to the car, Dougherty noticed the Impala's gas gauge loomed dangerously close to empty. He proceeded to the filling station on the edge of town and pulled up to the first available pump. He immediately recognized the attendant as Roger Meacham, a former classmate who took a couple of the same industrial arts classes as him. Meacham was a bit of a square who never swore and had the annoying habit of framing every conversation as a lecture, probably since he hoped to be a teacher one day. Meacham could not imagine a better life for any man than being a high school teacher. You only worked nine months out of the year, your summers were free to do as you pleased, and many of your colleagues were bright, attractive female teachers. Meacham's saving grace was that he landed Dougherty a part-time job at the filling station when Dougherty ran low on money his first year of college.

"Bill Dougherty, where the heck have you been?" Meacham said when he arrived at the driver's side of the car.

"Vietnam," Dougherty replied, casually. "Fill her up."

"No kidding? Vietnam?" Meacham said. He whistled as he started pumping gasoline into the Impala's tank.

"What about you?" Dougherty said through the open window. "What's new?"

"I'm graduating in May with a BA in industrial arts. Hope to land a teaching job in the area. I've been dating a girl at Duchesne College in Omaha. We're getting married this summer. I'm putting in some extra hours during the break, to save up for the wedding. I get off work in a few minutes, and then I'm going to see her."

Dougherty turned his head and looked back at Meacham through the open window. "If you can believe it, there's a girl at Duchesne who's been writing to me in Vietnam. I should go see her sometime," he added, off-handedly.

"Well, yeah," Meacham said, strolling over to the window. "If she's been writing to you in Vietnam, and you're here in Nebraska, then you should definitely go see her. What's her name?"

"Lena Weiss," Dougherty replied. "She's from Grand Island."

"Well, I'll be darned," Meacham said. "That's where Shirley lives. I'll bet my gal knows her. Give me a minute, and I'll ring her."

Before Dougherty could protest, his former classmate sprinted over to the pay phone next to the office. Dougherty had thought about Lena since arriving home, but on each occasion, he decided against reaching out to her. If he showed up on the nursing student's doorstep, the act might appear desperate and put an end to her letters. Dougherty also worried that Lena could never live up to his idealized version of her.

A few minutes later, Meacham returned to the car, beaming. "It's all set. Shirley knows Lena real well, and she's going to call her now. By the time we get to Grand Island, they should be ready. I'll ride with you," he said, as he climbed into the passenger seat of the Impala. "If we both drive, we'll be consuming twice as much fuel, and at thirty-one cents a gallon, who can afford that?"

Grand Island was the largest town in central Nebraska. The Union Pacific railroad reached the community in 1866, which connected it to major markets in the West and Midwest and attracted several large companies to the area, including a meat packing plant, a munitions factory, and several manufacturers of agricultural equipment.

Meacham guided Dougherty through a series of residential streets until they pulled up in front of a nice home in the wealthiest neighborhood in town. "Shirley's dad is an executive at the New Holland plant," he said. "They make tractors, combines, and other farming equipment, mostly for the domestic market but some exports, too."

Everyone in Nebraska knew what New Holland made, but Dougherty nodded politely.

"I can't believe Lena's been writing to you in Vietnam," Meacham's fiancé said the moment she slid into the back seat of the Impala. "I'm Shirley," the stylish brunette with professionally coiffed hair added, patting Dougherty on the shoulders. "You're gonna like Lena. She's a doll."

"Shirley girly, Billy boy here spent the last year flying around the jungle in a helicopter," Roger said.

"How exciting," Shirley replied. "Turn right here," she added, the first in a series of commands issued from the backseat. Soon they arrived at a much smaller but well-kept house on Walnut Street. "You should go up to the door," Shirley instructed Dougherty. "Roger, you come in the back with me so Lena can ride up front with Bill."

"Roger Dodger," Meacham said and saluted, which caused Shirley to snort. Dougherty sheepishly made his way to the front porch and rang the bell. He was surprised when a short young woman with dark curly hair and glasses answered. She was cute, but not what he expected from the Germanic name, Lena Weiss.

"Hi, there. I'm Lena," she said. "Welcome home."

"Hi, Lena. I'm Bill. Bill Dougherty. I bumped into Roger in Kearney, and he mentioned he was dating someone at Duchesne. I told him about you writing to me in Vietnam and he suggested we come down here. I hope you don't mind."

"I don't mind at all. In fact, I'm glad you did," Lena said, grabbing her coat and scarf. "It's been awfully boring being stuck at home during the break."

As they walked toward the Impala, Lena waved to Shirley and Roger snuggled together in the back seat, then turned and looked up at Dougherty. "When I was writing to you, I tried to picture what you looked like. You're much taller than I imagined," she said.

Shirley suggested they go downtown so that she and Roger could do some shopping while the "pen pals" talked at a restaurant. Dougherty and Lena sat opposite one another in a booth. They drank coffee and shared a piece of lemon meringue pie while they made casual conversation.

"I have a sister, Barbie, who's older than me," Lena said. "She still lives at home and works as a secretary at the Coca-Cola bottling plant. My mother is a seamstress, and my father is in charge of maintenance at the munitions plant. He can fix anything. His hobby is repairing old cuckoo clocks from the Black Forest. We have dozens of them around the house. You should hear it when they all go off at the same time," Lena said and laughed. "The clocks drive my mother cuckoo, but she tolerates it because she knows how much they mean to my father. I guess that's real love."

Lena took a small bite of pie. Dougherty studied her delicate features and missed the cue that it was his turn to speak.

"Tell me about yourself," Lena said, breaking the awkward silence. "How did you end up in the army?"

"I enlisted right before the start of my junior year at Kearney State College," he said, then paused while the waitress refilled their coffee cups. "I was dating a girl there, but it didn't feel right being in school while our country was at war. My father served in World War II, and my grandfather served in the First World War, so I guess you could say there's a tradition of service in our family. My dad was in the navy, but he encouraged me to join the army. If I had waited, I probably would have gotten drafted into the infantry. By enlisting, I was able to go for helicopters, which I like. You're studying to be a nurse?" Dougherty added, desperate to change the subject.

"Yes, I graduated from high school last May and started nursing school in Omaha a few months after that. This past fall I did my practical experience at the Grand Island VA Home."

"How was that?" Dougherty said, impressed Lena worked with veterans when so many other people their age protested the war.

"I liked it, but it was hard. Many of the vets I cared for fought in Europe during the First World War. Sometimes they told me their stories—the horrible things they experienced in the trenches. They live with those horrors every day. Nobody thinks about the soldiers fifty years after the war, hooked up to an iron lung or battling an infection from an artificial limb that rubs a stump until it bleeds. They're brave men who gave everything for our country. And now, most of them are at the end of their lives, broken and alone, living in a drafty old VA home with a second-year nursing student caring for them.

"It's sad to me," Lena continued. "Once or twice a year we wave our flags and wear our poppies, then it's back to business as usual. But when soldiers come back from war, it's like throwing a big handful of stones into a pond: each one sends a ripple across the water that effects everyone around them. That's the real cost of war—the ripples—not just the men who died on the battlefield."

Lena's observations stunned Dougherty. She had thought more about life after war than he had. He wanted to ask Lena about the ripples, but before he could formulate a question, Roger and Shirley returned.

Lena reached over and touched Dougherty's wrist, then turned the face of his Bulova watch slightly so that she could read the time from across the table. He thought the gesture was incredibly intimate, one Lena performed naturally, as if his wrist was an extension of her own body.

"I better get home," Lena said to the group. "I'm supposed to go to Mass tomorrow with some friends from Duchesne."

"Sure," Dougherty replied, disappointed the date was ending.

When they returned to the Weiss house, Dougherty walked Lena to the door.

"Some of my friends in Litchfield are having a little party on New Year's Eve. I'd be happy to come pick you up if you'd like to go."

Lena considered the offer for a moment and then smiled. "I'd like that," she said.

Every year, Nick Murphy hosted a New Year's Eve party at his family's farm. During his senior year of high school and his first two years of college, Dougherty had attended the get-together with Astrid. Lena received a lukewarm reception from his friends at the party, who were glad Dougherty was home from the war but seemed to resent someone new on their friend's arm.

Later in the evening, after everyone had several drinks, Nick suggested they all play spin the bottle, something the group of friends had done every year since they were sixteen. Nick cleared a few magazines and candy dishes off the coffee table and placed an empty Coca-Cola bottle on the walnut tabletop. Everyone in the room laughed when he furiously spun the bottle and it slowly came to rest, pointing directly at himself. He shrugged his shoulders and kissed Marnie Brewer, his girlfriend, who did not seem to object.

Marnie spun the bottle next. Everyone in the room appeared mesmerized as the glass bottle slowed. People shouted when the bottle finally stopped. The neck pointed at Mason Wilder from Ord, who walked over and kissed Lena.

Dougherty could tell the kiss made Lena uncomfortable, but she was good natured and wanted to make a positive impression on his friends, so she went with it.

When Lena spun the bottle, it came to rest pointing at Ronie Dahl, a graduate of Litchfield High who had a crush on Dougherty while he was dating Astrid. Ronie made a show of her selection by walking slowly around the room, pausing briefly at each male, as if considering the possibility. Finally, she stopped in front of Dougherty, placed her hand around his neck, and kissed him more passionately than he was expecting.

Dougherty wanted to stop the game. He even suggested they play something else, but the intoxicated crowd urged him to continue. Reluctantly, he spun the Coca Cola bottle, and the glass neck came to rest pointing at Luther Chop, a big farm boy who lived in Cairo, a town near Litchfield the locals pronounced "Care-O." Without hesitation, Chop marched directly over to Lena and kissed her more deeply than Wilder had, nearly bending her in half during the intense lip lock.

Dougherty grabbed Chop by the back of his shirt and pulled him away from Lena. "Knock it off," he said, pushing him back. "I see what you all are doing."

Nick and a couple of others stepped between Dougherty and Chop to prevent the situation from escalating. Before the war, Dougherty would have thought twice about picking a fight with someone Chop's size, but after a year in Vietnam, he had no reservations about mixing it up with a local farm boy.

"What the hell's wrong with you?" Nick shouted at Dougherty.

"What's wrong with all of you," Dougherty shouted, looking briefly at everyone in the room. "Come on, Lena, let's get out of here," he said, as he pushed his way through the crowd.

"I'm sorry about that," Dougherty said once he turned the Impala south onto Highway 2.

"It's okay," Lena replied. "They were just messing with us."

Not wanting to end the evening on a sour note, he turned into the Dead Water Recreation Area two miles southeast of Litchfield. The gravel road dead-ended at a meadow of rye grass beside a small lake. The glow from the Impala's headlights illuminated a few weathered picnic tables at the edge of the inky black water. Dead Water provided a teenage boy with the ideal spot to drink a few beers with his buddies or make out with his girlfriend.

After putting the car in park, Dougherty stared down at his hands on the steering wheel. "They were getting back at me because I wasn't with my old girlfriend. Everybody liked Astrid. No offense. They would like you, too, if they gave you a chance."

"Why did you and Astrid break up?" Lena said.

"She was mad that I enlisted last summer while she was working up in the Sand Hills. We had a big fight. She said I was just doing what my father told me. She and my dad never got along. The whole time we dated it felt like a tug of war between the two of them, with me in the middle, being pulled both ways."

"You talk an awful lot about your father, but I've never heard you say anything about your mother," Lena said.

"She left home when I was thirteen."

"I'm so sorry," Lena replied. "That must have been very difficult for you."

Dougherty nodded. "The day she left us, my father was waiting for me in the living room. I knew something was wrong. He never got to the house before dinner time. He was sitting in his chair, staring at the wall. I asked him where mom was, and he said she was gone and wasn't coming back. 'Where is she?' I yelled. 'How the hell should I know?' my father replied. 'Gone with Barry Haller. Says she loves him more than us.' When he said that, I ran out into the cornfield. My mother was supposed to take me to Ravenna after school that day, to help me buy my first razor. I remember thinking, *How am I ever going to learn to shave without her?*

"After a while, my father found me. Told me to follow him. When we got to the house, his truck was backed up to the front porch. There was a wooden crate in the bed. He told me to go inside and gather up everything that belonged to my mother and put it in the box. 'Every shred of clothing, every photograph she's in, every tube of lipstick and can of hairspray in the box,' he said. I didn't know what was going on. I thought maybe we were going to mail the stuff to her. 'Go,' he shouted. So I ran into the house and started gathering up her things—dresses, hats, shoes, aprons, gloves, books, pictures, beauty products—all of it went in the box. I was crying the whole time, but my father made me keep going. When I made one final search of the house, I checked my room. There on my pillow was the razor we were going to buy together, still in the box. She got it for me before she left."

"It's awful," Lena said, "but at least you had something to remember her by."

Dougherty shook his head. "I put that in the box, too. Then my father climbed into the bed of the truck, put the lid on the crate, and pounded a dozen nails in it. We drove into town but didn't stop at the post office. He kept going to the cemetery. Pulled the truck right up beside their double lot. Had me help unload the pine box, then he handed me a shovel. We dug a big hole in the spot where my mother would have been buried. When it was big enough for the crate, we carried it over to the edge and set it down. He stared down into that hole and said, 'If you were counting on your mother to show you how to be a man, you were barking up the wrong tree. We're gonna bury this box, and in my book, that makes you strong.' After we lowered the crate into the hole, he grabbed a shovel and started covering it with dirt. I didn't know what else to do, so I grabbed the other shovel and helped him."

"What was it like, growing up without her?" Lena said.

"I felt like the person who knew me best had disappeared and taken the blueprint to my life with her. I didn't have any close friends. The only person I had to help me figure stuff out was my father. He worked all the time and drank too much."

Dougherty stopped talking, and Lena remained silent, not because she was horrified by the story, but because she was so moved that someone had finally shared something deep and personal with her. Lena knew that real things like this happened in the world, but they never happened in her sheltered life in the well-kept house on Walnut Street. Here was a man who had lost his mother, loved a woman, and was fighting in a war, and he was telling her his deepest secrets.

Lena also believed that events in life happened for a reason. Her friend, Connie, suggested she write to a soldier in Vietnam, and she did. Her friend, Shirley, called and said her fiancé bumped into that same boy in Kearney, and he wanted to see her and so she saw him. And God, or some other force of the universe, had placed her in this car on this evening with this same young man. In Lena's mind, this was where she was meant to be.

Lena removed Dougherty's hand from the steering wheel and held it in her small, warm hand. "I'm sorry," she whispered. They leaned against each other, staring out at Dead Water Lake, neither saying a word until the first hint of daylight broke across the Nebraska skyline.

Dougherty refrained from calling Lena after their New Year's date. The start of 1968 reminded him that he had a commitment to the US Army, and it wasn't fair to drag Lena into that arrangement. Still, he smiled when a letter with familiar handwriting, identical to the ones he received in Vietnam, showed up at his home in Litchfield.

"If you want to get together before you go back, just give me a call," Lena wrote. The letter included her home phone number.

Dougherty felt compelled to call Lena. He didn't know anyone quite like her. He wondered if her unbridled optimism was simply naïveté or something more profound. It certainly was uncommon for Nebraska, where pragmatism ruled the day.

That evening after dinner, Dougherty slowly made his way down the long hallway and knocked on the door to his father's study.

"Huh," Keith Dougherty grunted.

Dougherty turned the knob and leaned into the room where his father sat in a worn plaid chair with a glass of Jim Beam on the rocks resting on a TV tray. "Mind if I come in?"

Keith Dougherty motioned with his hand, as if helping a truck driver back up to a loading dock. For the first time in years, Dougherty set foot in his father's inner sanctum, another unexpected perk of his military service.

"How's business?" he said, hoping the question would not infuriate his father.

Keith Dougherty shrugged. "A little slow right now, probably due to the holidays. Had to lay a few guys off, but that's the way construction goes—feast or famine."

"I heard something about some trouble with the city inspector in Kearney."

Keith Dougherty waved off the comment. "Who said that? It's nothing. The man's bluffing. People have already moved in. They don't want their driveways and yards ripped up because of some stupid ordinance. He'll have to grant an exception."

Dougherty looked down at his feet, then nodded.

As Dougherty stepped back out into the hall, his father called him back.

"Hey, I don't want you thinkin' about this stuff while you're over there," he said. "Keep your mind on the war. We'll get this sorted out, and everything will be fine by the time you get home."

Dougherty nodded again. As he pulled the door shut, he heard the familiar sound of ice cubes clinking against the side of his father's glass.

Over the next several weeks, Dougherty fell into a routine. Most of his evenings were spent hunting rabbits and drinking with his father. Every few days, when he had enough dead rabbits for a decent payday, he delivered them to the mink farm in Grand Island and then used the proceeds to take Lena on a date. He found himself opening up to Lena in ways he never had with Astrid. The nursing student always listened to what he said and never displayed a hint of judgment.

A week before his leave was up, Dougherty arrived early at Emma's restaurant to spend some time with his grandmother before going back to Vietnam.

"Morning, kiddo," she said, as she poured him a fresh cup of coffee. "It's freezing in here. Would you be a dear and get a fire going in the wood burner while I get things squared away for breakfast?"

"Sure," Dougherty replied, taking his coffee over to the cast iron stove in the back of the restaurant. He found a nice assortment of kindling and split logs that were dry as bones from sitting next to the hot stove. He made a teepee out of some small pieces of wood and then retrieved a few old newspapers from a stack Emma kept nearby for fire-starting. Dougherty froze when he picked up an old edition of the *Sherman County Times* and noticed there was an article clipped out of it. He flipped through the stack of papers until he found several others with missing articles.

Emma came out to check on her grandson's progress with the fire and to top off his coffee.

"Whose cuttin' up your papers, Grams?" Dougherty said.

"Oh, that would be your grandfather. He doesn't have much else to do, lying in bed all day. He clips out some of the articles and keeps them in shoe boxes under his bed. Then he gives me the papers, so I have something to get that old thing going each morning," she said, gesturing at the stove with the coffee pot.

Dougherty nodded. "You said Maxine is still helping with Grandpa. It occurred to me that I don't even know where she's from?"

"Berwyn," Emma said. "Lived there her whole life."

"That's out near Broken Bow, isn't it?"

Emma nodded. "For seven years, she's made that drive five days a week."

Dougherty struck a match and held it to the edge of the crumpled newspaper in the stove; words and pictures disappeared in the flames. "I've been meaning to spend some time with Grandpa before I leave. Maybe I'll run up there now."

"I know he'd enjoy that," Emma said. "He doesn't get much company. Just Maxine."

Emma and Norris Dougherty lived in town, an easy five-minute walk from the restaurant. Dougherty paused outside the gate to the faded white bungalow. Returning to the house reminded him of his mother. Before Candace Dougherty left, she was the one who checked on Norris throughout the week. Emma paid her for it, and she saved most of the money to attend beauty school. During summers, Dougherty tagged along with his mother. He and his grandfather played cards or listened to the radio while Candace prepared lunch and cleaned. Dougherty loved his grandfather but was ashamed to admit that he felt uncomfortable spending time alone with him. Perhaps it was the dark, musty room where Norris passed his days or his grandfather's condition that scared him—that maybe one day he would be trapped in a bed, unable to move, hands that shook, and eyes that seemed unable to focus.

"Hi, Gramps. How are you doing?" he said as he peered into the room.

Norris Dougherty shrugged. "Not bad for an old man, I guess. How 'bout you?"

"I'm ok. Just built Grams a fire over at the restaurant. Wanted to get out of there before the place fills up." He walked slowly to his grandfather's bedside and slid onto the same wooden chair he occupied as a boy. From this closer vantage point, he saw the two or three days of grey stubble Norris always seemed to wear on his wrinkled face and the remnants of his teeth, yellow and worn down from years of chewing on a pipe.

"Grandpa, I know you're the one whose been sending me the articles about Dad. Why?"

Norris looked down at his lifeless body beneath the sheet, his lower lip trembled. "I love your father . . . but the war changed him. When Keith got home, he fell into the bottle. I seen it happen to a lot of good men. He became angry and controlling. Everything had to be his way, and he wasn't always in the right frame of mind to make decisions, if you know what I mean. He had nightmares about those Kamikaze planes that tried to crash into his ship. When he was still living with us, I'd hear him shout things in his sleep like, 'Here they come!' or 'Over there! Over there!' He married your mother soon after he got back from the war, and they had you in '47. Pretty hard for a man to go from killing people to changing diapers. I should know."

Dougherty nodded.

"Your mother's a good woman," Norris said. "She cared for me like a daughter for nearly seven years. I don't blame her for leaving. But ever since then, your father's been lost. He's livin' his life like a man punchin' his way out of a swarm of bees—he might get through it, but not without getting stung plenty of times. I don't want to see that happen to you, Bill. That's why I sent you the articles. Thought maybe it would open your eyes a bit. I could see the way you looked up to him. You played football for him, worked construction for him, joined the army to please him. If you choose to do those things, that's fine. I just want you to know who you're following and make sure that's where you want to go, especially now that you're in a war."

Dougherty heard the front door open.

"Maxine," Norris said. A moment later, a stout, middle-aged woman with short brown hair entered the room.

"Our secret's out," Norris said.

"I told you he would figure it out," Maxine replied. "Sorry, Bill. Your grandfather made me do it. I go into Broken Bow a couple of times each week, so it was easy to drop off the envelopes. I'll leave you two alone," she said, zipping up her heavy winter coat. "I've got to run some errands. Need anything before I go?" she said to Norris, who frowned and shook his head.

When the two men heard Maxine leave the house, Norris turned his attention back to his grandson. "What were we talking about?"

"You said you wanted me to know about my father, especially since I'm in a war."

Norris nodded. "War. Seems this country sends every generation off to fight. They wrap it all up in the flag and some patriotic words, but it's hell. There's no other way to describe it. I fought in France during the First World War. We battled the Germans fifty miles outside of Paris at Belleau Woods. Our side lost ten thousand men in three weeks, and we were the *winners*. To this day, I still remember the smell of mustard gas and rotting flesh. The sight of men stabbing each other with bayonets. It wasn't even human, Bill. We were like demons tearing each other apart. Maybe you know what I mean. I hope you don't," Norris said, looking up with tired eyes.

"Was it wrong that he joined the navy?" Dougherty said, having difficulty processing this new information from his father's father.

"I'm not sayin' it was wrong. The world was at war. We owe your father and men like him a lot. But it would be wrong if he joined just because of me. I want you to understand, Bill, that you can belong to something, or you can believe in something, but just know, the price of that is a piece of you."

"The articles," Dougherty said. "Did my father burn down the church?"

Norris looked down at his shaking hands. "I can't prove it, but he may have. As a postman, your father knew every piece of property in the area. I remember him talking about that lot before the fire. Said it would make a good place for a home."

"Could be a coincidence," Dougherty said.

Norris nodded. "Could be."

"What happened at the post office?"

"Word around town was that your father took some money from the till."

"If he needed money, why wouldn't he just ask you?"

"Too proud, I imagine," Norris said. "Your father follows his own logic. He could have *borrowed* some money from the post office, intending to pay it back, and in his mind that wouldn't be stealing, even if a month passed."

"What should I do?" Dougherty said to his grandfather, as he stood up to leave.

"Don't take everything your father says at face value. Find your own way," Norris said.

"I'll try," Dougherty replied quietly, then leaned over the bed and hugged his grandfather. "I'll see you at dinner on Sunday," he added. "I'm bringing someone special I want you and Grams to meet."

Norris nodded. "Bill, I don't think your grandmother would approve of me sharing those articles with you. If you don't mind, let's keep it between us," Norris said with a grim smile.

On Sunday afternoon, Dougherty paced the living room floor while he waited for Lena to arrive. His father watched a special news report about the war in Vietnam: a Marine Corps base in Khe San was under heavy attack by the North Vietnamese Army.

"That's nowhere near me," Dougherty said at one point during the broadcast. "Khe Sanh is all the way up in I Corps, on the border with North Vietnam," he added, staring out the window.

"Enemy must be getting desperate," Keith said and snapped off the television set. "They'll be sorry if they mess with the marines," he added.

Dougherty smiled when Lena pulled up to their house in a big Ford sedan. This would be his last chance to see her before she returned to school, and he returned to Vietnam. At Lena's request, he dressed in his uniform that day, and she wore a bright yellow sweater that stood out in the dreary Nebraska winterscape. After a late lunch at his grandmother's house, he drove Lena around town so she could see where he attended school and played football. They concluded their tour on Cemetery Hill.

As they entered the burial grounds through a rusty iron gate, Dougherty broke the silence. "Lena, before I came home, I signed up for another tour in Vietnam. That's why I didn't call you after our date on New Year's Eve. Now I'm wishing I hadn't extended, but I can't change that. I have nine more months in Vietnam and then about nine months stateside."

"Nine months isn't so long," Lena said, trying to sound optimistic.

Having just served twelve months in Vietnam, Dougherty understood that nine months could feel like nine years, and that was assuming he survived his time in Thailand.

"Your letters meant a lot to me," he said. "I always looked forward to getting them."

"I'll keep writing them if you like," Lena replied, smiling.

"I want to show you something," Dougherty said. He led Lena through the cemetery to a set of headstones with his parents' names on them.

Keith and Candace Dougherty had picked a scenic spot for their permanent resting place. It sat at the highest point of the cemetery, where a person could see for miles in every direction—from the corn fields of Buffalo and Sherman Counties in the south and east, to the fingers of the Sand Hills in the west. Candace Dougherty's stone included both her birth date and the date of her departure from Litchfield, as if it were the date of her departure from the world.

"My father paid to have that date chiseled on there," Dougherty said.

"It's sad that your father didn't let you keep anything that belonged to your mother."

"I guess it was the only way he could deal with it, to completely erase her from our lives. In some ways it helped me, too. It forced me to move on," Dougherty said, staring at the ground where he helped bury his mother's possessions.

"I got you something," Lena said, reaching into her pocket. "A late Christmas gift," she added, holding up a silver, oval-shaped medal with the image of a bearded man holding a staff and carrying a child on his shoulders. Lena unclasped the sterling chain, reached up, and fastened it around Dougherty's neck. When Lena removed her hand, he noticed the words on the small silver medallion.

SAINT CHRISTOPHER – PROTECT US.

"Saint Christopher is the patron saint of travelers. Just because I'm not Catholic doesn't mean I can't believe in saints," Lena said and laughed. "I'm actually Lutheran, but Duchesne is a Catholic school and most of my friends are Catholic, so I go to Mass with them. That's how I learned about the saints. They're ordinary people who do extraordinary things. I like the idea that there are special people out there watching over us," Lena said.

Dougherty stepped closer and Lena put her arms around his waist. Then he leaned down, and they kissed.

As the sun descended over the Sand Hills, Dougherty knew it was time to leave, but he had one final revelation to share. "Lena, my mother wrote to me in Vietnam. She wants me to visit her in Los Angeles."

"You should go," Lena replied, placing her hand on Dougherty's chest. "I can't imagine having a son and not seeing him for seven years."

Following the conversation with his grandfather, Dougherty had the same thought. "Maybe it's time," he said, looking at his mother's headstone one final time before they left her grave site.

16

CALIFORNIA DREAMING

A FEW DAYS LATER, Dougherty's father drove him to the airport in Kearney. "Keep one foot on the ground, Boke," the old man said after he pulled into the parking lot. It was surrounded by mounds of plowed snow that had built up during the long, harsh winter.

Doughtery shook his father's hand and stepped into the frigid air. He hoisted his duffel out of the truck bed and waved farewell as Keith Dougherty drove off in the bitter Nebraska morning. Dougherty's feet crunched snow and ice as he slowly made his way to the terminal; each breath vaporized in the sub-zero temperatures.

At the ticket counter, Dougherty arranged to fly military standby to Chicago, where he could catch another standby flight to Los Angeles. During his layover at O'Hare, he called his mother's Santa Monica number and informed her that he would be at the Los Angeles International Airport in a few hours. She suggested they meet in the restaurant at the Theme Building on the grounds of LAX. "You can't miss it," she said, then wished him a safe flight.

When he stepped into the warmth and sunshine of Los Angeles, Dougherty felt as if he had emerged on another planet, a sensation reinforced by his mother's choice of meeting places. The *LA Times* described the iconic Theme Building as a "big white concrete-and-steel spider."

Parabolic arches supported a round, glass-walled dining room seventy feet off the ground that looked, to Dougherty, like a flying saucer from a science fiction movie. The restaurant offered panoramic views of the LA skyline, and patrons could visit the observation deck on the roof to watch planes taking off and landing at LAX.

When he entered the futuristic restaurant, Dougherty easily spotted his mother from across the dining room. She wore a white skirt and matching white cape that made her red hair pop like a flame. She looked as glamorous as a movie star, and he noticed other patrons turning to catch a glimpse of this woman who might be famous. A young boy of three or four sat beside his mother in the booth and stabbed a bowl of ice cream with a tiny spoon.

"Please, sit down," Candace Haller said, motioning to the empty chair across from her. "I can't believe how much you've grown. You're a man now, and a soldier," she said. "Your father must be so proud." As she took in the sight of her son, her eyes began to brim.

"Thank you for coming," she said, as she wiped her eyes. "I wouldn't have blamed you if you never wanted to see me again. I left you when you were a boy, and nothing I can say or do will ever fix that."

Dougherty heard his mother's words but could not divert his attention from the young boy across the table, a doppelganger of himself at the same age. It never occurred to Doughtery that his mother might have another child.

"This is my son, Dean," Candace said, turning to the disinterested boy. "I couldn't find anyone to watch him on such short notice, so I had to bring him with me. I'm sorry you're finding out about your half-brother this way," she added, understanding the additional pain it must have caused her oldest son, to see a younger version of himself beside his estranged mother.

When Dougherty struggled to find words, his mother filled the awkward silence. "How's it going over there? This war seems so dangerous, especially for you, flying in helicopters."

"It's not so bad," Dougherty replied. "More dangerous for those on the ground."

A waiter appeared at their table, and Candace ordered a latte. He

167

asked his mother what that was, and she explained it was a coffee with steamed milk. Dougherty ordered a regular coffee.

"You must have questions," Candace said.

Dougherty had a million questions, but all he could think to ask was, "Why did you leave?"

Candace exhaled. "It's a long and complicated story. I've imagined telling it to you a thousand times, so if this sounds rehearsed, I apologize."

The waiter arrived with their coffees, and once he departed, his mother composed herself and continued. "I never really belonged in Litchfield. I was always the outsider from Lincoln. I happened to be visiting a cousin in Ravenna one summer when I met your father outside the roller rink. That was during the war. He had just joined the Navy and asked if I would write to him while he was away. I was flattered that this older man with a convertible wanted me, of all people, to write to him. So, we wrote dozens of letters, back and forth.

"When your father returned from the war, he came to see me in Lincoln in his uniform. He was a good-looking man, and he had some medals on his chest. He proposed to me on that visit. I don't know, it all just felt so romantic, like a movie, and my role was to say 'yes.' Also, I didn't have a very good situation at home, so I suppose I was looking for a way to escape."

When the young boy started banging the table with the spoon, Candace removed it from his hand and deposited it in the bowl, which she slid out of his reach. This caused the toddler to burst into tears. Candace retrieved a toy truck from her bag on the floor and handed it to the boy, who immediately stopped crying.

"When we got back to Litchfield after our honeymoon in St. Louis, I knew right away that I had made a mistake. I spent hours alone while your father was at work, feeling like the real me was disappearing in those endless rows of corn. Your father was having nightmares about the war, and soon after we were married, he started drinking, heavily. I wanted him to get help, but he refused. He said people with problems in their head were just weak.

"I was about to leave him. I had it all figured out. My cousin from Oklahoma was going to pick me up while he was at work, and I was going to go live with her in Tulsa. But then I got pregnant . . . with you," Candace said, and smiled. "And that changed everything. I poured all of my heart into you. We did everything together, and that made it okay, because I had a purpose.

"When you were four, I got pregnant again. That's when your father decided we needed a place closer to town."

"The fire," Dougherty said. "Do you think he burned down the church to get the lot?"

"I can't prove it," Candace said, "but I think he did. I was so distressed about the whole thing that I had a miscarriage. And then you started school, and I was alone again. About that same time, your father lost his job at the Post Office. You probably heard him say he had a falling out with the postmaster. That is true. They got into a big fight when he accused Keith of taking some money from the register. But he did it, Bill. Your father took twenty dollars from the till. I think he was planning to pay it back, but they found the shortage before he could return the money. That's why he got fired and started working construction.

"After that, I fell into a deep depression. That's when your grandmother hired me to care for your grandfather. It probably saved my life. Norris was like a father to me. He was the only one in that town that I could really talk to.

"With the money your grandmother paid me, I eventually had enough saved up to go to school to become a beauty operator. I convinced your father the extra income would help us. I think Norris worked on him, too. In the end, he agreed. My classes were at night, and your father didn't want me driving alone. When he found out Barry was also taking classes in Kearney, he offered to loan him one of his pickup trucks if Barry would drive me to class on Tuesday and Thursday nights. We had the best conversations during those drives. I didn't realize a man and a woman could have conversations like that, just talking about anything and everything.

"Barry usually talked about Los Angeles and how he planned to move out here after graduation. The first time he suggested I come to LA with him, I just laughed. But he repeated the offer each week until we had the accident. You may remember that. It was a miracle we survived," Candace said, looking down into her coffee cup. "When Barry and I crawled out of that truck, it was like a wakeup call for me. I remember looking over at him kneeling on the ground. He had a cut on his forehead that was bleeding into the snow. That's when I told him I would go with him.

"The hardest part was the thought of leaving you. Of course, I didn't want to. I convinced Barry that we could bring you with us. We were all packed up and ready to go, waiting at the house for you to get home from school. That's when Keith showed up unexpectedly. He pieced it all together pretty quickly and threatened to kill us if we tried to take you from him."

Dougherty raised his eyebrows in disbelief.

"I believed him," Candace said, nervously rotating the coffee cup in her hands, "especially after he broke Barry's nose. I knew you would be ok with Norris and Emma . . . and even your father needed someone. I don't love him, but I don't hate him, either. So, Barry and I left that day without you."

As he studied the young boy beside his mother, Dougherty felt Candace Dougherty had simply hit the reset button on her life by trading Keith for Barry, Nebraska for California, and himself for Dean. "Was it the right decision?" Dougherty said.

Candace Haller thought about the question for several moments, nearly responding twice before stopping herself to consider her response further. "One thing I've learned from being a beauty operator is that just fixing someone's hair a bit differently or applying some makeup doesn't really make that person any different. The same problems are still there, just covered up. Sometimes, the only way to really make a change is to start over.

"I will say that LA is just as magical as Barry described it. We saw The Beatles at the Hollywood Bowl a few years ago. We spend Sundays on the beach at Santa Monica Pier, and I take Dean to Disneyland at least once a month. They have an area of the park called Tomorrowland where you can ride a rocket to the moon or voyage on a submarine deep beneath the sea. It's marvelous. In California you always feel like you're moving into the future. Just look at this place, she said of the modern, circular glass restaurant in which they sat. In Litchfield, I was Keith

Dougherty's wife, but here, I'm Candy Haller, hairdresser to the stars," she said, smiling.

Candace turned serious again. "Even though I love it here, there's an emptiness inside of me that seems like it can never be filled . . . because I abandoned you. And that makes me a monster."

Dougherty stared at his mother, not believing she was a monster, but not ready to absolve her, either. Instead, he changed the subject. "When I was home during leave, I noticed something that never occurred to me before. He hasn't called me 'William' or 'Bill' since you left, just 'Boke' or 'son.'"

Once again Candace's eyes welled with tears. "I'm sure it's because I picked the name William. I always loved that name. He probably stopped using it because it's dear to me."

Candace dabbed at her eyes with a napkin. "I must look a mess," she said, trying to smile. "I want to show you something," she said, reaching into her shoulder bag to retrieve a scrapbook, which she set on the table. She began flipping through pages of newspaper clippings about her oldest son—box scores from baseball games he had played, articles about football games he had quarterbacked, photos from the Old Settlers Picnic and high school graduation, even the two articles about his service in Vietnam.

"Your Grandpa Norris sent these to me," she said. "It was our secret. I went to see him right after the confrontation with your father. He was the only one I felt I could tell. He promised to help raise you and send me updates when he could. I think he felt bad about how Keith had treated me."

As he stared at his mother solemnly examining each article in her sacred book, Dougherty allowed himself to remember what they had once shared. In that moment, he felt his heart opening like the door to a crypt. Candace could sense it, too, a glimmer of hope that maybe one day there could be a world where they existed in each other's lives again.

"Mommy," the young boy blurted, looking from Candace to the unfamiliar man. The child's interjection surprised them, and when Candace turned her attention to her younger son, the connection with her firstborn was lost.

CHAPTER 16

"I have to go," Dougherty said, looking at his watch for emphasis. He didn't have to leave—he had several hours before his flight departed— but he needed to go because the past and present were colliding, and the pain of the moment threatened to consume him. When he stood, Candace raced around the table and embraced her son. She sobbed, uncontrollably, and held him tightly, as if she were trying to transport them both back in time. Dougherty awkwardly patted his mother's back and attempted to console her, using a set of human responses that had lain dormant for seven years. The young boy stared at them both, wide-eyed, as if they were characters at Disneyland.

Finally, Candace looked up at her son. "Anything is possible in California," she said, desperate to believe it herself. "You could start a new life here, just like I did. There's so much opportunity, and we would help you anyway we could." Sensing she may have gone too far, too fast, Candace squeezed her son's arms, tightly. "Maybe it's wishing for too much to have you here, but if there's EVER anything I can do for you, please . . . you must let me know," Candace said, staring into her son's eyes for some acknowledgment.

Dougherty nodded. As he turned to leave, the young boy saluted him. Dougherty stared at the toddler for several moments, then he returned a crisp salute and instructed Dean to take care of his mother.

Dougherty caught a short flight to Oakland, the Army's primary staging point for troops headed to Vietnam. The Army had erected hundreds of double bunks in a giant aircraft hangar, with restrooms at one end and a huge set of aviation doors at the other. When Dougherty arrived, he was told to find an empty bunk and that each morning, after formation, a clerk would call off a list of names. If your name was called, then you reported to the hangar doors and boarded a plane. If they didn't call your name, you went back to doing nothing. Uncle Sam was herding cattle. The arrangement gave Dougherty plenty of time to think about the reunion with his mother. He was not ready to forgive Candace and move on as if nothing had happened. Los Angeles might be the future; it may have saved her life, but his mother left him in the past, to fend for himself. Also, she had a new son now, and he suspected Dean would be her priority. Dougherty was not proud of the jealousy he felt toward the young boy, living an idyllic life that he had been denied.

On his second day in Oakland, Dougherty waited in line for two hours at a bank of pay phones with dozens of GIs lined up at each one. When his turn finally arrived, he placed a call to Duchesne College. A girl answered the hall phone in the dormitory and when he asked for Lena, the girl said, "She's out with someone."

"Who?" Dougherty demanded.

"I don't know. Some guy," the girl responded.

Dougherty slammed the phone down and returned to his bunk.

The following morning, he heard his name called during formation, and he boarded the next plane bound for Vietnam.

TET

AFTER FLYING FROM OAKLAND TO HAWAII, Hawaii to Guam, and Guam to South Vietnam, William Dougherty and dozens of other GIs touched down at Bien Hoa on the morning of January 30. Dougherty bumped into Mancuso and Sam on his way to the barracks.

"I thought you'd be in Thailand by now," Dougherty said, relieved to see a familiar face. He dropped his duffel and affectionately petted Sam until a look of sheer pleasure lit up the dog's face.

"Sheffield kept me here 'til you got back. You ain't gonna believe this, bro, but our team for Thailand is you, me, Briggsy, and Chalfant. That's why we went to the 'Fill-peens' together. I saw it on a sheet in Ops. I never would have signed up for this fuckin' thing if Sheffield told me I was goin' north with Chalfant."

"Damn," Dougherty said. "I can't believe it."

"Yeah, we're SOL," Mancuso said. "Shit out o' luck," he added, in case his friend didn't get it.

Dougherty had believed he would fly with Captain Ruby in Thailand; Sheffield even hinted at it during their meeting. Now, faced with the grim prospect of doing the nearly impossible with his life in the hands of Balfour Chalfant, Dougherty felt a wave of despair wash over him.

"Of all the people to go on a suicide mission with . . . fuckin' Ball

174

Four Chalfant," Mancuso said and trudged off toward the mess hall. Sam abandoned the gunner and followed Dougherty back to the barracks where he found his favorite corner in the room, turned around several times, then settled on the floor to rest in the heat.

Dougherty noticed a portrait of Jesus Christ on the wall above Godbolt's bunk. Someone had wired a wooden cross to the door of Jack's metal locker, and a pair of white, porcelain praying hands sat on the wooden crate beside a black Holy Bible with roughly twenty passages marked by tiny scraps of paper. At first, Dougherty wondered if Godbolt had rotated home and Swanson assigned the company chaplain to bunk with Coffey as a joke. But then he spotted the photo of Jack's baby girl on the wall beside Jesus and concluded his friend got religion while he was home on leave.

Dougherty slowly unpacked the duffel bag—his body in Vietnam, his mind in Los Angeles, and his heart in Nebraska. He tried to process Mancuso's news about flying up north with Captain Chalfant. Perhaps, after he arrived in Thailand, Ruby would make one of his famous spot decisions and assign Dougherty to his own ship.

"Good thing you're back," Swanson said from the doorway. "Get your stuff together. You're flyin' tonight."

"The hell I am!" Dougherty retorted.

Swanson's face broke into a grin, "I'm just messin' with yah, Doc. You're out of the rotation. We have a C-130 goin' up to Thailand in a couple of days. I've got you and Mancuso on that flight so you can join the others."

"Any idea who I'll be flying with in Thailand?" Dougherty said.

"Not a clue," Swanson replied and shrugged. "That's up to Captain Ruby."

Dougherty suspected the Ops sergeant knew the plans for Thailand like the back of his hand, but the man had a job to do, so he let it drop.

Exhausted by his four-day journey from Litchfield to Bien Hoa, Dougherty turned in at seven that evening. Operations assigned Coffey and Godbolt to Firefly, which gave the jet-lagged airman the peace and quiet he needed. In downtown Bien Hoa, as Dougherty drifted off to sleep, seven VC in a truck rode by the compound where the company's pilots lived and shouted, "Yankee, tonight you die."

Mortars started raining on Bien Hoa Air Base at three in the morning. One of the first rockets struck the Raider shack, causing the roof and walls to collapse like a house of cards. Dougherty's platoon had rotated from ESB to Firefly a few days prior, and the building sat empty that night. The enemy artillery, which began at a distance, moved across the flight line toward the living quarters. One rocket hit the motor pool across from Dougherty's barracks, and a few pieces of shrapnel stuck in the wood-sided exterior of the living quarters.

Dougherty jumped up from his bunk when the attack started, wearing nothing but his undershorts and dog tags. Following the direct hit on the motor pool, he decided to run to the nearest bunker. As he stood in the door another rocket landed nearby. Dougherty dove into a drainage ditch beside the barracks. Rocket flashes and explosions lit the sky. The sound of gunfire filled the smoky air. Someone shouted, "Sappers inside the wire," which meant that Viet Cong guerrillas with satchels of explosives had breached the concertina wire fence surrounding the base and were depositing their charges in strategic locations.

As he lay in the mud, a Jeep skidded to a stop in front of the barracks. "Raiders, Raiders, let's go," the driver shouted.

Dougherty raced back to his room for his boots, flight suit, and helmet, which he placed on the soft top of the Jeep now filled with people. He climbed onto the back of the vehicle, placing his bare feet on the protective bar around the tail lights. The driver took off, hauling ass down the taxiway toward the flight line where the Raider Huey gunships sat in their revetments.

VC snipers fired at the speeding vehicle from the Bien Hoa water tower, which sat adjacent to the US military base. Amid the hail of gunfire, the driver turned sharply, causing the jeep to skid sideways. As if in slow-motion, the vehicle tipped up, balanced on two wheels, then slowly rolled over, sending the passengers flying in all directions. Everyone scrambled for cover. Dougherty scurried behind a nearby berm.

When a rocket exploded near the tarmac, the blast momentarily illuminated the runway. Dougherty spotted his clothes beside the overturned Jeep, his flight helmet lying on the ground like a decapitated head. In that moment, Dougherty decided the worst fate would be to die in his underwear, so he sprinted toward his clothing, scooped the items into his arms, and continued running to the Jeep for cover. Once behind the overturned vehicle, Dougherty slipped on the flight suit and boots while snipers on the water tower continued shooting at the men on the runway. He watched in disbelief as the blast from another incoming rocket lifted a collection of metal trash cans off the airfield and slammed them back down to the ground in unison.

When the VC started their mortar attack, the Raider Firefly team with Godbolt and Coffey was returning to Bien Hoa to refuel and rearm. Captain Jerry Pearle, who led the Playboys through their transition from Hueys to Cobras, had been tapped as the company's new Operations officer in December. Pearle filled in when missions were short a pilot, a practice that became more common after half the Raiders departed for Thailand. Pearle had assigned himself to lead the Raider Firefly team that evening. In the days leading up to the attack, the pilot witnessed a heavy movement of enemy personnel protected by the TET cease-fire agreement that prevented US forces from firing on VC and NVA soldiers in groups of less than fifty. He suspected something was up and invited a senior officer to fly in the co-pilot's seat. He also had a South Vietnamese officer onboard to observe enemy movements and authorize strikes.

When the three Hueys landed on the Scabbard, the men hiding on the runway raced to their ships. Dougherty ran past the high ship and the light ship to the right door of the deck ship where Jack Godbolt sat.

"Do you need relieved?" he shouted.

Godbolt shook his head from side to side. "Help us rearm us. They're everywhere."

Some of the men raced to the depot beside the tarmac and grabbed armfuls of rockets, which they dispensed at each ship. Dougherty and another crew chief connected the detonation wires once the rockets rested in the pods. Several men grabbed ammunition for the gunners and crew chiefs, who frantically fed the rounds through their door boxes and into their weapons.

During the rearming, the remaining men topped off the ships using a fuel truck parked beside the runway. It was not lost on the airmen that if a rocket struck the truck filled with JP4, it would incinerate every helicopter and human in the vicinity. A few minutes later, Pearle waved everyone away, then he and the two other Hueys lifted off. From the sky, Pearle easily spotted the VC rockets streaking toward Bien Hoa from an area east of the base. He led the heavy fire team to the location where the three Huey gunships concentrated their rocket and machine gun fire on the position, eradicating the threat.

Minutes later, a huge fireball erupted over the US base at Long Binh. Dougherty later learned that enemy sappers had blown the facility's ammo dump. Since Pearle commanded the only airborne Hueys in the Long Binh area, the tower immediately ordered them to help secure the perimeter around the ammo dump. Once they expended their remaining ammunition, the three ships returned to the Scabbard to re-arm.

Dougherty ran to Jack's door, again. "The whole country's under attack," Godbolt shouted. "The radios are goin' crazy."

Once rearmed, Pearle's team lifted off again. This time they proceeded to the east end of the Air Force runway to support the 82nd Airborne Division, which was receiving heavy machine gun fire. The enemy had breached the wire through a cemetery near the barracks that housed the US Rangers—a poor choice by the planners of the attack. Pearle and his team expended their weapons on the position, creating dozens of fresh corpses amidst the ghostly white headstones.

As he touched down to rearm a third time, Pearle spotted an Air Force colonel attempting to bring order to the chaos on the flight line. Pearle waved the man to his ship and encouraged him to ride along and evaluate the situation. The officer hopped into Pearle's Huey, which soon lifted off to engage enemy forces in heavy firefights around the base. Once the enemy understood the threat facing them from above, they directed much of their fire toward Pearle's ship, filling it with bullet holes. Pearle and his crew fought like hell. Even the Air Force colonel fired his side arm out the Huey's open doors in a desperate effort to increase the ship's fire power in the face of the enemy barrage.

Dougherty and the other enlisted airmen waited on the flight line for their pilots to arrive, but none did. Finally, the small group of crew chiefs and door gunners decided to pull the M-60s off their helicopters and man the bunker at the end of the flight line. From that position, the men could defend against a direct advance on their Hueys. After several tense hours in the bunker, several gunships from the 68th Armed Helicopter Company returned to the adjacent flight line. Dougherty and a few other men raced to the Hueys, offering to fly, but no one wanted relieved. Instead, he joined the cooks and clerks who rearmed the ships and provided hot coffee and sandwiches to the crews.

In the early hours of the attack, the pilots from the 334th remained trapped at the Villa in downtown Bien Hoa until two heroic enlisted men hopped into a three-quarter ton truck and escaped the base. Their daring mission to retrieve the stranded officers succeeded, and at daybreak, the first group of Raider pilots arrived on the flight line. Upon seeing the truck, Dougherty sprinted to the revetment with the M-60 and jumped into his aircraft. As his ship lifted off, Dougherty noticed craters on the flight line. One Huey received a direct hit from a VC rocket: the magnesium in the ship's frame glowed white hot. The bodies of dead enemy soldiers littered the grass field that extended to the perimeter fence east of the runway. Patches of grass continued to burn.

Once airborne, Dougherty's pilot received an urgent dispatch from a slick operating in the area.

"Aircraft over Bien Hoa," the voice said. "I'm going to drop smoke on a target for you." Dougherty spotted the canister falling from the nearby Huey. Moments later, smoke poured skyward from a white rectangular building in downtown Bien Hoa.

A FAC plane arrived on the scene and reminded the gunships they could shoot anything between the railroad tracks and the river, which Dougherty realized turned most of their home city into a free strike zone. Moments later, he spotted several people running into the white building with a cross on the front and smoke billowing from the canister on its roof. As their helicopter approached the church, angry tracer fire zipped toward their ship. Dougherty opened up with his M-60, while his pilot fired a salvo of rockets into the building, which imploded a moment later.

The pilot banked away from the demolished church and flew just above the rooftops across the city. Dougherty and his door gunner fired at anything that moved. Upon returning to the flight line, they flew in low over the Air Force side of the base. Dougherty opened fire on a man squatting behind a tombstone in the cemetery where Pearle's team helped repulse the initial advance hours earlier. Unbeknownst to Dougherty, the man was already deceased, locked in rigor mortis in a crouching position. Dead bodies lay everywhere—at the fence, in the field, and on the tarmac.

By midmorning, other helicopter gunship crews worked the area, wiping out the snipers on the water tower and other pockets of VC and NVA now trapped in Bien Hoa. Dougherty heard chatter on the radio about a group of enemy combatants pinned down between the Oriental River and the base. MACV had gun boats on the river, Armored Personnel Carriers (APCs) from the 9th Infantry Division on the road, and helicopter gunships in the air. When the VC ran toward the river, the gunboats fired on them. When they ran toward the road, the armored vehicles shot at them. When they ran into the trees between the river and the road, the helicopters fired rockets at them.

"We're giving these guys a pretty rough time," the commander of the APCs said over the radio. "Looks like they're trying to surrender."

"How many are there?" Dougherty heard an authoritative voice say over the radio.

"Quite a few, sir, but fewer all the time," the commander of the APCs replied.

"No *Chieu Hoi's*," the voice said, meaning *no prisoners*. Moments later, Dougherty heard intense gunfire through his headphones.

Dougherty and his platoonmates flew nonstop for two days, mostly around Bien Hoa. With each passing hour, the enemy's strength diminished. Troops patrolling the area found split pieces of bamboo pounded into the ground at various locations, all pointed in the general direction of Bien Hoa. The VC used these primitive launching tubes to fire their rockets at the base.

In the days after the offensive, Dougherty learned the VC and NVA attacked more than a hundred cities and villages during TET, and the fighting continued in other parts of the country, including Hue, Khe Sanh, and Saigon, where the enemy briefly occupied the US Embassy. The enemy even attacked Tan Son Nhut Airbase and advanced inside the perimeter of the massive installation that served as home to the MACV headquarters. Dougherty wondered if his friend Dag Larsen survived the attack. He recalled how he had told Astrid that her brother was safe in Saigon. Now this war had made a liar of him, too.

After the initial attack, the US Army refused to let any of the local workers back onto the base. After several weeks of intense operations, when the smell of overworked men and unattended bathrooms became unbearable, the brass allowed the "house girls" to return, to clean the barracks and wash the men's uniforms. After the locals returned, the debris scattered throughout the base mysteriously disappeared.

Allowing the pilots of the 145th Combat Aviation Battalion to live off base in the relative comfort of the Villa proved to be a serious tactical mistake, as aircraft were unable to respond in the wake of the attack. In retrospect, had the VC also attacked Honour-Smith compound, they could have wiped out nearly all of Bien Hoa's air capability. It was a fortunate oversight that only delayed a heavy air defense by hours instead of days. After TET, the pilots, nurses, and Red Cross Donut Dollies all moved from the Villa to a cluster of buildings located within the perimeter of the US base. These new living quarters sat as close to town as one could get while remaining inside the wire.

Several weeks after TET, Captain Ruby and his team returned from Thailand. Their secret objective, their sacred cause—whether it was liberating American POWs or severing the Ho Cho Minh trail at its source or striking a blow deep within Northern Vietnam—represented another casualty of the country-wide offensive.

Jerry Pearle received the Distinguished Service Cross for Gallantry for his heroics during the battle of Bien Hoa. He also received a promotion to the rank of major. The man who led the first platoon of Cobras in Vietnam had also helped save Bien Hoa during the TET Offensive. The young officer's career was taking flight.

18

THE JOKER

BY THE END OF FEBRUARY, US forces defeated the last remnants of VC and NVA resistance in Hue, the old imperial capital in Central Vietnam, and despite some ongoing fighting in Khe Sanh and the Cholon district of Saigon, MACV declared an end to the TET Offensive. At Bien Hoa, the US Army used bulldozers to dig mass graves for the enemy corpses that littered the base. Dougherty watched General Westmoreland on his black and white TV, trying to spin the TET Offensive as a victory for the United States by pointing to the enemy's losses, which were significantly higher than US casualties. However, the psychological damage from the TET Offensive extended far beyond the physical loss of life. Graphics showing the numerous coordinated attacks throughout South Vietnam, as well as images of the US Embassy in Saigon under siege, appeared on televisions across America, where a skeptical public now had irrefutable proof that the Johnson Administration had lied about its progress in the war.

Since the Raiders flew continuously throughout February, the last month of Jack Godbolt's tour passed in the blink of an eye. Normally, when a member of the 334th was short, Operations rotated that person to light duty for his final two or three weeks, as nothing would deal a more crushing blow to company morale than the loss of a man about to

DEROS. Following TET, Swanson had no choice but to keep Godbolt in the air until the day before his scheduled departure.

On his final morning in Vietnam, after he shaved and showered, Jack Godbolt placed his football, basketball, and flight helmet on the neatly made bunk, signifying he had, as First Corinthians instructed, "put away childish things."

Since Godbolt did not consume alcohol, and the Raider shack lay in ruins, Jack's platoonmates skipped the typical going away bash on the eve of his departure. Instead, Dougherty requisitioned a Jeep from the motor pool and drove his friend across the base to catch his flight home.

"Pray with me, Brother Bill," Godbolt said after setting his duffel bag on the tarmac.

Knowing he might never see Godbolt again, Dougherty indulged his friend's request and lowered his head.

Godbolt chose Psalm 23:4 as his prayer for William Dougherty.

The Lord is my shepherd; I shall not want. He maketh me to lie down in green pastures: he leadeth me beside the still waters. He restoreth my soul: he leadeth me in the paths of righteousness for his name's sake. Yea, though I walk through the valley of the shadow of death, I will fear no evil: for thou art with me; thy rod and thy staff they comfort me. Thou preparest a table before me in the presence of mine enemies: thou anointest my head with oil; my cup runneth over. Surely goodness and mercy shall follow me all the days of my life: and I will dwell in the house of the Lord forever. Amen.

Godbolt retrieved an object from one of his bags. "I have a gift for you—something to remember me by," he said, extending the white ceramic praying hands he had purchased on the black market in Saigon.

"I couldn't," Dougherty said, aghast at the thought of returning to the barracks with the religious figurine. When Godbolt refused to retract the offering, he had no choice but to accept the praying hands.

"Thanks, Jack," Dougherty said with as much sincerity as he could muster.

"I'll pray for you, William," Godbolt said, extending his right hand. When Dougherty accepted the handshake, the gunner pulled him in for a hug.

"We've been to hell and back, brother. Anything is possible through Jesus Christ," Godbolt whispered in Dougherty's ear. "I plan to enter the lay ministry when I get back home," he added, after he released Dougherty from his embrace. "Who could have imagined that when I got here a year ago?"

As Godbolt walked toward his Freedom Bird, it occurred to Dougherty that his friend now applied the same discipline and determination to religion that he once reserved for sports and soldiering. The house of the Lord would be the new playing field where Godbolt aimed to score converts rather than touchdowns. Dougherty imagined his friend testifying before congregations throughout Ohio, telling them how a Huey passed through his light one night and Jesus entered his heart in the jungles of Vietnam.

When Dougherty returned to the barracks, Mancuso had already moved his stuff into the room and was pinning up his nudie posters on the plywood walls. Swanson had suggested the new living arrangement since Mancuso would be flying with Dougherty and, as much as possible, he planned to assign Coffey as door gunner on their wing ship. Having people bunk together who flew the same schedule minimized disruptions and maximized sleeping hours.

Coffey burst into laughter the moment he spotted Dougherty with the praying hands. He offered his roommate a beer in exchange for the ceramic statue, which he placed on the wooden crate beside the wall featuring Miss February in the spot once reserved for Jesus of Nazareth. It now appeared as if the hands prayed to the Playboy centerfold.

"I like it," Coffey said of the new decor. "Godbolt was getting a bit too churchy for me."

Following Godbolt's departure, Dougherty found himself spending more and more time with Coffey. One day after flying search and destroy missions together, the crew chief and gunner decided to walk to the Air Force side of the base for a bite to eat. A South Vietnamese girl working behind a small lunch counter next to the flight line asked what they would like.

"I'll take a ham sandwich," Coffey said to the girl, who immediately started cutting a French baguette to make Chuck's order.

"No, no, what are you doing?" Coffey said. "I want GI bread."

"No GI bread, today," she replied, referring to the homemade American-style bread, and continued cutting the baguette.

"I said, I want GI bread. None of that French shit."

"Sorry, no GI bread. All out," she added without looking up from her work.

Coffey removed a grenade from his pocket. "I said I want some fuckin' GI bread."

The girl stopped cutting and set the knife on the counter. She looked up at the grenade in Chuck's outstretched hand and slowly raised her own hands as if to surrender.

"So sorry, no GI bread," she pleaded, keeping her eyes fixed on the deadly explosive device.

Coffey stared at her for a long moment, then pulled the pin on the grenade. Two Air Force enlisted men dropped their sandwiches and dove under a nearby picnic table. Dougherty dropped to the concrete slab as Coffey lobbed the grenade over the counter.

A few seconds later, when there was no explosion, Dougherty noticed Coffey laughing and pointing inside the kiosk. Dougherty stood up and looked over the counter at the girl huddled on the floor, crying. The grenade rested on the ground in a pool of liquid. The girl had wet herself.

"I removed the powder," Coffey said, laughing.

"ASSHOLE," Dougherty shouted and stormed away from the lunch counter.

As he walked back to the Army side of the base, Dougherty decided against returning to the barracks. He knew Coffey would pester him and ply him with beers until he forgave the misdeed, and he was not ready to do that. Instead, Dougherty returned to the revetment to open a letter from Lena he stashed in his flight bag weeks ago. As Dougherty peered beneath his seat in the helicopter, he noticed a bullet hole in the Huey's frame, inches from his open door. Dougherty inserted his right index finger into the tiny opening. The round, most likely 50-caliber, had traveled on a trajectory from the ground up toward his body. If the Huey had been a millisecond slower or the shooter's finger an instant quicker, the bullet surely would have struck the center of his body.

How many other such close calls? Dougherty wondered as he considered all of the rounds fired at his gunship during the hundreds of missions he had flown over the last fifteen months. The fact that he was still alive seemed to defy all odds.

The following week, while they were flying a search and destroy mission, word came over the radio that B-52s were about to start a bombing run over western Vietnam and all aircraft should vacate the area.

From the sky, Dougherty had witnessed on numerous occasions the endless line of craters created by the countless bombing runs over Tay Ninh Province, an area US forces frequently targeted due to its proximity to the Ho Chi Minh Trail. Over time, most of the craters filled with rainwater and now appeared the size of fishing ponds back home in Nebraska.

Captain Ruby served as aircraft commander of the lead ship that day and ordered his team to put down at Tay Ninh to wait for the all clear. Captain Chalfant, who piloted Dougherty's ship, instructed his crew chief and gunner to refuel and rearm while he and Briggs went with Ruby and Hocking to Operations. After tending to the aircraft, Mancuso decided to take a nap in the Huey, while Dougherty walked through the dry brown grass next to the flight line to have a cigarette a safe distance from their ship.

Soon Dougherty heard a rumbling, and the ground started vibrating. He turned and spotted the arc light on the horizon from the B-52s dropping their payload. He heard stories of dead bodies found in these areas with blood trickling from their ears and noses—the sheer force of the blasts literally concussed people to death.

Dougherty turned away from the bombing and walked over to a chain link fence. Beyond the fence ran a service road, and beyond that was another grassy area that extended to the outer perimeter of the base. Dougherty noticed a living quarters down the road, to his left. As he lit his cigarette, several nurses on the perimeter road passed by. Dougherty knew he looked like shit, but still, in his flight gear and at a lean six-foot-two, he was a good-looking man. One of the nurses, who slightly resembled the actress Lauren Bacall, turned to her friends and said, "I'll catch up with you." The others continued down the road toward the barracks, while the blond nurse walked back toward the enlisted airman.

"How's it going, soldier?" she said.

"OK, ma'am," Dougherty replied, acknowledging the woman's rank as an officer.

"Bullshit," she replied, motioning to the cigarette. "Can I have a drag?" she said. After a moment, Dougherty's brain kicked in and he passed the lit cigarette through the fence. She took a long pull on the Marlboro and exhaled. "I see the wounded coming in from the field. Don't tell me it's going OK."

Dougherty nodded.

The nurse took another drag and passed the cigarette back through the fence. "Where are you from?"

"Litchfield, Nebraska, ma'am," Dougherty replied. "Population nothing."

The woman smiled and gave the young airman a flirtatious look he had only ever seen on the big screen. "Population nothing minus one," she said.

Dougherty smiled. "How 'bout you, ma'am?" he said.

"Chicago. I'm a Midwesterner, too. I miss the cold. You can drop the *ma'am*," she added.

Dougherty nodded. He hoped the cigarette would burn forever—anything to keep the nurse there, talking to him—but he couldn't think of anything to say and so they just passed the cigarette back and forth. Each time they traded the Marlboro, Dougherty's fingers lightly brushed the woman's fingers. It was the only human contact he'd had in weeks, and it felt wonderful.

"Is there a special girl waiting for you back in Litchfield?" the nurse said.

Dougherty shook his head. "I thought there was someone. I was home during Christmas, and we spent some time together. I thought it was good, but I guess not."

"This war is hard on the people back home, too," she said.

Dougherty nodded.

"When was the last time you heard from her?"

"I tried to call her on my way back here after leave, but she was out with some guy. Then I got this letter," Dougherty said, reaching into his flak jacket, "but I haven't opened it, yet."

"Why not?" the nurse said, looking perplexed.

"I guess I couldn't take it if there was any bad news in there."

The woman held out her hand. "Here, let me read it to you."

"What?" Dougherty said, looking at the nurse as if she had taken leave of her senses.

"It will be better this way. I'm a woman, and it will be better if you hear this from a woman. If it's a breakup letter, I'll be the one breaking up with you. Then I'll walk down this road, and you'll never see me again."

She motioned with her hand for the letter to be passed through the fence. Dougherty folded the envelope and inserted it through one of the chain links. The nurse took one last drag and passed the cigarette back. Then she opened the envelope and removed the letter.

"Look at me," she said when she caught Dougherty staring at the ground. "You need to look at me while I tell you this."

Dougherty dropped the butt of the cigarette on the grass and stomped it out with his boot. He looked directly at the nurse and nodded.

February 7, 1968

Dear Bill,

I hope this letter finds you safe and well. I saw in the news that your base was attacked right after you went back to Vietnam. No one has heard from you, and we are all worried. I know you are probably busy with the war . . .

My hall mate said 'some guy' called for me the day after you left Nebraska. I guess she told you I was out with someone. Please let me explain. Before you came home on leave, I was dating a fellow from Omaha. I was out with him that night. But I went out with him to break up. I told him I couldn't see him anymore because I met someone else during the holidays.

When we started writing last year, I began to care about you.

But when I met you in-person this winter, I realized I also love you . . . with all my heart. I hope you feel the same way.

    I don't want you to worry about me because I'll be waiting for you to come home.

     Love always,

     Lena

The nurse lowered the letter. "I hope that wasn't too painful," she said. Dougherty remained speechless.

"There's a picture. She's pretty," the woman said, studying the photograph of Lena in her school uniform. "And a nurse. I like her." The woman passed the letter and photograph back through the fence and announced she had to go. "You take care of yourself," she said.

"Thanks," Dougherty replied, a broad smile forming on his face for the first time in weeks.

The woman smiled once more, then turned and walked away. Dougherty stared out toward the airfield and feigned indifference, but he watched the nurse go down the road from his peripheral vision. She looked back one final time, and he pretended not to notice. Then she quickly turned forward and continued toward her barracks.

Dougherty knew he would never see the woman again, but he considered her small gesture incredibly kind. For five minutes, he felt like a human being again. *That was good nursing*, he thought, as he walked back to the gunship.

A few days later, when Dougherty and Mancuso tuned in for their favorite TV show, *Laugh-In*, a pre-recorded news special aired instead. They watched in shock as President Lyndon Johnson announced to the world, "With America's sons in the fields far away, with America's future under challenge right here at home, with our hopes and the world's hopes for peace in the balance every day, I do not believe that I should devote an hour or a day of my time to any personal partisan causes or to any duties other than the awesome duties of this office—the presidency of your country. Accordingly, I shall not seek, and I will not accept, the nomination of my party for another term as your president." Dougherty's thoughts turned to Captain Ruby and how devastated the Texan must be by LBJ's decision.

Around the time of Johnson's historic announcement, Coffey purchased another vinyl disc for the record player he acquired while on leave in Hong Kong. For his second record, Coffey selected *The Legend of Bonnie & Clyde* by Merle Haggard. The song, inspired by the movie of the same title, had a siren in the middle that sounded like the base siren signaling incoming mortar attacks. At various times, usually late at night, Coffey quietly set up his portable record player in the hallway of the barracks, cued the *Bonnie and Clyde* record to the siren portion of the song, and cranked up the volume. Then Chuck laughed, hysterically, as the platoon scrambled in their underwear, searching for the door. In the wake of TET, the siren was believable, even expected, so Coffey fooled them every time.

When the enemy started shelling Bien Hoa again, during its Mini-TET campaign, everyone in the barracks assumed it was Chuck's record player. No one except for Coffey sought shelter during these attacks until after the mortars exploded. Following several nights of mortar attacks, Coffey declared a cease fire with his record player so that everyone knew the sirens represented a real threat.

As the nightly shelling of Bien Hoa continued, the 334th moved its Emergency Stand By teams to Operations, to minimize the time it took for crews to race to the flight line and get airborne. Invariably, the mortars stopped falling the moment the Huey gunships lifted off. Determined to catch the enemy attackers red-handed, the 334th moved its Emergency Stand By teams to bunkers beside the runway, to reduce the response time even further. In these instances, the VC simply shortened their mortar attacks. Finally, at great expense, the 334th kept a Light Fire Team in the air over Bien Hoa from dusk until dawn. On these occasions, the enemy did not attack at all. After two weeks of mortar-free nights, the ESB crews returned to Operations, and the shelling resumed.

One evening in late May, during an ESB shift, Dougherty and Coffey sat together in Operations, a deck of Bicycle playing cards on the table between them. Coffey stared intently at the deck, as if attempting to use psychic powers to determine the face value of the top card. Finally, the gunner drew the first card, flipped it over, and studied it. Then, using his thumb and index finger, Coffey spun the card around so Dougherty could see.

"The Joker," Coffey said. "People think the Joker's funny, but he ain't funny. There's somethin' sinister and wild about him."

Dougherty noticed that Coffey's maniacal grin bore a slight resemblance to the figure on playing card beside his face. Dougherty picked up a *Life* magazine and started flipping through the pages.

"There are two Jokers in every deck, but there's a reason people take them out before they play," Coffey continued. "A Joker don't follow any rules. People runnin' the game can't stand it when a motherfuckin' Joker keeps breakin' the rules."

Dougherty looked up from the magazine as Coffey brought the card close to his right eye, to examine its edges. "Such a thin layer of paper hides the card's true identity," he observed, as if in a trance.

"You ok, Chuck?" Dougherty said, as he set the magazine on the table.

Before Coffey could respond, an air raid siren screamed in the night. Within seconds, mortars shook the ground. The siren seemed to flip a switch in Coffey's brain. As the others raced out of the room, Coffey swept the deck of playing cards off the table with his arm, then watched as a few of the cards momentarily lifted into the air, then autorotated to the floor like helicopters. Coffey jumped up from the table and sprinted out the door. With rockets landing all around, he screamed, "Kill, kill, kill." During the frantic race to the flight line, Coffey shoved a passing lieutenant out of his way and shouted, "Kill, kill, kill" at the fallen officer.

When the ESB team failed to locate the source of the mortars, which stopped the moment the two Huey gunships lifted off, Captain Ruby ordered the Light Fire Team back to base.

"Oh, shit," Ruby said over the intercom when he spotted a Jeep with blinking lights on the runway. The lieutenant Coffey had knocked down, as well as the CO and several MPs, waited on the flight line for the returning gunships.

Captain Ruby quickly exited the Huey to defuse the situation.

"I know my gunner got a little excited earlier, but he wants to apologize," Ruby said. "Where's Coffey?" the pilot shouted when he spotted Dougherty on the tarmac.

"He's in the aircraft," Dougherty replied, removing his flight helmet.

Captain Ruby turned to face the lieutenant. "My gunner's going to apologize to you once he gets out here."

Coffey emerged from the ship, brandishing his M-60 with a band of ammunition dangling from it. "It's all just a game and this is the toy," Coffey said, holding up the machine gun.

Everyone on the flight line instinctively took two steps back.

"It's all a fuckin' game and this is the fuckin' toy," Coffey said louder.

"Whoa, just calm down and tell the lieutenant you're sorry," Dougherty said, taking a step toward his friend.

Coffey shook his head. "I ain't gonna apologize to no Jokers. It's all a fuckin' game and this is the fuckin' toy," he said, waving his M-60 in the air with one arm.

One of the MPs stepped forward and Chuck lowered the weapon. "Hold it right there," he said. "You ain't takin' me out of the deck."

"Calm down, Chuck," Dougherty said, holding out his hands. "The Jokers are already out of the deck. Just put the gun down." From the corner of his eye, Dougherty noticed the other MP circling behind the Huey, beyond Coffey's peripheral vision. "Look at me, Chuck. No one's going to mess up your game," Dougherty said, holding his gunner's attention.

A moment later, the MP lunged from behind the helicopter toward Coffey's right arm and wrestled the weapon away while the second MP rushed forward and tackled the crazed gunner to the ground.

"It's all a fuckin' game," Coffey shouted, as the MPs rolled him onto his stomach and handcuffed his wrists behind his back. Each man grabbed one of Coffey's arms and lifted him to his feet. "Let go of me, you mother fuckin' Jokers. It's all a fuckin' game," Coffey shouted, as the MPs dragged him to their Jeep.

The airmen on the tarmac watched in silent disbelief as the blinking lights from the Jeep disappeared down the flight line. "Did you know this man was on the edge like this?" Major Sheffield said to Dougherty.

"Sir, he's been like that ever since I've known him. He's a good gunner and a decent guy, but he just gets a little flipped out once in a while."

Sheffield raised his eyebrows, indicating that was the understatement of the year.

The next morning, when Dougherty returned to the barracks, he was surprised to see Coffey in his bunk.

"They think I'm crazy," the gunner said after Dougherty entered the room.

"You are crazy," Dougherty replied, setting his flight gear by his locker. "And you've been taken off flight duty."

"They put me under house arrest, but this ain't a house. That makes them crazy," Coffey said and laughed. "I served with Captain Carpenter when he called in a napalm strike on his own men."

"You gotta pull it together, Chuck, or they're gonna lock you up," Dougherty said quietly.

After resting in the barracks for a few days, Coffey grew bored and tried to return to flight duty. He periodically showed up on the tarmac wearing his flight suit and carrying his helmet, but these misguided efforts invariably ended in a shouting match with the pilots, who ordered him back to the barracks.

Each time the disturbed gunner wandered away from the flight line, Coffey could be heard shouting, "Don't tell me what to do. I was with Captain Carpenter when he called in a napalm strike on his own men."

Within a week, the army discharged Coffey and sent him home. Before storming out of the barracks, the gunner placed a solitary playing card, face down, on his bunk. When Dougherty flipped it over, the Joker stared up at him with a sinister grin. "It's all a game," Coffey had scrawled on the face of the playing card. Dougherty turned the card on its side, a razor's edge that revealed nothing, then tucked the Joker into the chest pocket of his fatigues.

19

MENAGERIE BENEATH THE MAT

IN EARLY JULY, COLONEL NIKOLAI SARKIS, the yet-to-be-promoted commanding officer of the 12th Aviation Group, ordered every armed helicopter company under his command to provide one gunship each to support Operation Daniel Boone in the vicinity of the Parrot's Beak, a portion of Cambodian territory in the shape of a bird's bill that extended into western Vietnam. Daniel Boone squads were small units of US and South Vietnamese Special Forces guided by Cambodian mercenaries, known as a "Bodes," that performed cross-border reconnaissance in search of the elusive Ho Chi Minh Trail. When Major Sheffield relayed the colonel's order to the members of the 334th, Captain Ruby immediately volunteered for the mission. "Pick your crew," Sheffield instructed the Raider Platoon leader before dismissing the company.

"You up for this?" was all Ruby said to Dougherty as the other men dispersed.

Dougherty nodded.

"Count me in, too, Cap'n," Mancuso said, pointing at himself for effect.

Ruby nodded at both men and walked away.

On the day they departed for the Parrot's Beak, Dougherty sensed his pilot's somber mood from the absence of friendly chatter over the

194

intercom that normally kept everyone on board confident and relaxed. Instead, Captain Ruby and the crew of The Green Monster flew in silence over the free-strike zones in Western Vietnam. Dougherty and his shipmates flew so far south and west that they almost certainly crossed into Cambodia at times, a suspicion supported by the unusual architecture and unique boats they spotted from the sky.

As their fuel gauge crept closer to empty, Captain Ruby finally located the Daniel Boone squad from a set of coordinates Hocking had written on their windshield with his grease pencil.

"I don't see a damn thing except for jungle," the copilot said into his helmet mic.

Then a deep voice spoke over the radio. "Raider 2-6, this is Boone squad leader. We're popping smoke on the LZ, over." Moments later, a ghostly white vapor escaped from a small opening in the thick, triple-canopy jungle directly ahead of their position. Ruby carefully maneuvered their Huey toward the smoke.

Hocking keyed his mic, again. "They want us to land in there? That'll be like flying into the devil's asshole."

Ruby remained silent and maintained a steady path toward the ominous portal. As they descended into the abyss, wispy white smoke raced by the ship's open doors like souls ascending to heaven. Dougherty felt as though a dark force pulled their Huey deep into the bowels of the jungle, a sensation reinforced by the smell of decaying organic matter emanating from the flora and fauna surrounding them. When the ship's skids touched ground, their rotors pushed a wall of white smoke in all directions.

Captain Ruby opted to keep the ship's rotors turning to minimize their departure time. The aircraft commander unbuckled his seat belt and turned toward the enlisted airmen in the cabin behind him. "Stay sharp," the pilot said, then hopped out the door and jogged around the nose of the helicopter to consult with two American Special Forces advisers who had walked over to the landing zone during their descent.

As the smoke began to dissipate, Dougherty noticed glowing white fungi that looked like eyeballs protruding from the trunks of leafy green trees surrounding the makeshift landing zone. Exotic, colorful blooms oozing milky fluids emerged from thick stalks as if vomited into the surrounding bed of dark sludge. Dougherty noticed a large viper's head staked to a nearby tree with a Bowie knife; its mouth, open wide, exposing deadly white fangs. Someone had pinned the serpent's decapitated body, at least six feet long, beside the head with a second blade. As more smoke cleared, Dougherty spotted a stack of dead monkeys in a bed of ferns beside the LZ; their bodies contorted; their fur matted in blood. When the last traces of smoke vanished, a squad of emotionless men in camouflaged fatigues and face paint appeared. They casually cleaned weapons and sharpened knives as they rested beside a line of standing prisoners, hands bound, connected by a single rope wrapped around each man's neck. As Ruby chatted with the American advisers, a Cambodian mercenary wearing a necklace of human ears appeared in the clearing. The ARVN in charge proceeded to interrogate one of the suspected Viet Cong guerrillas. When the *Chieu Hoi* failed to produce satisfactory answers, the South Vietnamese soldier motioned to the newly arrived Bode with the necklace. He yanked the prisoner's pants down and attached wires from a field telephone to the man's testicles. The ARVN continued his interrogation.

"Crazy motherfuckers," Ruby said into his helmet mic after he climbed back into the cockpit. "They want us to take a prisoner up and drop him once we get above the treetops. They said that will get the others talking. I told them no fucking way. We're going to patrol the area, and they'll call us if they need gunship support." As Ruby slowly ascended toward the opening in the canopy, Dougherty watched in horror as the mercenary cranked the field telephone, sending a jolt of electricity into the interrogated prisoner's body that caused him to scream in agony and drop to the ground. The man's sudden fall pulled the other prisoners down with him.

"Jesus Christ," Mancuso said, watching the scene from Dougherty's open doorway.

As they emerged from the hell hole, it occurred to Dougherty that everyone would later be able to say that no American or South Vietnamese soldier had tortured the man and that would not be a lie. This was not war as he knew it, with front lines and rear areas, officers and enlisted men,

missions and orders. This was something primitive and crudely improvised.

Later that day, Captain Ruby received a radio request to pick up an
injured member of a South Vietnamese Army platoon that happened to
be humping through the area.

"We got a damn Marvin Arvin with a sprained ankle," an American
voice said wearily over the radio. "We're tired of carryin' his ass. Next
time you're low on fuel, drop down and pick this guy up."

Ruby flew toward the coordinates provided by the voice on the radio
and soon, Dougherty spotted the ragtag squad stumbling down a dike,
carrying one of their members on a makeshift stretcher. The dejected
troops did not give off the vibe of a deadly force on the prowl; rather they
looked like men on death row making a slow and painful march to the
gallows. Without hesitation, Ruby descended toward a small clearing at
the end of the paddy dike. As the Huey's skids touched earth, the ARVN
troops at the front of the line raced toward the open door to board the
helicopter. Dougherty pushed and kicked the unhinged men as they attempted to board his ship, but occasionally one slipped by him. In these
instances, Mancuso pulled the unsuspecting man out the other open
door. A large black Special Forces sergeant soon pushed his way through
the crowd and started grabbing South Vietnamese soldiers by their collars
and pulling them back.

"GET BACK IN LINE YOU SONS OF BITCHES," he shouted.
"THIS BIRD AIN'T FOR YOU. GET BACK IN LINE, GODDAM-
MIT! I'LL SHOOT YOU MYSELF IF YOU DON'T GET BACK IN
LINE," the sergeant screamed.

Finally, the injured man was brought forward and loaded into the
cabin of the Huey. Dougherty and Mancuso continued tossing rucksacks
out their open doors as the ship slowly lifted off. When a couple of desperate ARVNs made a last-minute effort to board their ship, Ruby finally
lost his patience.

"They want on here, I'll put 'em on here," the pilot said over the
intercom. Instead of lifting higher into the air, he maneuvered the
ship forward down the dike, forcing the weary soldiers further down
the line to duck and jump into the shallow water of the adjacent rice

paddies. Dougherty noticed the sergeant laughing hysterically at his displaced troops.

"SERVES YOU RIGHT, YOU GODDAM SONS OF BITCHES," he shouted.

Once airborne, Dougherty and Mancuso turned their attention to the ARVN on the floor, who stared up at them with wide eyes as if the tall Americans might be his captors rather than his allies.

"What's this?" Dougherty said, picking up a Thompson submachine gun beside the injured troop. When the man tried to grab his weapon, Mancuso stepped in.

"Easy, bro, you won't be needin' that," the gunner said. "We're the only swingin' dicks with guns on this ship," he added.

"How the hell did this guy get a Tommy gun?" Dougherty said over the intercom. "Al Capone was using these in Chicago forty years ago."

"Beats the hell out of me," Mancuso said. "All kinds of crazy shit out here, maybe even gangsters."

When Ruby landed at a fire support base, the crew chief and gunner pushed the ARVN out of their ship. The Vietnamese man pleaded for his weapon as he hopped on one leg beside the helicopter, but Dougherty refused to return the vintage machine gun. Instead, he tossed the man's rucksack onto the tarmac, then Ruby and the wing ship lifted off to find a refueling station.

On more than one occasion, their Daniel Boone squad disappeared for two or three days at a time, and when they did, Captain Ruby and his crew performed round-the-clock search and destroy missions in the area. From his open door, Dougherty shot water buffalo in open fields during the daytime and crocodiles on muddy riverbanks at night. Sometimes he spotted from the sky the carcass of an animal he shot days before, its flesh rotting in the brutal tropical climate, the occasional white bone exposed and picked clean by vultures. In these instances, he shot the vultures atop the dead animal. One time Ruby flew over a peasant ushering a flock of ducks with two ten-foot bamboo poles. Dougherty sprayed the area with the Tommy gun, scattering the birds and leaving the man in a snowfall of feathers.

Whenever exhaustion overtook the crew of The Green Monster, Captain Ruby landed at the nearest firebase or outpost and the men slept in their seats for five or six hours until the pilot fired the igniters and they lifted off again.

Occasionally, "people sniffers" mounted to US aircraft flying over the Parrot's Beak detected the ammonia smell emitted by human bodies. The ever-present FAC plane then relayed coordinates of the smell to the Daniel Boone squads. If Dougherty's ship happened to be in the vicinity, Captain Ruby turned out the Huey's running lights and flew to the designated location. One time when Ruby turned on the lights, they spotted dozens of peasants harvesting pineapples in the dead of night. Ruby turned out the lights and their Huey departed without firing a single shot—no one willing to massacre the unarmed farmers. Another time when Ruby flipped the switch, their ship hovered directly above a canal with a line of sampans as far as the eye could see. Dougherty and his shipmates expended their weapons, quickly rearmed at a nearby fire support base, then returned to the area to shoot up the endless convoy of sampans some more—a process they repeated until only splintered wood, pineapples, and bodies floated in the canal.

After landing at a remote firebase that evening, Ruby threw off his helmet and walked away from the ship. When Hocking went to check on the pilot, Dougherty dug a flask of Jim Beam out of his flight bag, took a sip, and passed it to Mancuso, who was grateful for the drink.

"I think the cap'n is losin' it," Mancuso said, pointing with the flask. "I'm pretty sure those were the same farmers who were pickin' pineapples a couple nights ago."

In the moonlight they could see Hocking trying to talk Ruby down as the agitated pilot paced back and forth in front of their ship.

It occurred to Dougherty, as he watched the two pilots talking, that TET was the start of Ruby's descent. The enemy's country-wide offensive had displayed the kind of initiative the young Texan repeatedly called for, and it was clearly gnawing at him. TET also effectively canceled the Thailand mission—Ruby's preordained date with history. And ultimately, TET ended LBJ's Presidency and any hope the young captain held for reuniting with his Commander-In-Chief after the war. Ruby hoped to fabricate something spectacular from the Daniel Boone mission, but it was becoming increasingly apparent to all on board that there was nothing glorious or honorable to be achieved in this nightmare.

The next evening, after they landed at an abandoned outpost near the Cambodian border, Ruby left the ship to be alone with his thoughts. After finishing a can of C-rats, Dougherty decided to check on his platoon leader, who was standing alone at the edge of the jungle. Recalling the viper pinned to the tree, Dougherty grabbed the bolo knife hanging from the back of his seat and walked over to where Ruby stood with his back to the Huey. Not wanting to startle the pilot, he announced his arrival from several paces away.

"You ok, Captain?" Dougherty whispered.

When Ruby did not respond, Dougherty stepped forward until the two men stood side by side, facing the impenetrable jungle. Captain Ruby looked down at the knife in Dougherty's hand, then returned his gaze to the jungle. "This war has no clear direction," he said. "We just fly around killing people, hoping if we kill enough of them, they will quit."

"Yes, sir," Dougherty replied. "Seems that way."

"We don't know a damn thing about these people, so we make things up. Tell ourselves they're *evil* or *invisible.* We're losin' this war because we don't *see* them. How can you fight someone you don't see?"

"I reckon you can't, sir," Dougherty replied.

The two men stared silently at the jungle for several more minutes until Captain Ruby spoke again. "Doc, do you think there's a part of us that never changes?" Ruby whispered.

"Yes, sir," Dougherty replied. "That part of me that doesn't ever change seems to be my problem. And the good parts of me, well, they seem to be the ones slipping away."

The pilot leaned toward Dougherty and spoke so quietly that it sounded like a gentle breeze passing through the jungle. "So much of who we are is who we think we are and how strongly we believe in that myth," the pilot said, then walked back to the ship.

After several more days of continuous flying, with no showering and limited sleep, Dougherty believed he and his shipmates had morphed into strange creatures that appeared more animal than human. Their elongated bodies and large helmeted heads seemed reptilian; their gloved hands like claws; their eyes invisible beneath dark visors. The crew rarely communicated in complete sentences, just gestures and grunting sounds. Dougherty recalled what his grandfather had said about fighting against the Germans during the First World War, and how men from both sides had transformed into demons.

The next day, while flying low around a free-strike zone near the Cambodian border, Dougherty thought he saw the ground shift. He considered the Vietnamese masters of camouflage—a belief reinforced when he spotted a building or bunker from the air, only to circle around and never find the thing again because the angle had changed. But this optical illusion defied logic.

"Ground's moving," Dougherty grunted over the intercom, pointing with a gloved hand out his open door.

"Shoot it," Ruby barked.

Dougherty fired a quick burst of rounds from his M-60 into the area. A water buffalo suddenly appeared as if conjured from thin air. The wounded beast staggered ten feet forward, then dropped dead. Dougherty fired another series of bursts into the ground, which sent dozens of pigs and ducks scurrying in all directions. Next came an ox, several chickens, a pack of dogs, and finally, the rabbits. Ruby flew in a tight, circular pattern with his crew chief's left door continuously facing the target. Dougherty fired every one of his three thousand rounds into the thatch, until dozens of dead animals littered the area, and the ground shifted no more.

Dougherty dropped to his knees, ripped off his gloves, and snatched the nylon flight bag from beneath his seat. He clawed through the sack until he found the offering from Colonel Sarkis. With shaking hands, Dougherty unsealed the deck of playing cards and thrust it out of the Huey. He leaned against the door frame and watched as fifty-two Aces, all Spades, fluttered and turned in the breeze. For a moment, the cards remained in formation like a flock of migrating fowl. An instant later, the paper wings dispersed, some rising, others falling, but all turning—red, white, red, white—like wounded birds scattered by gunfire.

Captain Ruby flew to the nearest fire support base so the crew could refuel and rearm. When they returned to the area less than two hours later, they found nothing. No dead animals or playing cards. It was as if they collectively dreamed the whole experience.

"How?" was all Dougherty said to his shipmates over the intercom.

The horror of that mat wasn't the slaughter: Dougherty had experienced that before, in spades. He imagined a community of farmers had spent countless hours weaving together strips of bamboo and palm fronds to conceal their livestock and themselves. They put their faith in that desperate plan, and in an instant, the bullets from his gun ripped through the veneer of their improbable shelter. And Dougherty would never know exactly what lay beneath the mat. Women? Children? Babies? A few? Dozens? An entire village? It was that potential for infinite horror that was horrific to Dougherty.

When their detachment with the Daniel Boone squad finally ended, Captain Ruby knew he could not take the crew of *The Green Monster* back to Bien Hoa in their present state. Instead, they landed at Firebase Dakota to wash up; the cool water transforming them from demons to animals. When they stopped a second time, for food and fuel at Tay Ninh, they transformed again, from animals to something resembling the men who had embarked on the mission ten days prior.

On the final leg of their journey, Dougherty leaned back in his seat and closed his eyes. Cool air washed over him as images from the menagerie beneath the mat played on the back of his eyelids. Halfway home, with eyes still closed, Dougherty keyed his mic. "Wanna grab a drink later?" he said to Mancuso.

"I'll have one, bro, but that's it," the gunner replied with great effort. "I'm a single digit midget," Mancuso added, referring to the fact that he had less than ten days until his deployment ended and he headed home. "Gotta keep my ass clean. Don't want anything to fuck up my DEROS in the bottom of the ninth."

"You're so short, you could walk under a fuckin' door," Dougherty said.

Mancuso laughed. "Eight and a wake up, bro" he replied, "then I'm takin' that Freedom Bird back to the motherfuckin' US of A so I can make doors and get laid."

Nine days later, Mancuso walked into the plywood living quarters where Dougherty reclined on his bunk smoking a Marlboro and sipping a glass of Jim Beam. Not wanting to disturb his friend, Mancuso proceeded to roll up his nudie posters, which he slid into a cardboard tube for safe transport. Once he finished packing, Mancuso placed his bags beside the door and walked over to Dougherty's bunk.

"I'm outta here, bro," Mancuso said. "You stay safe until they ship you home. You hear me?" he said, his eyebrows raising slightly. "When you get back to civilization, if you ever need a job, call me. We could always use a good man like you at our door factory." Mancuso concluded his rehearsed speech by handing Dougherty his father's business card.

> Vinny Mancuso, President
> Mancuso Doors, Inc.
> New Brunswick, New Jersey

Dougherty studied the card, touched by the gesture. "Thanks, Louie. I just might call you."

The two men shook hands and hugged. As he looked over Mancuso's shoulder, Dougherty spied Miss February, his door gunner's favorite poster, spread out on the bunk.

"Keep one foot on the ground, Louie," Dougherty said.

In the weeks after Mancuso's departure, bad weather moved into the area as the monsoon season arrived early in III Corps. Day after day, torrential rains washed over Bien Hoa, creating temporary lakes on the flight lines that eventually subsided but left every crevice on base filled with muddy standing water.

Despite the heavy rains, Operations expected flight crews to be ready to go in the event the weather cleared. One such evening, Dougherty served as Major Pearle's crew chief on the high ship of a Firefly team. In the pre-dawn hours, bad weather quickly rolled into their area of operation; Dougherty and his shipmates were startled by the sudden and intense rain pounding their helicopter. The Huey's feeble wiper blades attempted to swat away the flood of monsoon waters that cascaded down their windshield. With each passing klick, the cloud cover and precipitation worsened as the three Hueys raced east, hoping to outrun the storm.

When visibility reached zero, the pilots switched over to Instrument Flight Rules, and the three ships fanned out to avoid a mid-air collision. Pearle maintained radio contact with Lieutenant Allen, an inexperienced pilot who recently joined the 334th. Pearle attempted to calm the young pilot as wind and turbulence moved their Hueys effortlessly, like plastic bags floating in the breeze.

"We've got mountains in the area," Pearle announced over the radio, referring to the southern reaches of the Annamite Range. This prompted a lengthy exchange among the three pilots about the approximate location and elevation of those peaks.

As the three Hueys struggled toward Bien Hoa like salmon swimming against the current of a raging river, a fresh bank of dense fog rolled off the Central Highlands—the final straw for Major Pearle.

"Raider 2-6, Raider 2-2, this is Saber-6. We are changing course for Tan Son Nhut. I'll contact the tower and have them put us on radar," Pearle said.

"Saber-6, this is Raider 2-6. I'm returning to Bien Hoa, twenty-five kilometers southwest," Captain Ruby responded.

"Negative, Raider 2-6," Pearle replied. "Proceed to Tan Son Nhut." Pearle then radioed the tower and asked the air traffic controller to place all three Hueys on radar, to guide them to Saigon where they could safely land and wait out the storm.

"Saber-6, this is tower at Tan Son Nhut. I'm picking up two aircraft on radar, but not a third, over."

The fog and clouds extended to the ground and rolled through the open doors of their Huey. Dougherty noticed that Pearle repeatedly wiped the display panel with his sleeve so he could see his instruments.

"Raider 2-6, this is Saber-6. Change course for Tan Son Nhut, immediately. We are ALL going to Saigon," he stated, emphatically.

"Negative," Ruby replied. "Safer for me to land on the Scabbard than to change course now, over."

"Dammit, Ruby, I am ordering you to Tan Son Nhut," Major Pearle said.

After minutes of agonizing silence, Captain Ruby's voice finally crackled over the radio. "I'm under the fog. I can see the lights of Bien Hoa. I'm heading home."

"Roger, 2-6," Pearle said with resignation, knowing the decision was already made and that there would have to be a conversation later, perhaps even disciplinary action. "We're on IFR going to Saigon, over."

"Must not be so bad on the Scabbard," Pearle said to his crew over the intercom.

A few minutes later the radio squawked again. "Saber-6, this is tower. Winds out of the north, forty knots. Barometric pressure is dropping fast. We have some bad weather rolling into the area, but you are free to land."

As they approached Tan Son Nhut, Dougherty's ship received one final radio transmission from Captain Ruby. "We're about to turn Shell," the Texan said, referring to the Royal Dutch Shell refinery just south of the Bien Hoa Air Base. The facility, which housed petrochemicals and fuel in large storage tanks, served as a convenient marker for helicopters coming and going from the base.

"Watch out for the powerlines, 2-6," Pearle replied, although he knew Ruby would remember the Huey that flipped on those lines a year before and crashed to the ground—rotors down, skids up, killing all four crew members on board.

"Copy that," Ruby replied, and then the line went silent.

After the two Hueys safely landed in Saigon, Pearle immediately radioed Captain Ruby's ship, but there was no reply. Following several more attempts, Pearle threw off his helmet and raced into the nearest building to call Bien Hoa on the land line. Operations informed him that Raider 2-6 never arrived.

By dawn the storm had passed. Pearle and Allen lifted off from Tan Son Nhut and flew north toward a set of coordinates in Long Khanh Province that a fire support base radioed in during the night as the site of a possible helicopter crash. In the early morning mist, Dougherty and his shipmates spotted a Huey gunship nestled into the side of a small but steep mountain, far north of Bien Hoa Air Base.

A foot patrol from the fire base had reached the crash site shortly before the two Hueys arrived; a small group of soldiers clustered around the downed aircraft. Dougherty spotted other troops climbing the rugged hillside to join the rescue effort.

The steep, tree-covered terrain prevented Pearle and his wing ship from landing, so they flew back and forth over the crash site. On their second pass, a radio operator from the rescue team arrived on the scene.

"There's debris everywhere," the voice from the ground said. "The rotor is mangled. There's no way this bird can fly. We're going to have to sling the ship out or blow it up."

After a few minutes of complete silence that seemed like an eternity, the radio operator continued his assessment. "The two gunners in the cabin are okay. Shaken up, but they should be able to walk out. The co-pilot is hurt pretty bad, but he's alive. We're going to have to stretcher him out."

Hocking is alive, Dougherty nearly said it aloud, relieved his friend had survived the crash.

After a few more minutes of silence, the radio operator spoke, again. "Negative objective on the pilot," he said.

It sounded so innocent in code, but everyone on board knew that "negative objective" meant "pilot found dead."

He may have succumbed to vertigo—that disoriented feeling of thinking up is down and down is up—or target fixation, which occurs when a pilot is so focused on a specific point that he loses track of altitude and obstacles. Or perhaps another bank of fog rolled in at just the wrong moment. Whatever the cause, Captain Ruby flew straight into the side of the mountain, and the mistake had cost him his life.

When Major Pearle realized there was nothing that could be done from the air, he ordered the Light Fire Team back to Bien Hoa. At that moment, Dougherty could have switched off the radio feed to his headset to avoid further painful details, but instead, he forced himself to continue listening.

"The front of the Huey is completely crushed. This guy's legs are pinned in the wreckage. It's going to take us hours to get the body out. A piece of the windshield is stuck in his throat. Looks like he bled to death," the voice from the ground concluded.

Dougherty reached up and switched off the radio. Then he closed his eyes, leaned back in his seat, and wept behind his dark visor.

When Dougherty returned to the barracks that afternoon, he found his belongings in the hallway outside his plywood room. With Mancuso and Coffey gone, three other Raiders, whose names now appeared on his door, decided they should have the nearly vacant quarters while the short-timer could find another room with an empty bunk for his final month in-country.

Dougherty hurled his flight helmet into the plywood wall. "THAT'S IT. I'M DONE," he shouted.

A few men appeared in the hall.

"THAT'S MY FUCKIN' ROOM. TWO TOURS. I'VE BEEN HERE LONGER THAN ANY OF YOU MOTHERFUCKERS AND THAT'S THE WAY YOU TREAT ME?"

When a sleepy straphanger opened the room's door to check on the ruckus, Dougherty grabbed the man by his undershirt and pulled him into the hallway. As he reared his fist back, several Raiders jumped in and restrained the outraged crew chief.

The platoon sergeant pushed his way through the melee and grabbed Dougherty by the arm. "LET'S TAKE IT OUTSIDE," he shouted.

When Swanson finished explaining the incident to the Operations officer, he asked Major Pearle what he should do.

"Doc's been here nearly two years," Pearle said, staring out the window of his office. "He's flown over eight hundred missions and his DEROS is next month. Let the man be. Give him something to do in Command Quarters but leave him alone. Besides, more Cobras are on their way. The Raiders will be all-Cobra by the end of the month, and then they won't need Huey crew chiefs. What we really need are Cobra mechanics," Major Pearle added.

"More straphangers, sir?" Swanson replied, momentarily forgetting Pearle had just lost a fellow pilot he admired deeply.

"I mean people who can keep these fuckin' Cobras in the air so we might win this goddamn war," Pearle snapped.

"Yes, sir," Swanson said and saluted the Major's back.

"Sergeant," Pearle said, turning to face the Ops sergeant before he left the room.

"Yes, sir?"

"Be sure to collect all of Dougherty's weapons, including that knife he carries, and send everything over to Supply for safekeeping."

THE ROTOR'S EDGE

FOLLOWING THE INCIDENT IN THE BARRACKS, Operations grounded Dougherty and assigned him to the Command Quarters graveyard shift, which required him to sit in the Orderly Room throughout the night, playing Solitaire and answering the phone on the odd chance that it rang. One time, the Military Police in Singapore called to say a member of the 334th who was on leave was being detained for drunken disorderliness. Dougherty confirmed the man was a member of the company, approved for R&R, and presumably they let him go.

During his CQ shifts inside the corrugated metal Quonset hut, Dougherty listened to Johnny Grant's *Small World* on a transistor radio. Every night, without fail, the host played *Dock of the Bay* by Otis Redding. Dougherty felt the song's despondent lyrics and Redding's soulful voice perfectly captured the mood of his current assignment—stuck at the end of the dock, with nothing changing and no prospects on the horizon.

CQ offered Dougherty an opportunity to catch up on his reading. Mostly, he read magazine articles, including some about the peace protests back home and the assassinations of Civil Rights leader Martin Luther King Jr. and presidential hopeful Robert Kennedy. Occasionally, Dougherty tried to write a letter to his mother or Lena, but each time, the paper ended up in the metal waste basket beside the desk.

209

To kill time, Dougherty worked on his short-timer's calendar. Each day he filled in a dozen or so of the numbered segments on a drawing of an army helmet resting on a pair of boots with a lit cigarette protruding from beneath the helmet. Each numbered segment corresponded to a day spent in Vietnam, and the idea was that the owner of the calendar was so short on his remaining time in-country that all you could see were his helmet and boots.

One night, while searching for office supplies, Dougherty stumbled upon a scale the base doctors used when conducting physicals. He removed his boots and stepped onto the scale, then adjusted the metal arm until it balanced. Dougherty weighed a solid one hundred and seventy-five pounds when he arrived in-country. He couldn't believe the number he was seeing. The tall Nebraskan weighed one hundred and thirty-five pounds. Others must have noticed Dougherty's emaciated frame, too, because one night, the black sergeant who ran the mess hall and answered to the unimaginative moniker "Chef" visited the orderly room.

"Casper, I brought you some of my gumbo," the lifer from New Orleans said, as he slid the plate across the desk. "Ya like a damn ghost over here," he said, taking a seat across from Dougherty. "I gotta be up, gettin' everythin' ready for breakfast, but you, you like a damn ghost hauntin' this place."

After that, Chef stopped by the Orderly Room most nights with something for Dougherty—a plate of donuts, some scrambled eggs, or even just a cup of coffee. A conversation with Chef wasn't really a conversation at all. Chef rambled on about whatever happened to be on his mind that day, and Dougherty listened. There was no telling what Chef's topic might be on any given night. It could be the fine art of mashing five hundred pounds of potatoes for a single meal or how he used to hang out on Caffin Avenue in the Lower Ninth Ward of New Orleans, listening to Fats Domino practicing inside his house, or the time he got a promotion for removing a stain from a Colonel's uniform. There was no point in interjecting or trying to change the subject. You just had to let the man say his piece, and when he decided he was done, Chef would leave.

Following his grounding, Dougherty spent more time with Sam, who waited outside CQ each morning for him to finish his shift. Occasionally, Dougherty scooped the mutt up in his arms, amazed the pup he rescued from Nha Be was now a full-grown dog. Sam always followed Dougherty to the mess hall, where he waited outside until the human finished his breakfast and reappeared with some scraps of food.

Because he worked all night, Dougherty slept all day. He typically awoke around three in the afternoon when the Firefly crews stirred in the barracks. After shaving and showering, Dougherty picked up his mail and took an early dinner in the mess hall before reporting to the orderly room. One afternoon, a week before his DEROS, he received a letter from home with his father's handwriting on the envelope.

"Short-timer," Chef said that evening while watching Dougherty work on his calendar.

"Six and a wake-up," Dougherty replied, without looking up from his coloring.

"What's the deal with you guys who just wanna get out? Why would you ever want to leave the army?" Chef said. "Decent pay. Three square meals a day. Roof over ya head. No sir, I ain't leavin'. Not until I get my pension from Uncle Sam. Then I'm gonna take that money and open a restaurant in the Lower Nine."

Chef has a plan, Dougherty thought. And then it occurred to him that he had sent most of his pay home for nearly two years. Although he hadn't opened his bank statements in months, Dougherty suspected he had accrued a tidy sum. Dougherty originally planned to use that money to buy a new Ford Mustang convertible, but now he considered that perhaps he had some other options. He could go back to college or put some money down on a house or maybe even start a small business. It was the first positive thought he'd had about the future in months.

"What's this?" Chef said, picking up the correspondence from Keith Dougherty.

"Don't touch that . . . please," Dougherty said, not ready to open the envelope but not wanting anything to happen to it, either.

"Must be pretty damn important," Chef said, setting the envelope back down on the desk. "Well, Casper, I'm gonna go check on those boys cleanin' my grease traps. You carry on."

After Chef left, Dougherty stared at his father's handwriting on the white envelope. Finally, he retrieved a metal letter opener from the desk drawer and sliced through the top, revealing four folded blank sheets of paper that served as protection for a single cassette tape. Dougherty examined the cassette in the dim light of the office lamp, as if it was an artifact from one of Astrid's archeological digs.

Since returning to Vietnam for his second tour, Dougherty had not produced a single audio recording for his father and had long since stashed the tape player in the bottom of his locker. Dougherty wanted to listen to the cassette, but there was some risk involved with leaving his post. If the officer of the day happened to show up during the five minutes it would take to retrieve his Panasonic from the barracks, he would be in big trouble. But what could they do to him? He was leaving Vietnam in a week. Dougherty peered out the front door of the Quonset hut, and when he spotted no one, he walked briskly to his room and back.

After setting the tape recorder on the desk, Dougherty turned the volume down on the transistor radio. His hands shook as he inserted the cassette into the device and pressed *play*. Soon, Keith Dougherty's deep, distinct voice reverberated through the still night like a ghost.

> *Hello, Boke. It's been a while since I heard from you. I've got some good news to share. I was gonna wait until you got home, but then I figured, why wait? Congratulations, son. You are now a fully invested partner in Dougherty Construction.* (The sound of ice cubes clinking against glass.)
>
> *It's a good thing you put me down as a co-signer on that account we set up at the Litchfield Bank and Trust. I had to take some money out to pay those sons of bitches in Kearney for the driveways. That was ten grand, which gets you a fifty percent stake in the company. I know that was most of your savings, but with that nonsense in Kearney behind us, we can really grow this business into something special.*

Dougherty pressed the *stop* button on the recorder and rewound the tape. He listened to his father's message a second time, and when it ended, he rewound the tape and listened again.

"Son of a bitch," Dougherty shouted, pounding his fist on the metal desk. He recalled seeing a statement from the Litchfield Bank and Trust in his stack of mail. Dougherty grabbed the steel blade from the desktop and sliced into the envelope. He removed the statement, which showed his father's withdrawal for $10,000 and a remaining balance of $21.13 in his account. He crumbled the paper into a ball and hurled it into the metal trash can. Dougherty nearly threw the recorder across the room, but restrained himself, and pressed *play*. The voice continued, quieter, less confident.

> *Maybe one day you'll have kids of your own and you'll see, there*
> *are times when you really need THEM, just like you needed me when*
> *your mother left. . . .* (a long silence).
> *I need you to come home . . . to take over the family business and*
> *bury me when the time comes. There's no one else I can trust with that.*
> *Keep one foot on the ground, Boke.*

Dougherty pressed *stop* on the recorder. "It was always about you," he said aloud.

Three days before his DEROS, Dougherty visited Supply to retrieve the weapons Swanson had deposited there after his grounding—the bolo knife he bought from the Negrito and the Samurai sword he received from Lowrie.

"They're gone," the Supply Sergeant said through clenched teeth that gnawed on an unlit cheroot.

"What do you mean they're gone?" Dougherty snapped.

"I mean, they ain't here, and no, I don't know where they went, and yes, you are shit out of luck."

"I bought that knife with my own money and the sword was a gift from my gunner. I'm goin' home on Friday, and I want my stuff," Dougherty said louder.

The cigar chewing man smiled, revealing a missing front tooth. He leaned forward and placed both hands on the counter, offering Dougherty a wide-open shot at his steel jaw. "Listen to me Dock-Her-Tee. You ain't gettin' on that plane with anything bigger than a shavin' razor. Now get the hell outta here before I call the MPs."

Two days before his DEROS, Dougherty walked into Operations wearing flight gear.

"Doc, what the hell are you doing here?" Swanson said with a stern look on his face.

"I want to go up one last time."

"Not a fucking chance. With two days left, you are bad luck, mister," the Ops Sergeant replied, firmly.

"You owe me one, Sarge," Dougherty said, holding his ground.

After some more back and forth, Swanson finally relented. "Chavez, looks like you get a day off," the Ops Sergeant shouted across the room. The Latino crew chief from East LA gave the thumbs up sign. "Doc, I'll let you fly, but not out west. I'll give you Dong Nai River Recon for a farewell spin, but that's it. Final offer. Take it or leave it."

During lift-off, Dougherty experienced the same thrill he felt that day at Fort Eustis when he went up in a Huey for the first time. The pilot flew down the center of the Dong Nai at high altitude, never once dropping down to the banks to draw enemy fire. Swanson instructed the man to make this the sort of low-risk flight he might give a news crew or visiting dignitary. Although September was the rainy season, it happened to be a beautiful morning. The river beneath their ship glittered as if filled with millions of tiny diamonds that refracted light in all directions. Eventually, a lone Swift Boat disrupted the calm—its wake rippled across the surface of the water and shattered the illusion. Dougherty touched the Saint Christopher medal around his neck as he watched the tiny waves cascading toward shore.

As their Huey motored toward the coast, Dougherty observed the unfamiliar gunner in the ship's right doorway. He thought about the different men who rode in that seat with him— Lowrie, Coffey, Godbolt, and Mancuso. All four men gone now, and yet, he realized, his father was only half-right. People would always leave him, but sometimes they would return, too, like his mother. And maybe they returned in ways other than being physically present—through their words and wisdom. Lowrie had taught him about Bushido and how to live by a moral code. Godbolt had showed him how to run through holes before they closed. Mancuso believed in having a plan and sticking to it. Even Coffey offered the lesson of letting go, sometimes.

On the return flight, as Dougherty gazed across the horizon to the south, his eyes were drawn to the numerous waterways, like arteries, emerging from the heart of the land. He often mocked Vietnam's disoriented rivers that doubled back upon themselves and seemed to lead nowhere. He considered these wandering tributaries a metaphor for Vietnam itself—a country that did not appear to know where it was going. For the first time, Dougherty realized he was the fool for ever doubting their path. These rivers always ran to the sea, just in their own time and in their own way.

In the steady *wump, wump, wump* of the rotors, a calmness and clarity settled over Dougherty. For a long time, he stared at the image burned into his right forearm. Ever since he was a child, he believed the eagle on his father's forearm was lifting the heavy anchor—an act of incredible strength—but now, he saw the anchor as a tremendous burden, pulling the bird down from the sky. Dougherty slowly removed his flight helmet and held it out in front of himself. He studied the reflection in his dark visor. The image of a tired, bitter man stared back at him. In that moment, William Dougherty understood he had been soundly defeated in Vietnam—every mission he flew, every bullet he fired, every life he extinguished another step toward that inevitable loss.

On the day of his DEROS, when he returned to the barracks after breakfast, Dougherty spotted a brown manila envelope resting on his bunk. He opened the unexpected piece of mail, which contained a Bronze Star with V device for Valor. The envelope also contained a citation, which vaguely described the time he had spent with Captain Ruby, Mr. Hocking, and

Mancuso, supporting Operation Daniel Boone. It was signed by Briga-
dier General Nikolai Sarkis. The CO of the 12th had finally landed his
long-awaited promotion, presumably for dispatching his gunships to the
hellish mission on the Cambodian border.

So this is how it ends, Dougherty thought. *No top brass shaking my
hand, thanking me for a job well done. Just an envelope left on my bunk.*

When he lowered the citation, Dougherty noticed he was not alone.
Sam had jumped up on the bunk and sat, as if at attention.

"For incredible bravery in the face of mortal danger, I am awarding
you this Bronze Star," Dougherty said and pinned the medal on the dog's
collar. Then he stepped back and saluted. Sam smiled, his tongue hanging out, drool dripping from his mouth.

"Keep your ears down, boy, and you just might survive this war,"
Dougherty said, affectionately petting the dog one last time. Then he
slung the duffel bag over his shoulder, picked up the porcelain praying
hands from the crate beneath Miss February, and left the barracks without looking back.

When he stepped outside, Bien Hoa Air Base already seemed different, like the set for a play he was not in or might not attend. Dougherty
knew this was the end of something. He could feel it slipping away, like
the last bit of water swirling around a bathtub drain. Just then, a busload
of new recruits slowly rumbled to a stop. A fresh-faced young man stared
down at him through the bus's chicken wire-covered window. The young
man reminded Dougherty of himself when he first arrived in-country:
eager, confident, and ignorant. After two tours of duty in Vietnam,
Dougherty no longer thought of himself as a log transformed into lumber. The spinning disc had made too many cuts. If he held to that belief,
he would be nothing but a pile of sawdust by now. If he learned one thing
from his enemy, it was that sometimes, when the blade is coming at you,
the best thing you can do is move out of the way.

As the bus rumbled away, Dougherty retreated to the row of la-
trines behind the barracks where a straphanger had already removed the
half-barrels and ignited the human waste in each can. Dougherty set his
duffel bag down and held the praying hands out above the nearest barrel.
A moment later, he released the ceramic figurine: the base of the porce-

lain statue embedded in the muck, then the ghostly white hands slowly descended into the flames of hell.

Dougherty reached into his pocket and removed the final audio cassette from his father. He pulled the thin ribbon from the plastic cartridge until he held a small pile of twisted magnetic tape in his hand. This, too, he tossed into the burning barrel of shit.

Feeling lighter, William Dougherty walked across base and boarded the Freedom Bird that would take him back to the United States.

21

RIPPLES

SEPTEMBER 19, 2018

Dougherty stood frozen in the center of the hotel room, unable to speak, his blood pressure dangerously low—a side effect of the Carbidopa-Levodopa he took five times a day for Parkinson's disease. *Welcome to Stage 4,* he thought.

Before taking his mid-morning meds, Dougherty had turned on the room's flat-screen TV and found a twenty-four-hour news channel. Unable to move, he now stared at the anchor as she discussed flooding in south central North Carolina after Hurricane Florence dumped thirty-six inches of rain on the area. Pre-recorded drone footage showed cars stranded on submersed roads and people in small motorboats riding through a community that looked as if it was constructed in the middle of a massive lake—church spires, telephone poles, treetops, roofs, and road signs all sprouting from the murky standing water.

"You know someone who lives there, don't you?" Lena called out from the bathroom where she was fixing her curly gray hair in the mirror.

When there was no reply, Lena peeked around the bathroom door and spotted her husband standing stiff as a board in the middle of the room. The retired nurse hurried to his side, gently led him over to the bed, and lowered him to a seated position on the mattress.

"Locked up, again?" she said, rhetorically. Lena lifted the tail of her partner's shirt and rubbed some ointment into his shoulders and lower back. "Give the pills a little time and your blood pressure will come back up," she said.

It all started eight years ago, when Dougherty noticed he had lost his sense of smell. Then his daughter Hannah, a speech pathologist, detected some subtle communication impairments and expressed concern about the early onset of dementia. She referred her father to a neurologist, who subsequently diagnosed him with Parkinson's Disease; his condition possibly caused by exposure to Agent Orange in Vietnam.

At first, Dougherty thought the Parkinson's wasn't too bad, but then came the shaking, the loss of balance, and the stiffening of his entire body. Now, he regularly saw three specialists per month and took sixteen pills a day, all to maintain some semblance of a normal life. He spent most of his waking hours in a recliner, watching television and trying to hold on to the good memories.

As Lena finished her massage, the Florence coverage switched to footage of National Guardsmen unloading cases of bottled water and boxes of relief supplies from an olive-green helicopter in Lumberton, North Carolina, Lowrie's hometown.

Two hours later, Lena had her husband dressed in his black suit and stationed beside her beneath an oversized umbrella outside the New Brunswick Holiday Inn Xpress. After leaving North Carolina, Hurricane Florence visited West Virginia, Pennsylvania, New York, and now, two days later, her heavy rains were falling over New Jersey.

"When's the taxi coming?" Dougherty said.

"I ordered an Uber," Lena replied, glancing at her iPhone. "It will be here in seven minutes. A white Kia. Emir is our driver," she added.

Seven minutes later, a white Kia Optima pulled up in front of the hotel. The passenger window automatically descended and a smiling, dark-skinned man with short black hair and a beard leaned over from the driver's seat. "Lena?" he said.

Fifteen minutes later, their Uber parked in a handicapped space in front of the Royce Funeral Chapel. Emir helped Lena pull her husband out of the backseat and onto the sidewalk, where the driver handed him his cane.

"How much do we owe you?" Dougherty said to the young South Sudanese man.

Emir looked at Lena and smiled. "It's all covered, sir. Have a blessed day."

"Thank you, Emir," Lena replied, taking hold of her husband's left arm. "I am definitely giving him five stars," she said to her husband, as the white Kia and its talkative driver pulled away.

The front parlor of the Royce Funeral Chapel appeared like so many other places offering final arrangements—a sign-in book on a small table at the entrance and numerous floral bouquets and wreaths interspersed amidst a gathering of solemn people in their Sunday best.

As they scanned the crowd, a distinguished elderly gentleman, trim in his expensive suit, approached. "Jerry Pearle," he said, extending his hand.

"William Dougherty," Lena said on behalf of her husband.

It only took Pearle a moment to place the name and face, despite his former crew chief's gray hair and withered body. "Doc," he said fondly, while maintaining the firm handshake.

Dougherty was not surprised to learn that Pearle had served as a representative in the New York State Assembly in the 1980s before taking a job as an investment banker. After working on Wall Street for more than thirty years, Pearle had recently retired as director of a well-known mutual fund. These days, he served on a few boards, dabbled in philanthropy, and worked on his tennis game.

A moment later they were joined by a tall, well-built man who exuded reverence.

"Brother Bill," Jack Godbolt said, then embraced Dougherty without waiting for an invitation to do so. "It's wonderful to see you."

An elderly but fit Afton Brown emerged from behind Godbolt. "Doc, I'm glad to see you're still climbing."

"A. B.," Dougherty said, shaking his friend's hand. "Did you ever get that degree?"

Brown adjusted his wire-rimmed glasses. "I got three of them," he said. "My sister, too. I'm Professor Emeritus of History at Morehouse

College. Retired last year after thirty-five years of teaching."

Another familiar face emerged from behind Brown. "Good to see you, Doc," Dick Swanson, the company's former Operations sergeant said. Swanson had kept tabs on various members of the 334th through-out the years and proceeded to laundry-list a mixed bag of outcomes, in-cluding marriages, divorces, promotions, firings, miraculous recoveries, and early deaths. Dougherty already knew that Coffey had died of liver cancer in the '90s, but he did not know that Jim Hocking lived in a VA home somewhere in western Pennsylvania.

"Is Vic coming?" someone in the group asked Swanson.

"I don't think so," Swanson replied, shaking his head. "I spoke to him yesterday. Florence beat the hell out of them. His place got flooded pretty bad."

Three middle-aged men who bore a striking resemblance to Mancuso joined the conversation. "We're Louie's sons," said the one who appeared to be the oldest. "Are you Bill Dougherty? My father talked about you all the time. He told us stories about flying with you."

Dougherty nodded. "I was sorry to hear about your father's heart attack."

"Pops liked his pasta and cannoli," the youngest of the three said.

"And cigarettes," the middle son added. "Smoked like a chimney right up until the end."

Dougherty could tell his friend's sons hoped for more details from their father's past, and he feared the Parkinson's might deny them that.

"He talked a lot about doors," Dougherty blurted out, and the three young men laughed. "And going back to Jersey to start a family. We flew together and roomed together at Bien Hoa. He was a brave guy. I always knew he had my back."

"Mancuso Doors won't be the same without him," the eldest son said.

"I think we're ready, friends," a priest announced to the crowd, and the mourners began shuffling through the double doors leading into the chapel.

Once everyone was seated, the priest said that the family wanted Louie's friends from the army to have a few minutes at the casket before the service started. Pearle, Godbolt, and Swanson went first, while Lena helped her husband to his feet. As they inched their way down the aisle, Dougherty did not notice the man who entered the chapel late and followed them to the casket. When Lena spotted the man, he winked at her, and even without knowing Lowrie, she understood that was her cue to return to the pew.

Lowrie put one hand on Dougherty's shoulder and squeezed his friend's arm with the other. "How you doin', buddy?" Lowrie said, as if he had just returned from a short R&R.

"Not so good," Dougherty replied, only able to turn slightly toward his friend.

"Jeez, you look worse than Mancuso," Lowrie whispered, and Dougherty smiled.

The two men stared in silence at the inflated but familiar body of Louie Mancuso resting in the ornate white casket.

"Looks like he had a pretty good life," Lowrie said. "Good friends. Good family. Seventy years and a room full of people at the end. That's all a man can hope for. If this was a Lumbee funeral, we'd sing in his honor."

Dougherty nodded.

"You ready to do this?" Lowrie said.

Dougherty nodded and his friend led him back to the pew.

During the service, Godbolt spoke on behalf of the men Mancuso served with in Vietnam. He spoke fondly of his brothers in arms, shared a few stories from their days at Bien Hoa, and somehow made it all seem like the work of Jesus. As he was wrapping up, Godbolt looked at Dougherty and told the mourners he would like to finish with one of his favorite pieces of scripture.

"The Lord is my shepherd. I shall not want," Godbolt said, and Dougherty felt a tear slide down his cheek.

When the service ended, Dougherty and Lena exited the funeral home while Lowrie stayed behind to ask the staff to call him a cab. Neither Lowrie nor the Doughertys planned to go to the cemetery in the rain.

"Remember our deal," Lena said, referring to the pact she and her husband made to never end up in a place like the Royce Funeral Chapel. Instead, they planned to have themselves cremated, their ashes scattered in Bali where they celebrated their fortieth wedding anniversary with their family. That was before the diagnosis, and it was the best week of

Bill and Lena's life. They played with their grandchildren in the surf and sand and marveled at the beautiful family they had created.

The couple had done well. Although his father depleted his account, Dougherty saved enough money during his final year in the army to buy Lena an engagement ring. They married and honeymooned in Los Angeles shortly after his enlistment ended. Before leaving LA, Dougherty's mother loaned him ten thousand dollars to start a small construction equipment rental business in Albuquerque, New Mexico, which he sold in the 1990s to buy a larger one in Phoenix, Arizona. He found himself on the front end of both of those cities' booms and made a tidy sum, which proved to be just enough to put their four children through college, help them get started in their adult lives, and ensure he and Lena had enough to live comfortably until the end of their days.

Lowrie emerged from the Royce Funeral Chapel with a loaner umbrella and joined the Doughertys at the curb.

"How are you?" Dougherty said.

"Well, I can fish in my living room thanks to Florence, but other than that, I can't complain. Got married after the war. Raised three kids. Lost my beautiful wife Rhoda fifteen years ago to breast cancer, which was rough. Retired after forty years with the phone company. Got my pension. Got my Social Security. Got my grandkids and a mutt back home to keep me company. I sit on the tribal council and mentor Lumbee vets when they come off active duty. I guess I'm doin' ok."

Dougherty nodded, pleased his friend had forged a decent life after the war.

"There's something I've been wanting to ask you for fifty years," Dougherty said to his former gunner.

"Sure," Lowrie replied.

"When you left Vietnam, did you take the shotgun?"

Lowrie smiled. "I took it from the ship … and buried it in the landfill at Bien Hoa. I figured it could only cause trouble for you or me. But I left you my sword."

Dougherty smiled. "Remember that guy who ran Supply? Tough as nails sergeant, always chewin' on a cigar?"

Lowrie nodded.

"He took it."

"That bastard," Lowrie said. "Well, maybe he got Bushido," he added, and the two men laughed.

Dougherty wanted to ask Lowrie one final question—if what their country had asked them to do in Vietnam was wrong. But he refrained, since he knew his friend's likely response—that the high ground was already lost by the time they got there; that colonialism was a fancy name for slavery; and no matter how far their leaders tried to bend that around with their pretzel logic, they could never bend it far enough to make it right.

Dougherty studied Lowrie's weathered face and curly gray hair, wondering how he had let this good man slip out of his life for half a century.

"Need a place to stay for a while?" Dougherty said. "We've got lots of room in Scottsdale," he added, referring to their beautiful home on a golf course in one of the wealthier neighborhoods of the Phoenix suburb.

Lowrie shook his head. "Thanks, bud, but I've got a daughter in Charlotte. I'm flyin' there now. I'll play with my grandkids until the water goes down, then head back to Lumberton to clean up the mess."

When the taxi arrived, William Dougherty and Victor Braveboy Lowrie embraced for the first and final time. Lowrie climbed into the backseat of the cab and waved as his ride pulled away.

"Do you remember what you told me on our first date?" Dougherty said to Lena as they waited in the rain for their Uber. "That no one thinks about the soldiers fifty years after the war . . . and when they come home, it's like someone threw a handful of stones in a pond."

Now it was Lena who was crying. "The ripples," she said.

"I hope my ripples weren't too bad," Dougherty said as he leaned against his wife beneath the umbrella.

Four hours later, Bill and Lena pre-boarded their direct flight from Newark Liberty International Airport to Phoenix. A male flight attendant offered them drinks as they settled into their first-class seats.

Dougherty studied his wife's face as she fastened his seat belt and then her own. For half a century, this woman had kept him facing forward, moving from one life experience to the next—the birth of their four children, first days of school, sporting events, vacations, graduations, weddings, and the arrival of grandchildren. There were times throughout the years when he could feel the ripples at his back, close enough that they might overtake him, like when the business nearly failed in the 1980s and he started drinking heavily, or when his mother and Barry died in a car crash in LA a decade later. Still, Lena kept him ahead of those wakes, even inserting herself between her husband and the ripples if they ever got too close.

There were those rare occasions when Dougherty turned to face the past—burying his father on Cemetery Hill in Litchfield after Keith Dougherty lost a short battle with brain cancer, and returning every Memorial Day to plant flowers on his parents' graves. Lena also approved the occasional event for Vietnam veterans. Several days before those gatherings, Dougherty retrieved a dusty box from the attic that held his flight helmet, photo albums, and other memorabilia. But immediately after those events ended, Lena made sure the box went back in the attic and her husband faced forward again.

There was an understanding between them: they were going to run this play until the clock ran out, and then Lena and their four children and their five grandchildren would release Dougherty's ashes on a beautiful beach in Bali. Cremation was Lena's stroke of genius—ashes float and cause no ripples. The fine carbon matter absorbs water until it breaks apart and then disappears.

Dougherty held tightly to Lena's hand as their plane accelerated down the runway. When the ship escaped gravity's pull and lifted into the air, William Dougherty closed his eyes and rested, knowing he had finally boarded his Freedom Bird.

ACKNOWLEDGMENTS

FIRST AND FOREMOST, I would like to thank Rick McCurry for sharing his life story and allowing me to manipulate it for this work of fiction. *First With Guns* is highly informed by Rick's childhood in Nebraska and his two tours of duty in Vietnam as a crew chief with the 334th Armed Helicopter Company, from January 1967 to September 1968.

Sincere thanks to Samantha Moyer, Peter Worthing, Ed McNertney, and Col (Ret) Scott McGowan, who read the manuscript at various stages and offered helpful feedback.

Thanks to Scott Miller for reminding me, "If you don't have a plan, someone is going to make a plan for you."

There are a handful of notable works that informed the manuscript and deserve special recognition. *The Only Land I Know: A History of the Lumbee Indians* by Adolph L. Dial and David K. Eliades is, in my opinion, the definitive source on Lumbee history and culture. Their book's section on Henry Berry Lowrie largely informed the story told by Victor Braveboy Lowrie in Chapter 4—"Paradise Lost."

Valerie Vierk, Mary Lee Pesek and Geoffrey Pesek wrote an excellent account of the Tiger Man titled "John Pesek—The Wrestler from Ravenna," which was published by the Buffalo County Historical Society. That work, along with Rick McCurry's experiences with John and Jack Pesek, informed Dougherty's story in Chapter 5—"The Tiger Man of Nebraska." Incidentally, there is a statue of John Pesek on Main Street in Ravenna, Nebraska, which I encourage you to visit.

The late Vietnam War scholar, Stanley Karnow, also wrote a fine book on the United States' involvement in the Philippines titled *In our Image: America's Empire in the Philippines.* That work, along with Rick McCurry's experiences at the Jungle Environment Survival Training (JEST) camp in the Philippines, largely informed Chapter 13—JEST.

For those seeking a work of nonfiction about the exploits of the 334th Armed Helicopter Company in Vietnam, I recommend *Returning Fire: In the Beginning,* by Col (Ret) James E. "Pete" Booth.

At a time when I was feeling cut-off and exposed, the squad from TCU Press parachuted into the novel, threw the manuscript and me over their shoulders, and carried us safely through to publication. Molly, Kathy, James, and Dan, in the world of *First With Guns,* you are all Four Star Generals, and I salute you.

Finally, I would like to thank my family and friends. I went to war with this novel, and you waited for me to come home. ♥

ABOUT THE AUTHOR

JAMES EDWARD ENGLISH received a BA in English from the College of William & Mary and a MA in history from Texas Christian University. English has published articles and opinion pieces in *Ability* magazine, *China Report*, *Asian Politics & Policy*, the *Fort Worth Star-Telegram*, and the *Miami Herald*. He is the author of *Galia's Dad Is in a Wheelchair* (TCU Press), a children's book about disability in Haiti. *First with Guns* is his first novel.

English works at Southern New Hampshire University and lives in Manchester.